One

March 1817

MOST PEOPLE HOPED TO SPOT FAMILIAR FACES IN A crowded ballroom. Augusta Meredith prayed to see only strangers.

For nearly a week, her prayers had been granted. In winter's waning days, the *ton* kept its distance from Bath. The resort city's fashionable years were in the past, and so the cream of society avoided it, favoring the rural delights of hunting or the sophisticated pleasures of London.

Not that Augusta had ever been part of the *ton*. But like a moth before an ever-closed window, she had fluttered around its bounds long enough that someone might recognize her.

Thus far, though, the crowds in Bath's Upper Rooms presented her only with strangers—merchants and cits and hangers-on. A lower social class; exactly the sort of people Augusta knew best. Exactly who she was. In Bath, she didn't have to pretend to be someone else.

Though larger than any ballroom Augusta had seen in London, the Upper Rooms were just as crowded with slowly churning waves of people. But there was one great difference: here Augusta inhabited the center, not the edge.

"Mrs. Flowers, m'dear!"

The voice floated above the din in the high-ceilinged room, and Augusta turned toward it. "Mrs. Flowers!" The call came again; this time, the shouting man waved his arms too.

Augusta returned his wave with a graceful flicker of her fan, then flipped it open to hide her grin.

Well, maybe she did pretend to be someone else.

The shouting man was heavyset and young, probably less than her twenty-five years. Every time he had spoken with Augusta, he had been tipsy; since she could not recall his name, she had mentally dubbed him Hiccuper. He shouldered toward her, making slow progress through the crowd. The pale-walled, elaborately plastered ballroom stretched high and long, yet dancing figures filled it to the brim. Babbling voices bounced from the barrel-vaulted ceiling, raining from the wrought iron–faced walkway across the room's end.

Bath was a city of carefully calculated comforts, from the regimented hours for bathing and taking the mineral waters to the location of the nightly assemblies. Everything was orchestrated to bring strangers together in harmony. And through this sort of artificial harmony, Augusta would slip into the escape she craved.

Hiccuper had almost reached her; no doubt he

intended to escort her into the winding figures of the dance. When the steps brought them together, he would leer at her breasts; when the dance was over, he might try to persuade her to accompany him home.

All part of the plan she put into action when she entered a false name in Bath's social registry, the Pump Room's guest book. By writing "Mrs. John Flowers" instead of "Miss Augusta Meredith," she became a widow instead of an unmarried woman, shedding the social manacles of an heiress who drew her fortune from trade.

And she didn't intend to carry out her plan with someone like Hiccuper. Augusta Meredith might hope for no better, but Mrs. Flowers could.

Hiccuper was still feet away, swept into a conversation with friends, when another voice spoke in her ear. "Mrs. Flowers, what good fortune to encounter you here in Bath. Do you know, you greatly resemble a young lady of my acquaintance."

A male voice. A *familiar* male voice.

Damn. Her luck had just run out.

Still hiding behind her fan, Augusta turned toward the voice. From its cursed tone of humor, she at once recognized it as Josiah Everett's—and yes, here he stood, plainly dressed, handsome, and full of wicked glee. He was the worst sort of person she could have encountered: one who knew her too well to be fooled by her deception, but not well enough to take part in it.

"Mr. Everett." She forced a smile. "How unexpectedly delightful to see you. I would have expected you to remain in London for business reasons."

Like Augusta, Everett orbited society at a distance but had a few friends among the *beau monde*'s permissive fringes. Although of respectable birth, his means were straitened. He worked for his bread, serving as Baron Sutcliffe's man of business.

This much Augusta had gleaned from the gossip that scattered whenever Everett made his occasional forays into society. She knew little else about him.

"I almost believe your delight in our meeting to be sincere." Everett bowed. "You are correct, I am generally in London at this time of year. At the present, though, a particular errand requires my attention in Bath. A happy accident, would you not say?"

Was that amusement in his dark eyes? Probably. Humph. He always looked amused.

"But what of you, Mrs. Flowers?" he pressed. "Your name tells me you have been recently married. Permit me to congratulate you."

"Oh, I am not married at present, Mr. Everett." A true statement. She fluttered her fan, an elaborate affair of lace and ivory and painted silk, before her bosom. Earlier this evening, a certain Mr. Rowe had informed her the gesture looked elegant.

As though a woman with hair the color of a persimmon, and no birth to recommend her, could ever truly be elegant. But elegance had its limits, and Augusta had grown used to enticing men with her figure instead.

Everett refused to be enticed; he only folded his arms in his plain, black coat. "Dear me. Ought I instead to offer condolences? Has Mr. Flowers departed this earth?"

Augusta snapped her fan closed. "Is there something you require of me, sir?"

"Merely a confirmation." Everett's dark features held a sardonic expression. "My condolences, then. I did suspect you to be a *widow*"—he paused over this final word—"since half the men in this ballroom are caterwauling your praises."

"Only half?" She arched a brow. "How sad. My popularity is declining."

Everett's smile grew. "I haven't been present long. It might be more."

"And what are these caterwauling men saying of me?"

He lifted his gaze to a chandelier, one of five elaborate gilt affairs that lit the stretching room and cast down as much heat as they did light. Outside, night hung like dark velvet over the clerestory windows. "I believe," he drawled, "that someone said your bosom could launch a thousand ships. That seems a bit much to ask of a bosom, though. It is not a dockyard."

"Certainly not for you," Augusta muttered. It was, however, her best feature. Her indigo silk's low-cut bodice was trimmed in gold cord and lace, a fashion flattering to a young woman with more curves than subtlety.

"Perhaps I shouldn't have told you what I'd overheard." Everett was looking at her again, dark brows slightly lifted as though he were challenging her. "Then again, if you're a widow, you can handle a bit of scandalous talk."

"Mrs. Flowers!" Hiccuper had pushed his way through the crowd at last, panting boozily. "Mrs. Flowers, m'dear."

"Ah, Mr.…." She covered her uncertainty over his name with a titter. "How good to see you."

"You must dance with me, Mrs. Flowers. They're forming a cotillion." The young man leaned closer, the odor of perspiration and cheap sherry as sharp as a slap. When he breathed out, setting the curls at Augusta's ears into a dance, she went stiff.

Avoiding Everett's gaze, she simpered, "I'm sorry, dear sir, but I've just agreed to dance with this gentleman." She waved her fan in Everett's direction with languid disinterest, hoping he had manners enough not to give the lie to her words.

Indeed, Everett spoke up at once. "So sorry, *dear sir*, but perhaps you may have a later dance. Mrs. Flowers, shall we take our places in the set?" He held out a gray-gloved hand.

With a parting wave, she left a surprised Hiccuper behind and joined Everett in pressing through the crowd. "Thank you for covering my little falsehood—"

"One of several."

"But," she added in a slightly louder tone, "you don't really have to dance with me. I could develop an urgent requirement for tea. Or a rest."

"I certainly *do* need to dance with you, if that's the sort of man who follows you around discussing your bosom." Everett frowned back at Hiccuper. "Your *dear sir* smelled as though he hadn't washed for a week. Has he bothered you before?"

"No. No one bothers me."

Everett slanted a sideways look at her, then set his jaw.

It was a rather nice jaw, clean and strong. As though

his veins carried Mediterranean blood, his skin was a dark olive, his hair black and slightly curling. Within his gray gloves, his hands had a firm, pleasant grip.

How unfortunate that such a fine form belonged to such an unnerving man, with such a pestilent wit.

Though at the moment, his usual satirical expression had settled into solemn lines. "It is, of course, your affair if you want to throw away your time on men who compare you to a dockyard."

"*You* were the one who made that comparison." She tried to tug her fingers from his grasp, but an elderly man with grizzled side whiskers jostled against them. To steady her, Everett drew her closer. The contact surprised a hitching breath from Augusta; at Everett's side, she caught a faint, spicy scent. Sandalwood?

Again, he looked at her sidelong. "Yes, well. I certainly wouldn't deny you could find better company than me. Though at least I wash every day. That's something, I suppose."

"That's something," she repeated. Under the guise of stumbling against his arm, then catching her breath in the crowd, she inhaled again. *Yes.* Sandalwood. A faraway scent, as unusual as it was masculine. Because it had to be imported from afar, from sultry corners of the world like India or Hawai'i, the golden oil was costly.

As the heiress to a cosmetics fortune, Augusta knew fragrances as well as most women knew fashion. Sandalwood was an unusual choice for any Englishman, much less one of limited means.

She had just learned something else about Josiah Everett: he was a man of at least one surprise.

Maybe he would hold one more, if she could

persuade him. Rising to her toes, she whispered in his ear, "Mr. Everett. How can I convince you to keep my secret?"

⤛⤜

Encountering Augusta Meredith was not the first surprise that had befallen Joss since his arrival in Bath three days before, though it was certainly more pleasant than the ones that had preceded it.

Hearing Augusta Meredith referred to as "Mrs. Flowers"? Another surprise, and this one less pleasant. For a dreadful, swooping moment, he thought she had finally got herself married off.

But no. It seemed the name and the widowhood were equally fictitious, part of some plan of hers. As, no doubt, was her warm breath in his ear. Her husky whisper. The faint floral scent she wore, so delicate and sweet he could almost taste it.

How can I convince you to keep my secret?

He ought to require no convincing at all; he ought simply to do a lady's bidding. But as he knew quite well, secrets came at a great price. That was, after all, why he was in Bath to begin with.

So he reserved a definite reply, at least until he could determine what sort of scheme the lady had in mind. "At the moment, my dear Mrs. Flowers, you need do nothing but dance with me." He drew her to one side of a set. Throughout the enormous ballroom, couples were grouping, four by four, into the squares of the cotillion.

Joss hoped he remembered the steps. He hadn't danced since he was a half-grown boy, filling in the sets with maids and servants to help his second cousin, Lord Sutcliffe, learn the figures he would need to move about in high society.

How many years had Joss spent helping Sutcliffe with figures? Though he was only thirty-one years old, it seemed the task of a lifetime. Now, though, the baron needed his aid with figures of a different sort: amounts of money, curves of women.

But soon that would all be done, Joss's long servitude at an end. If he could get a few damned people to speak with him. So far, the so-called Mrs. Flowers was the only person who had given him more than a curious glance, or a dismissive one. And though her smile had been polite, he was fortunate her eyes were incapable of firing bullets.

He had hoped the fluctuations of Bath society, always bidding *bonjour* and *adieu* to travelers, would allow him to conduct his business more efficiently than in London. But no, even here, gazes skated over him. Maybe because of his dark complexion or the plainness of his clothing. To them, Joss did not appear as though he had anything to offer.

At least he made a better dance partner than an unwashed sot.

He looked down at Miss Meredith, standing to his right, impatient and fidgety under her lush tangle of red curls threaded with amber beads. Her bosom—which might not truly launch a thousand ships, but which was certainly worthy of a flotilla—rose and fell with fascinating force within her purple silk gown. Maybe she intended to use her pneumatic talents to befuddle him into agreement.

He was quite willing to let her try. "Take hands, my dear widow."

With a filthy look quickly turned angelic, she let him draw her into the small circle of their dance.

"I wonder at your grimaces, Mrs. Flowers," he murmured, sliding over the smooth wooden floor in some semblance of the correct balances and steps and *chassés*. "*You* invited *me* to dance, after all. Is this cotillion not the fulfillment of your ambition?"

Her light brown eyes opened wide, but a retort was arrested by the movement of the dance: the four women stepped inward, forming a cross with their joined hands. After they completed their steps and turns, the men did the same. Joss's three companions bore a familiar look of determined concentration; one man was actually counting the steps to himself.

This was Bath in miniature: a polite grouping of strangers thrust into close proximity. All unwilling to give offense, but unsure whether they ought to have anything to do with one another. Yet the people, like the ballroom walls, were plastered and painted. Hoping to impress.

Joss was no different, was he? Except that plaster and paint were beyond his means. He had only ever seen the *ton* from the outside, peering out from the corner of a ballroom or down from a balcony's dizzying height. This feeling of being melted and mixed into a crowd was unfamiliar and thus not entirely pleasant.

Before the dance dragged them apart again, Miss Meredith managed to hiss in his ear. "I will grant that I find you preferable to being pawed by a drunkard."

"You honor me. As I am not intoxicated, may I be permitted to paw you instead?"

Stepping, sliding, hopping again. This dance was not conducive to conversation. And Joss much preferred boots to the ridiculous glossy shoes required by Bath's master of ceremonies at formal assemblies. It was so difficult to find his footing in this sort of place.

When they next passed each other, Miss Meredith gave him a truly lovely smile. "You are welcome to try it and see what happens. Are you fond of all your fingers?"

"Indeed I am, my dear Widow Flowers, so I shan't put a hand on you except as part of this dance. You deserve every courtesy, having married and buried a husband since we last met—when was it?"

"Last summer." She frowned. "Just before the Duke of Wyverne's house party."

"No doubt you are right," he said lightly, as though he could not remember the exact dates. She had not been present at the ducal house party in Lancashire; he had noticed at the time. And he had wondered how bright her hair would appear under the cold northern sky.

A violin wandered out of tune; with a sweet rebuke, an oboe called it back. Joss stepped forward into the cross with the other men. Now the chain, in which his feet were supposed to do something intricate while he and Miss Meredith held hands. He settled for taking her fingers and shuffling back and forth just enough not to smack into the other dancers.

"As I said before, you have my condolences for your recent bereavement," he pressed mercilessly.

"This festive interlude must be an attempt to kick away your mourning. How brave and noble of you! Though it is a bit soon, if—"

"It's all a lie, all right?" she whispered. "Now stop talking. You know I'm not a widow."

Her sudden frankness surprised him into silence, as did the hard expression that crossed her soft features.

For a moment they simply shuffled gracelessly, hands clasped and bodies a breath apart. The pale swell of her flotilla-launching breasts, the fiery glints of her hair under the chandelier light had him wishing she were a widow in truth.

But she was a maiden. A *dishonest* maiden. And two generations of family scandal had taught Joss that, though dishonesty was sometimes permissible, dallying with maidens was not.

"I know you are not." Regret thickened his voice. "I would love to lie about who I am. I simply didn't think of it."

"If only you had, then we would be on equal footing. As it is, my reputation is in your hands."

"Mrs. Flowers, every time a woman dances with a man, her reputation is in his hands. That is why it is such an honor when a lady agrees to dance with a man."

"But I asked you to dance," she said. "Or if we are to be accurate, I informed you that you were to dance with me."

"Then I suppose *my* reputation is in *your* hands."

She looked at him with some surprise; then the dance separated them. There ensued an interminable winding and stepping and crossing, until finally the orchestra's sawing dwindled away. As Miss Meredith applauded with the other dancers, Joss caught her elbow and steered her to the edge of the room.

The crush was slightly less here. When Joss glared at a dandy seated on a small bench, the fellow scrambled away and Joss handed his partner into the seat. "Do tell me, Mrs. Flowers," he said as he looked down at her, "how have you passed off this new identity?"

A fan dangled from one wrist; she caught it up in her other hand and began teasing it open. It bore a painting of some curly-headed, Greek-looking youth, with white draperies and tiny wings and puffed-out cheeks.

"Zephyr," she said, noticing Joss's gaze. "The god of the west wind. An apt decoration for a fan, don't you think?" She waved it at him, and a welcome eddy of cool air brushed his features.

Joss ignored this attempt at diversion, lifting his brows.

She snapped the fan closed. "Very well. I'm visiting Bath in company with the Countess of Tallant. You have made her acquaintance, I think?"

"Yes, certainly." The young auburn-haired countess and her doting husband were a popular pair, sharing unshakable good humor.

"Lady Tallant is"—Miss Meredith paused—"not well. She's here to take the waters and does not plan to mix much in Bath society. So I was tasked with visiting the Pump Room after we arrived, to sign our names in the guest book and meet the master of ceremonies and whatnot. I took the opportunity to… not be me anymore."

"You are still you," Joss reminded her. "You simply called yourself something different. Why Mrs. Flowers, by the way?"

She coughed. "I saw a vase of flowers in one corner as I was introducing myself, and that was that."

"To think, if the master of ceremonies had made your introduction in a different room, Bath might now be admiring the charms of Mrs. Roman Statue."

Her attempt at a frown was a dreadful failure; in a moment, it flipped into a smile and a low chuckle. The sound was throaty and knowing, entirely different from the feathery giggle she had used with the portly drunkard who had tried to seize her for a dance.

That had been a maiden's laugh. This? This was the chuckle of a woman who liked the company of a man.

Only when her laugh fell silent, the smile vanishing, did Joss realize he had been staring at her in some wonder.

"So you'll keep my secret?" she asked in a brittle voice.

"That depends on why you possess a secret in the first place." Though his brows were getting tired from all the lifting, he kept the blasé expression on his face. "Why are you posing as a widow, Miss Meredith? Are you in some danger?"

Her features crumpled; then she straightened her shoulders. "Not at all." She looked up at him, and her smile almost reached her brandy-gold eyes. "It's as simple as this, Mr. Everett. I require a lover."

Two

I REQUIRE A LOVER.

Augusta had never permitted herself to utter these words before; no, until now she had kept the idea carefully locked away. The word *require* muscled forth oddly with its implication that her plan held more of necessity than desire.

Now that it had escaped her lips, it was clearly the right word.

And the effect of her statement was rather marvelous: Mr. Everett's mouth fell open. Actually *fell open,* as though her bosom had truly launched a thousand ships into the ballroom.

In an instant, he recovered his composure. "Why?"

Augusta drew herself up straight. "If you don't know the reasons people take lovers, I'm sure you could hire someone to explain them to you."

He folded his arms.

"You're not terrible looking," she added in a soothing voice. "You might even get someone to demonstrate for no charge."

His lips curled slightly. "That is *not* what I meant.

Why now? Or why do you *require* one?" His gaze
dropped to her midsection. "Is there some medical
urgency about the matter?"

"Not for the reason you suspect." Augusta considered. She could refuse to explain, could return to
Hiccuper and his ilk and hope that Everett would
indeed hold his tongue.

But he had no reason to, did he? Men never
behaved as they ought without some incentive.
And when he inevitably told, scandal would follow.
Augusta's hostess Lady Tallant, ailing though she was,
would be driven from Bath when her houseguest's
true identity leaked out.

Lady Tallant deserved better. And Augusta rather
thought Mrs. Flowers did too.

"Let us go somewhere private," she finally said. "I
shall try to explain."

"You honor me."

"Don't be so sure of that," Augusta said. "If you
recall, I hold your frail reputation in my hands."

When his smile turned to a grin, she had to look
away to suppress a sudden flutter. It ought not to be a
surprise that she had been found out, after all. And she
was not entirely sorry it was by him.

Her fingertips on his forearm, her heart thudding
quickly, she accompanied Mr. Everett through the
crush at the edges of the ballroom. They exited into
the Octagon Room, a butter-yellow polygon crowded
with connecting doors and fireplaces and watched
over by yet another of those giant crystal chandeliers.
Groups of chairs in dark-stained wood flanked each
doorway, and the pair settled in two of these.

Mr. Everett spoke first. "Now. Do tell me more about your unusual requirement, my dear fake widow."

Augusta watched the people trailing by: some laughing, some flirting, some trying to hide tears; others bored, drinking cups of punch, cooling heated brows with fans. None with a care for her or Mr. Everett at all.

Nor did she care for them, really. She still felt as though a window divided her from her surroundings, and she, naught but a moth, was trapped behind the glass. If she could never get through, was there any purpose in continuing to flutter her wings?

There must be. There had to be. Surely one day she would break the glass and…belong.

Surely the yet-unknown lover would help her to do this: to set aside a past in which she had been deceived, judged wanting without even knowing she was on trial.

Surely it would be a way not to be alone anymore. On her terms, at last and only.

Her breath coming shallowly, she stared at the parquet floor. "To claim a lover would be a much-needed victory."

"Over whom?" Everett's voice was quiet, or maybe the ringing in Augusta's ears was loud. "Not that it is any of my affair, I suppose."

What would be the worst that would happen if she told him? He might reveal Mrs. Flowers to be a fraud. The same was true if she told him nothing, though. Simply knowing her identity was enough to ruin her.

And she ached to tell him a bit more. To free a few more words from their prison—one that had turned her too much inward, monitoring the locks and chains upon dark and treacherous thoughts. She had a terror of solitude. "It would be a victory over myself."

"A victory well worth the pursuit. Yet you could marry and achieve the same…ah, carnal result."

She looked up at him. "Mrs. Flowers is not a prize marriage prospect. As far as Bath knows, she has no birth and little fortune. Nothing to recommend her but her noble friend."

"Right. Yes. That's why men flirt with you and praise your delightful appearance. Because you are friends with Lady Tallant."

"They are flirting with *Mrs. Flowers*," Augusta reminded him. "As a widow, she has more possibilities open to her than I do."

"*She is you.* Simply you, frosted with a few lies." Dark brown eyes held her gaze. "Do you not think you are worth marrying, then?"

"That is a remarkably impertinent question."

His gaze was steady. "And that is not an answer. Which is answer enough."

Aggravating man. "I do not think about marriage. I don't wish to marry."

"A lovely heiress such as Augusta Meredith? Surely you could find some land-rich blue blood with pockets to let. He would be delighted to take you to wife."

"Me? Or my money?"

A wry smile. "For most of the *ton*, there is little difference."

"Ah, but there is to me." Augusta rubbed at her upper arms above her long gloves, feeling chilled though this room was just as crowded as the ballroom.

"I cannot allow anyone to have that sort of control over me. Once I trusted a man too much, and he abandoned me. This time, I shall do the choosing. All I require is a lover. I will take him, then leave him, when I see fit."

Men did not mind this sort of treatment. Colin Hawford had proved to Augusta that sex had nothing to do with love, and that romance was only a veil for selfishness.

Hawford had seemed bright and strong at first, taking root easily in her life. Then he had grown not like a bloom, but a thistle. Able to draw blood when she least expected it. Impossible to eradicate from memory, even two years later.

She had always known her fortune would attract men. Foolishly, she had not realized they would conquer her body and her heart in a quest for her hand. For coin.

"If I married, I would lose myself," she told Mr. Everett. "I cannot take that chance."

For a moment, she felt lost again. Clenching her toes within her slippers, she pressed her feet to the floor. *Steady, Augusta.* She had been a fool, but she was wiser now, and protected by a false name.

Assuming Mr. Everett held his tongue.

At her side, he was silent for a long moment—silent and still. Finally, he said, "It seems to me you are still trying to lose yourself, Mrs. Flowers."

"Not at all. The false name is a shield to make it easier to get what I want."

His expression said *If you say so* as clearly as if he'd spoken the words. "Well. I am sorry a man unworthy of your trust crossed your path in the past. You seem to have your victory strategy well in hand, though." He began to rise to his feet. "Mrs. Flowers, I shall leave you to your plans, as I must be on with mine. I wish you all the best of luck in your search for a lover."

Before she could think better of it, Augusta clutched at his arm. "You would do, Mr. Everett."

He froze halfway to a stand, eyes fixed on Augusta's gloved hand on his sleeve. "I would do?" Dropping into his chair again, he added, "I presume you mean as a lover?"

"Yes."

He lifted his chin, looking down his high-bridged nose at her. "Because I am convenient? Or because I am entirely unworthy of marriage?"

His tone froze her fingers, and she withdrew her hand to her lap. "Because"—she raised her own chin—"you bathe regularly and are not bad-looking. As I mentioned previously."

"I may swoon."

"And also you know the truth about what I want. And why." Damnation, her throat was dry. She forced herself to hold his gaze. "It was not easy to tell you, but I'm glad I did."

His dark brown eyes looked into her lighter ones, unsettling yet thoughtful. When, after a tense pause, he relaxed against the back of his chair, the scent of sandalwood teased Augusta again.

"You honor me." For the first time, he sounded sincere. "But I cannot do as you ask."

"No matter how much I may—want that?" She stumbled over the words.

Everett gave a harsh laugh. "Worse yet. No matter how much *I* may want that."

"But if you and I both—"

"It's not a matter of desire, but decency." He pressed at his temple with the heel of his hand. "My own background has made me painfully aware of the importance of a man's character. As I know you to be a maiden rather than a widow, I cannot be a part of your ruin."

But I am already ruined. And not only in the way society might suspect. No, her ruin came from within, from the spiraling thoughts in which she so often became entangled.

"It's not ruin if I seek it," she said numbly.

"My apologies; that was a poor choice of words. I cannot share in your 'victory,' as you call it. As I possess little beyond my pretense to honor, I beg you, do not ask me to give it up. I may not be able to refuse you a second time."

"I see." In her lap, she laced her fingers bloodlessly tight, so she would have something to hold fast to. There was nothing left outside herself to cling to, though hundreds of people were less than a cry away.

A gray-gloved hand patted her forearm, once, twice, and then it rested there. "Ah, my dear fake widow. I don't know if you *do* see. I am the most damnably proud fellow you can imagine."

Where his hand touched her, a bit of warmth spread into her skin. She looked at the hand, wary, as though it might flee.

It did not, and Everett added, "Damnably proud. Why, when I arrived in Bath a few days ago, I neglected to call upon the master of ceremonies so that he might appraise me."

So mischievous and conspiratorial was his smile, Augusta was not prepared for it. She was beginning to feel warmer yet, warm all over, and the feeling flustered her. Under his palm, within her own glove, the skin of her forearm tingled. Somehow she replied in a sensible manner: "With so many strangers mixing in this town, the master of ceremonies must vouch for their reputations."

"A logical statement. But I did not choose to solicit the good opinion of a man I do not know, simply so he could make that good opinion known to other people with whom I am not acquainted. Thus am I served for my pride. I cannot conduct my business if no one will speak to me." Lifting his hand from her arm, he scrubbed it over his face. "I have paid half a guinea for the privilege of walking about a crowded ballroom in relative solitude. Except for your company, my dear fake widow. But that was only because you knew me already."

Augusta folded her arms, trying to preserve the warmth he'd imparted. "Mr. Everett, you must stop calling me *my dear fake widow.* The mockery is entirely too obvious for me to ignore."

"Ought I to refer to you as Miss Meredith, then?"

"No. If someone overheard you, my secret would be out. You can't call me that either."

"What shall I call you, then?"

"Augusta, I suppose." At his arched eyebrow, she explained, "It's the only name I've got left."

"No middle name that's less terrifying and

Roman-sounding?" When she shook her head, feeling a smile tug at her lips, he said, "*Augusta* it is, then. Thank you."

"Won't you say I can call you Josiah in return? We can tell everyone we're distant cousins if you like, so they won't wonder at it."

"God, no." She must have looked affronted, for he explained, "That is, 'God, no' to calling me Josiah. It's never suited me. Much too serious. You may call me Joss."

"Joss." She tested it out.

He nodded.

She nodded back. It felt…good. As though the window separating her from the world had opened, just a crack.

"We mustn't be cousins, though," he added. "I've already got one of those, and one cousin like Sutcliffe is more than enough."

How odd; she had thought Lord Sutcliffe extremely pleasant when she met the baron once in London. "Old friends, then?"

"I have far too few of those, especially in Bath. Everyone would guess it to be false."

Augusta considered. "You made a jest while we danced that your reputation was in my hands. What if that were so?"

"It *is* so. I said so."

She rolled her eyes. "You made a joke, but I speak in seriousness. You say you have some business to conduct. That is vague, but I assure you, I know a great deal about business. And because I am known to be Lady Tallant's guest—and because I paid my respects to the master of ceremonies—I can catch the ear of half the men in Bath."

"Only half? How sad. Your popularity must be declining."

He echoed her words of earlier, and she was tempted to put out her tongue at him.

"You forget, my dear—ah, Augusta," he corrected himself. "I have the most damnable pride. I do not care to be beholden to anyone."

"Oh, but you wouldn't be," she explained in a rush. "It would be in exchange for you keeping the secret of my true name. Not a favor at all; just a bargain."

He watched her narrowly from the corner of his eye. "Go on."

"I could help you with your business. You could help me find a lover." She fumbled for words. "Men won't lie to Mrs. Flowers about business matters, because they'll assume she won't understand. And men will not lie to Mr. Everett about what they really think about women. If any people we encounter are dishonest or dreadful, each of us can tell the other."

"You trust me to toss you into the bed of someone you hardly know?"

"You mistake the matter. I simply ask you to share any relevant information you learn. If there is to be any throwing of my person into a bed, I shall do it."

He blinked. "Had I to guess what, of all the sentences in the world, you might utter next, I confess that is not the sentence I would have selected."

"Ah. So I surprise you?"

"My dear fake widow—I mean, Augusta—after years in the employment of Lord Sutcliffe, it takes a great deal to surprise me." He raised his brows. "But yes, you do."

"And you surprise me, Joss. No, *don't* say I honor you, because I'm not sure I do. Though I do think you're unusual."

"You are right about that." Leaning his head against the wall, he looked up at the great crystal chandelier in the center of the ceiling. "I wonder how many of those crystals and candles would equal my annual salary."

"I…ah." Some reply seemed necessary, but Augusta had no idea what it might be. She was unaccustomed to thinking in terms of *salary* or *how many*. With a fortune as vast as hers, sums were meaningless. One simply bought and owned.

"Very well, Augusta. I shall tell you my business." He opened his eyes again, leaving his gaze fixed upon the tiny relentless suns of the chandelier. "Someone in Bath possesses information he ought not. For this information, he requires payment."

She understood at once. "You're being blackmailed."

"Not I, but my employer. I cannot be specific about the reason; you must see that."

Curiosity burned within her, but she managed to sound calm. "Of course."

"My employer has insufficient funds to pay off the blackmailer. To raise the money, I must sell an interest in the coal lands he owns in northern Somersetshire. Bath's foundries need fuel, so he hopes I shall find a buyer here. And I retain the fantasy that I shall find the blackmailer, somehow, and make such a payment unnecessary."

"I had no idea men of business handled such tasks."

"They do not, usually. I believe I am unique. Perhaps because I'm family of a sort." His brow furrowed. "Or because Lord Sutcliffe is not a typical employer. I assure you, I also carry out the usual sort of interference in his correspondence and engagements."

Joss pushed himself to his feet, then extended a hand to Augusta. "I shall not tell your secret, you know. Your business in Bath is your own, whether you choose to help me or not."

"I—" She cut herself off, not quite believing him, not knowing how to say so. She had not been well served in the past for her faith in a handsome young man.

"Not certain how to reply? You could say, 'Thank you, Joss. How very kind you are.'"

She muttered something profane.

"Dear me. That did *not* sound like 'Thank you, Joss. How very—'"

"Stop." She stood facing him, letting the crowd in the Octagon Room flow past in all directions. "Joss. Mr. Everett. In Bath, as Mrs. Flowers, I cannot use Miss Meredith's money or knowledge. At least let me share the latter with you. I cannot trust you without some collateral."

"You don't believe I shall hold my tongue? That's all right. It's not the worst thing that has ever been believed of me." His mouth made the shape of a smile, but there was nothing of humor in it.

It was an expression she knew well: a mind trying to ignore the tangle of its own thoughts, a face trying to hide what was on its mind.

Surely she could do business with a man whose face

took on such an expression. She could trust him as much—or as little—as she trusted herself.

"Then we have a bargain?" Augusta folded her arms, cold again. "Joss."

"Yes, I suppose we do."

Three

THE ASSEMBLY ROOMS CLOSED AT THE EARLY HOUR OF eleven o'clock; even so, Augusta expected to find the rented house in Queen Square all but bedded down for the night. Lady Tallant, Augusta's hostess and friend, had been instructed by physicians in both London and Bath to take a great deal of rest.

Lady Tallant rarely did as ordered.

Thus, when Augusta bade the servants close up the house for the night, then tiptoed up the stairs to her bedchamber—*damn*, she had forgotten that the third step creaked—she found the young countess stretched out on a settee, pretending to read.

"Lady Tallant. Emily." Augusta stopped short, then glanced around to make certain she had entered the correct room of the rented house. Yes, this was her chamber: dark brown wallpaper printed with trellises, and an equally dark flowered carpet stretching across the floor. Emily's room was done in shades of blue. "You ought to be asleep; you should not have waited up for me. Or did I wake you when I returned home?"

"Of course you didn't wake me." Without even

glancing at her book, the countess shut it and let it fall to the carpet with a muffled thump. "In London, this is practically midafternoon. I should be finishing my tea right now and thinking about which dress I'd like to wear for dinner."

Augusta said nothing. She simply raised an eyebrow, a trick she'd recently seen Joss Everett put to good use.

"You're trying to intimidate me. It can't be done, I'm sorry to tell you." Emily subsided against the settee, clutching her peach-colored dressing gown more tightly around her form. The lamplight gilded her brown hair and hid the too-pale cast of her complexion, though there was no disguising the shadows under her eyes. "I'm a countess and an invalid, and therefore, I can do whatever I wish. Besides, this was your first Bath assembly and I must hear all about it."

"You'll go to bed right away afterward?"

"I will if what you tell me is boring. If it's extremely boring, maybe I'll go to sleep right here."

Augusta relented with a smile and seated herself in a slipper chair facing Lady Tallant. About five years Augusta's senior, the countess had befriended her in London the previous season. Their polite chatter at a ball had turned into an invitation to call, and another, and another. That had been around the same time Augusta had first met Josiah Everett. Joss. A man of nicknames and unreadable, dark eyes and acid humor.

A man of kind hands and unexpected honor.

Augusta cleared her throat. "The rooms were crowded. I joined in several country dances."

Emily faked a snore.

"And," Augusta added, "I met an acquaintance of ours."

Emily's green eyes grew wide. "Indeed? Was it a handsome male bachelor sort of acquaintance?"

"Not exactly." The fire had been built high for Emily's comfort; Augusta stretched her slippered feet toward it with feigned nonchalance. "I mean—yes, he was a bachelor male. And some might think him handsome, too. Mr. Josiah Everett."

"*Some* might think him handsome? I suppose some might, at that. You offer no opinion on the matter, I note." Emily's lips pressed together with suspicious humor. "He has black hair, which is a point in his favor."

Emily's husband, Lord Tallant, was also dark-haired. Their marriage was a happy one, though the earl and the couple's two young sons had remained in London during Emily's convalescence.

Shrewd eyes met Augusta's. "And did he have the good sense to dance with you?"

"Yes, but only because I forced him to. And that was only because he was at hand when I needed not to dance with someone else."

"So neither of you wanted to dance together, yet you accomplished the matter all the same. Well done, my dear." Emily beamed, and the shadows under her eyes seemed less dark for a moment. "Mr. Everett enjoys a bit of intellectual sparring, if I recall correctly."

"About that." Augusta began tugging at the fingertips of her gloves. "I have a confession to make."

Emily raised herself to one elbow. "That you're pretending to be a widow named Mrs. Flowers? Or is there something else you wish to confess?"

A glove shook free and fluttered to the floor. "Uh. I. Yes, that's—that's basically all."

"Basically all," Emily repeated. "All right. I can be satisfied with that."

"How did you know?"

The countess gave an airy wave. "I bestirred myself to the Pump Room this morning to try the famous mineral water and thought I'd sign the guest book while I was there. The master of ceremonies informed me that my young friend had already seen to the matter and showed me the entry." She frowned. "The water is quite nasty, by the by. It looks like old milk and smells like old eggs. I must assume something so foul is doing my health some good."

"Yes," Augusta said vaguely. Anything she said might be too much, now that Emily knew Augusta had taken advantage of the countess's benevolence.

"Shall I ask why you are passing under a false name?" Emily's light eyes caught Augusta's for just a moment before Augusta bent, scrabbling for her fallen glove. *Coward.* "No, I shan't press you. We all need to flee ourselves sometimes. Though if you wish to tell me what has caused your flight, I shall be glad to hear it."

The second unexpected kindness of the evening, following Joss Everett's insistence that he would keep her secret. Which was, apparently, not nearly so much of a secret as it ought to have been.

Now, and many a time before, the countess would have been within her rights to cut Augusta's acquaintance. But Emily's goodwill was unstinting.

"Thank you, ma'am. I suppose I did need to flee myself, and becoming a widow seemed as good a way as any to do that." Augusta straightened, glove in hand, and blurted, "Do you ever regret marrying Lord Tallant?"

The young countess leaned back against the settee again, her gaze drifting to the plaster roundel on the ceiling, then to the fireplace. "I don't think," she began slowly, "there's an honest woman alive who doesn't sometimes regret her marriage. Human beings can be so irritating, and when both spouses are irritating at once—well." She smiled. "But I am fortunate not to be troubled, as so many are, by financial worries or by mistrust of my husband. So the irritating moments pass, and we are still married, and I am glad of it. The permanence of marriage is one of its finest qualities, if one is married to a good man."

And if one was not...marrying a bad man would make a prison of each day. How could a woman ever know? A man could fake a smile indefinitely, unless some accident forced him to show his true face.

It was better to leave marriage to women with less money and more power. A false widowhood was quite enough for Augusta.

"Ought I to worry about you? Are you troubled by regrets?" Emily's voice was quiet.

"No more than usual." Augusta made herself smile, meeting her friend's eye. A quick image of Joss flashed into her mind, how he had appeared regretful as he declined her offer. She was unsuited to a dishonorable liaison, he thought.

Yet once Colin Hawford had thought her unsuited to an honorable one. So really, she was suited for... nothing. Always, she had been in between. Caught between trade and society, between the life she'd been born to and the one her parents wanted her to have.

We all need to flee ourselves sometimes, said Emily. Yet Joss had insisted there was no way to do so; that Augusta was still herself, no matter how she might pretend to be a merry widow. And if he was right, there was nowhere she could go to get away. No name she might adopt that would let her be free.

Enough. Enough. She had dwelled on this enough for today.

"Shall I read to you, Emily?" she offered, noticing the weariness that tugged at the countess's lids.

"That would be lovely," her friend replied, shutting her eyes.

Augusta rose, picked up the volume Emily had dropped, and settled herself on the floor next to the settee. "It's William Blake. Is that all right?"

Emily nodded, a sliver of movement. "Read 'Infant Joy.'"

Augusta turned the pages until she found the correct poem. This edition reproduced Blake's paintings, and the words were tucked within an illustration of a fire-red flower cradling a mother and infant, a haloed angel blessing them.

"*I have no name*," she read.

> "*I am but two days old.*
> *What shall I call thee?*
> *I happy am,*
> *Joy is my name.*
> *Sweet joy befall thee!*"

"Stop," said Emily. "Stop. Stop reading."

Augusta looked up from the small volume. Emily's eyes were still closed, but a tear had trickled beneath her lid, tracing the hollow of her cheek.

"I think I ought to go to bed." The countess's voice was choked and flat. "I shouldn't have waited up so late."

To repay her friend's kindness, Augusta refrained from saying *I told you so*. Instead, she helped Emily to rise to her feet; she pretended not to notice the second tear that followed the first, or the ones that came afterward.

Emily's much-wanted daughter had no name, had never drawn a breath. And just as Augusta had held Emily's hand after the terrible loss a month earlier, she held it again now, leading her down the corridor and settling Emily into her own night-blue room.

Augusta helped the countess climb the steps to the bed, then drew the counterpane up to her thin shoulders. "I'm here, Emily. If you wish to talk, I shall be glad to hear it."

The echo of Emily's own offer seemed to rouse the countess. "You know why I asked you to accompany me to Bath, Augusta?"

"Yes." Augusta sat on the edge of the bed. "You wanted company during your recovery."

A pause followed, though the room was too dark for Augusta to read her friend's expression. "I did want company. But were it only that, I could have traveled here with my husband and sons. Though I now I miss them terribly, I never considered bringing them along."

"Why is that?"

"Because they remind me of what I've lost." Emily raised herself onto her elbows and stared at the glowing coal fire. "Of all the friends I could have invited, you were the one whose companionship I wanted. Because you understand what loss means."

Oh. "Yes," Augusta said again. Though this fire, like the one in her own room, was built up high, her fingers had gone numb. Her feet, her toes. The stone of her heart.

"You know," Emily said, "how loss can make a person feel mad. Or how it can show her sides of herself she never knew she possessed."

Augusta felt Emily's words not as a reprimand, but as a plea for understanding. "Loss can make a person reckless."

Loss could slash a person with a grief so deep, she might throw away all the good she possessed and let it burn. Not caring. Not wanting to care. Not wanting to feel anything; willing to pursue any promise of oblivion.

Yet that promise, along with so many others, had been broken. Oblivion had never yet been hers.

"You should go to sleep now," Augusta said, and Emily lay down again without a word of argument.

Simply revealing *what* brought them here had been difficult enough. Neither of them was ready to talk about *why* yet, or *how* they would move beyond this house, this time away from the world they knew.

As Augusta crept from the room and back down the silent corridor to her own chamber, the sardonic face of Joss Everett came to mind. He had named himself her ally, yet he had picked at her character.

Taunted her, even. Why? What did it serve? Maybe he felt she had taunted him first by implying he wasn't trustworthy.

She should have told him that no one was trustworthy. No one but Lady Tallant. And once upon a time, Augusta's parents, lost so suddenly.

Certainly not Augusta herself.

Handsome and unpredictable as he was, the idea of taking Joss Everett as a lover had a sort of brute appeal. But it terrified Augusta as much as it enticed her. He would not be satisfied to take her body and leave the rest of her alone.

It was better that he had said no. For his sake…and for hers.

৩৩

He couldn't believe he had declined Augusta Meredith's offer.

Joss regarded himself in the cracked glass over his battered trunk, tugging his cravat free with careful fingers. He hadn't the linens to spare for spoiled neckcloths, nor the coin for unnecessary starching and laundering. As deliberately as he had knotted the cloth earlier, so did he now coax free its folds and lay it flat.

His lodging was like his dress: outwardly adequate, secretly scrimping. He had taken a room on respectable Trim Street—but in the top story of the building, a narrow chamber to the side of the house. The walls and ceiling sloped beneath the mansard roof, and the plaster walls were unpapered, the floor of bare wood. Mildew had made a spot on the ceiling, and the room smelled faintly of damp during the near-ceaseless drizzle. Had this building belonged to a single family, Joss's room would be in the servants' quarters.

Well. That was what he was, wasn't he? For now. Maybe not for much longer, if he had his way.

If he had his way. He turned aside from the glass, disgusted with the blurred, cracked surface that made a horror of his face. Only too much would he like to have his way with Augusta Meredith. She wore costly bespoke silks as carelessly as other women might pin on a nosegay. She moved with determination, yet possessed a heartbreaking uncertainty. She was ripe for seduction; she *asked* to be seduced.

If he obliged her, though, she was the one who would suffer—either in the loss of reputation or the burden of an unwanted child. He could not take his pleasure only to leave suffering in its place.

That was, after all, how Joss had been knit into existence.

He crossed the room to his desk, wishing for more moonlight to leak into the lamplit attic space. So many letters for him to read; so many questions to answer. Yet instead of taking up his work at once, he shuffled aside the papers on his desk and found a thin octavo-sized ledger. The black leather binding was unstamped and plain, worn from decades of handling.

Why did he carry it about? Why did he bother to look at it? It was not as though he would find more enlightenment within its covers this evening than he had in the past.

Yet he flipped it open, skimming the curling Devanagari script of his grandmother's native Hindustani, the English translations his mother had later jotted in the page margins. Here and there was a spidery botanical drawing, the ink browned with age. He remembered some of these plants from his youth, when his mother still lived to tend them. Their names twisted and lilted over the tongue: *ghikumari*, which could soothe burns; *tindora*, the ivy gourd, which strengthened the blood and quieted palpitations. *Shikakai* and *reetha*, for cleansing hair. *Neem*, a tree too tall for the shelter of the glassed-in conservatory. Before a series of cold winters nipped it, its seed oil had been pressed for use in nearly every stillroom concoction, from drinkable tonics to skin creams to treatments for rheumatic joints.

And here was a drawing of *somalata*, a deceptively innocent-looking grass. It could ease the terrifying symptoms of asthma—or, as the present baron had discovered, it could stimulate the mind and body. Over the years, Sutcliffe had given over more and more of Sutcliffe Hall's conservatory to its cultivation, until it had edged out all other plants.

Decades before, when Joss's grandmother had the care of the conservatory, a much greater variety had grown. In her day, Jumanah, Lady Sutcliffe, had coaxed a small corner of India to flourish.

Apparently. Joss had never known her, for within a few years of her arrival in Somersetshire, the English winters had chilled her just as they had the *neem*. This small, handwritten book was all Joss had left of his grandmother, who had long ago stepped from the soil of Calcutta onto a boat alongside a cook, an *ayah*, and the English soldier she had wed in haste. She had served him as *bibi*; she now carried his child. His unexpected ascent to a barony required their marriage along with their swift journey to England. The future heir to the Sutcliffe barony—for did not all parents assume they would have a son?—must be born in wedlock.

In only one generation, though, their branch of the family tree snapped and fell. The hoped-for heir had been a girl—a daughter unprotected by settlements from a marriage contracted in haste, unshielded by a dowry. If her parents had lived, all might still have been well.

But they hadn't. And when their orphaned daughter Kitty met the worthless Jack Everett, scandal and ruin soon followed. Thanks to the forceful persuasion of her uncle, the father of the present baron, Everett had married her. Her son, Josiah, had not been born a bastard. That was the only selfless act Jack Everett had ever managed.

Cloaked and shielded in notes and coin, Augusta Meredith had no idea how vulnerable she was. How much she had to lose if she placed her trust in the wrong person.

No, Joss would have to watch her carefully. Another item to add to his list of *urgent, top secret, must do at once* tasks while in Bath. Where he had told Augusta *no*, someone else was sure to tell her *yes*.

People who had grown up with unstained birth and reputation could never comprehend how difficult a stain was to remove.

Shutting the book, Joss peered out the small window above the desk. The room overlooked a mews, and at the street level, watery moonlight revealed a boy hauling an empty Bath chair, likely ready to head home for the night.

Joss pried at the latch, opened the window, and called down to the boy in a hoarse whisper. "Will you deliver a note?"

With canny greed, the boy laid down his burden and agreed to a small fee. Squinting into his room—not much brighter than the street, as his lamp was turned low to save fuel—Joss located writing materials and scrawled a quick letter asking Augusta to meet him the following day. He folded it, sealed it, then twisted it around a coin and dropped it into the waiting hands of the boy three stories below.

"Do you know Lady Tallant's house?"

"Coo," said the boy. "Her what stays in Queen Square? The countess?"

"Indeed. That note is for her friend, Mrs. Flowers. And the coin—"

"Is for me. Right you are, gov'nor." With the admirable energy of the young, the boy tucked the note in a pocket and hoisted the handle of his chair again. And he was off, the echoes of their conversation still dying in the quiet street. The rattle of his chair wheels faded, leaving nothing behind except rows of houses with shuttered faces, their golden stone washed gray by the starless sky.

Tomorrow, if Augusta agreed to his request, Joss would meet her again. He would take her at her word: that she truly did trust him to sort through possible lovers for her, and that she could help him make the land deal that would free him for a new life.

He hoped she planned to be more forthright than he did.

Four

EIGHT O'CLOCK IN THE CURSED MORNING AND THE Pump Room was already crowded. An endless parade of Bath's denizens—the fashionable, the invalids, and the merely curious—passed before Joss on foot or in wheeled chairs.

The room was larger than any London ballroom he'd seen, nearly three stories in height and far longer than a cricket pitch. A wall of windows fronted the endless space, through which a weak and watery sun could be seen struggling to rise behind a misty rain. The surly weather could not keep these health seekers from their noxious-smelling mineral waters, though Joss thought they would receive much more benefit by keeping to their beds a few hours longer.

He certainly would have liked to do so. It was far too early to begin today's business, considering the previous day's work had not ended for Joss until hours past midnight. His errand in Bath didn't absolve him of his regular duties as Sutcliffe's employee. Though he'd told Augusta he managed the baron's correspondence and engagements, he also did a fair amount of soothing and currying, as though his cousin were a fractious horse. The comparison was especially apt considering how Sutcliffe had kicked over his traces recently.

Their requisite daily training was much more difficult at a distance, though Bath lay a scant eight miles from Sutcliffe Hall. Over the past few days, the baron had flooded Joss with frantic letters, desperate notes sent by mail and by express. Neatly block printed at first, then scrawled in a nearly illegible flood of slanted writing, the urgency leaping from the page.

> *Where are my favorite cuff links My brandy decanter is empty and I think the servants have been drinking from it Lady Sutcliffe wants more pin money What should I do if another of those threatening letters arrives When will you return to my house I need your advice*
> *Have you sold the land yet*

At least Sutcliffe managed to ask after Joss's real errand at some point. And at least he had franked all those letters so Joss wasn't responsible for paying the exorbitant postage.

Joss had learned to be grateful for life's small sanities.

Though this was easier at an hour later than *eight o'clock in the cursed morning*. He rubbed at gritty eyes, then again scanned the crowd for Augusta. "Mrs. Flowers" had replied in the affirmative to Joss's note the previous night, sending the same wiry urchin darting back through the streets with letter in hand and a demand for yet another coin. Joss had tossed the lad a shilling; too much by far, but by God, it felt like the first step toward freedom.

There. A flash of burnt-umber hair, vivid in the gray-chased morning gloom, peeped from beneath the edge of a bonnet. It must be she, for several men stopped to engage her in conversation. As each then continued on his way, his expression said that all was right with the world, for a pretty woman had passed the time of day with him.

Joss shouldered through the crowd making its lazy promenade about the room, stopping short before his quarry: Augusta, in a sedate printed gown beneath a warm brown pelisse. There was nothing about her clothing to draw notice, but her smile—that was extraordinary. Bright and sweet and cheeky, as though she found no greater pleasure than to stroll about a crowded room on a rainy morning, conversing with strangers.

She was not alone, he noted a moment later: Augusta pushed an iron-framed wheeled chair in which was seated Lady Tallant. Joss deepened his hasty bow. "Good morning to you both. My lady. Mrs.... ah, Augusta."

The countess looked a bit thin and weary, though her greeting was as warm as Joss remembered from past meetings. "Mr. Everett. Thank you for your kindness to our young friend last night at the assembly."

"It was my pleasure." Joss pasted on a devil-may-care grin. How much had Augusta revealed—of her own secrets, and his?

"The countess," said Augusta, "is aware of my widowhood."

"Such a tragic loss," agreed Lady Tallant, tugging a

tasseled shawl about her shoulders. "Poor Mr. Flowers, to be trampled by a hippopotamus."

Augusta choked. "I never said—"

"But you are young and lovely, my dear. I'm sure you'll marry again soon. Only take care to stay away from large mammals."

"I have been informed," said Joss, feeling a bit wicked, "that Mrs. Flowers has caught the eye of half the men in Bath. And as far as I know, there are no hippopotami—is it the Latin plural?—here to endanger them."

Augusta folded her arms, putting her delightful bosom on impressive display over a swoop of printed cotton bodice. "Are you two quite finished? Emily, you ought to take your mineral water."

The countess pulled a face. "The water tastes like rotten eggs and rust. I'd much rather stay here and tease you."

"I would be pleased to join you in such a noble task, my lady." Catching Augusta's eye, Joss mouthed *dockyard* and cast a significant glance at her person. Just to make those tawny eyes narrow. At once, she dropped clenched fists to her sides. Too bad.

Lady Tallant looked from Joss to Augusta with the sort of knowing smile that made perspiration break out between a man's shoulder blades. "Perhaps Mr. Everett can handle the task alone, at that. I do have a responsibility to my health." Waving off Joss's offered hand, she hoisted herself to her feet and began a slow, careful progress toward the marble fountain from which mineral waters were pumped and served.

"She looks well today," Augusta murmured, watching her friend walk away.

Joss had been thinking precisely the opposite, so he settled for a noncommittal noise.

Augusta steered the wheeled chair to a far wall of the room, waving off Joss's attempt to take its cumbersome weight from her. "You mayn't think Lady Tallant looks well if you have not seen her since last autumn. Since we have arrived, though, she has regained much of her spirit." Her features clouded, and she added, "Most of the time, that is."

"You are holding everyone's secrets," Joss said. "Your own, your friend's, and now mine."

"I suppose I am." She tugged at her pelisse, wrapping the gold-spangled brown more tightly around her gown and lovely figure. "I've never been permitted so much responsibility before."

Joss regretted the covering of the gown, but it was no more than he deserved for his earlier teasing. "And do you intend to use this responsibility for good or evil? I should have made this inquiry before entrusting you with my confidence."

Brandy-brown eyes met his. Held. "Are you never serious?"

"Rarely. Seriousness is a frustration and a liability in my position."

"How am I to know what you really think, then?"

"Must you know what I really think? I did not think that was essential among the fashionable. The opposite of honesty, in fact, is what makes high society run smoothly."

"That might be the case, but neither you nor I has been accepted into the bosom of society. If you cannot be truthful with me, then I can't help you. And you can't help me." She nodded in the direction of a lanky gentleman in conversation with the red-coated master of ceremonies. "If I'm on my own, perhaps I'll take that man as a lover. His legs look well enough. Or maybe I'll make a scandalous offer to the master of ceremonies. Or to one of the footmen at the next assembly."

"Augusta." Joss had no idea what to say next. The *ton* bantered and flirted; they never craved earnestness. Such was the world at whose edges he usually prowled.

"What does it matter with whom I make arrangements?" She asked. "If it makes no difference to me, it needn't to anyone else." Though her voice was unsteady, her features were serene. Somehow, she even managed to keep a little smile on her lips.

"Augusta." Joss reached out, touching her under the chin. He didn't turn her face toward him; he wondered whether she would turn on her own.

She breathed more quickly, but let the moment pull out long and slow as taffy. Her sweet, flowery scent caught at him, and the voices ringing against the stretching walls and ceiling of the marble room seemed a bit less overwhelming to his tired ears.

He shouldn't have declined her offer, gracelessly though it had been made. *You would do.* It was better by far than much of what he had heard in his life. *Mongrel*, said the village children who lived near Sutcliffe House. From his own relatives: *You're lucky we took you in. Be grateful for what you're given.*

Compared to that, *you would do* was practically a benediction. Even now, maybe, he could tell her

Yes—yes, take me, and I will take you. I'll be whatever you want in a man.

But if he did that, he would be trapped by everything he sought to escape. He would be nothing *he* wanted.

"Augusta," he said once more, quiet as a whisper. "I'm sorry. And it does matter to me."

Her eyes searched him, a flicker of lashes up and down. As she looked up at him, her jaw was set. Was that dismissal he read in her features?

It was nothing new. Nothing he hadn't seen or heard from Sutcliffe time and again.

And just as always when faced with dismissal, he smiled to show how little it affected him.

A heavy pause followed; then, to Joss's surprise, Augusta smiled back. A real smile, one that made her eyes crinkle and caused the most adorable little crease to cross the bridge of her nose.

Ahem. Not an adorable crease. An ordinary crease, of the same sort that fat old men got when they frowned at a newspaper.

Right.

Then she lifted a hand to catch his, pressing it away from her chin. "So you *can* be serious."

"When the moment requires it." He sighed.

"The moment did, most definitely, require it." As though dusting herself off, she brushed his gloved fingers from hers. "I agreed to meet you at this time and place, because this is when everyone in Bath comes to the Pump Room. Here, we are sure to find the people we seek."

"You to find your lover, and me—"

"I've been thinking about that," she said, as calmly as

though it were quite usual for a man and woman who hardly knew each other to discuss paramours in public. "Your cousin wishes you to raise money by selling land or coal or some such thing. But if he is truly being black-mailed, there's no guarantee another demand for money won't come. What would he do if that happened?"

If that happened…Joss wouldn't give a damn, because he would be free from the quagmire of Sutcliffe's life. "I cannot prepare for that eventuality, unless you think the blackmailer can be located and somehow be persuaded to stop. Which would be delightful, but blackmail-ers are rarely noted for their charitable impulses."

"They are not, that's true." Rising to her tiptoes, she whispered in his ear. "But there are many ways to persuade people without appealing to their better natures. All we need do is find the right method."

"*We?*" Joss shook his head slightly to dispel the tickling sensation left in his ear by her breath. "No, impossible. You cannot become involved in Sutcliffe's private affairs. I may have said you held everyone's secrets, but Augusta, I didn't mean it."

"I know you didn't. You weren't being serious at that time." With a smile that looked like bared teeth, she added, "But you're serious now, and I am too. We both want something far too much for wisdom. And so we need to help each other, or we'll both end by making a terrible mistake."

◈

Augusta blew out an impatient breath, waiting for Joss to do something besides blink down at her. If he ever would.

This was a man who hadn't wanted to dance with her. Hadn't wanted to become her lover. Hadn't wanted to do anything but satisfy his mild curiosity about her false name, then continue on his merry way. Really, he could not have been much clearer about his lack of interest.

Until he sent her a note last night, inviting her to meet him again. He might not have wanted to start the game, but for a short while at least, he seemed willing to play along.

"What sort of mistake are we in danger of making?" he said carefully.

Carefully, indeed. Because it was not a game at all, was it? She had no idea what was at stake for him, but it was certainly more than a job.

"Everyone in Bath comes from somewhere else," she replied. "We might do and say and be whatever we need to, free of London. If we're fortunate, we'll become what we want to. If we're not…"

"We'll be trapped. Again." He pressed at his temples. "Yes. All right. Clearly you have something in mind, so please oblige me by telling me what that is. As long as it's not some sort of hen-witted espionage caper."

Augusta sniffed. "I am never hen-witted. And I do not caper."

One of his eyebrows shot up.

"*And*," she added, "this is not a matter of espionage. It is a matter of business. I have made a list." Tugging a folded slip of paper from the inner wrist of her glove, she handed it to him. "Last night, I thought of three men whom you might approach about the sale of coal lands. And if you wish instead to find and throttle your cousin's blackmailer, I have listed the name of a man who can hunt that information."

"Quite an assortment." His eyes flicked over the list.

"That last man I mentioned has only just arrived in Bath. I had the news from the boy who ran our messages back and forth," she explained. "I had to pay him another half crown for the privilege of learning whom he had seen lodged in the Royal Crescent."

"A half crown? Highway robbery."

A half crown meant nothing to Augusta, whose reticule was full of coin, whose fortune grew monthly under the guardianship of doting trustees. So she only smiled and watched him read the names—once, twice, again—deciding.

Deep in thought, he appeared much less English. He did not look sideways to see her reaction as he read, did not puff out his chest or square his shoulders to impress her as she waited. He lacked the *beau monde*'s usual jittery joviality—or perhaps it would be better to say that he possessed a stillness entirely foreign to most men Augusta knew. His arched brows knit, and the crease between them carved his profile into something starker—a high forehead and high-bridged nose, full lips, and a stern chin.

And smoky dark and sweet, the scent of sandalwood that made her want to draw closer, to tuck her head into the line of his shoulder and breathe in deeply. A longing caught her, so sudden and enticing that she had to step away lest her body betray her by swaying too close.

No. He wasn't the man she needed. She needed someone pliant and agreeable and ultimately disposable.

He looked up from the paper. "I am impressed by this list, Augusta. How do you come to know of these men?"

"I read the guest book and saw that they were in Bath. I've been avoiding them all week so they wouldn't see me and call me by my real name."

Refolding the paper, he fixed her with a look. "That is not what I meant. How do you happen to be acquainted with them?"

"Oh. I've always known them." She tucked a strand of hair behind her bonnet ribbon, fumbling for an explanation. "They are powerful men of business. And I'm Meredith Beauty, or all that's left of it."

Dark eyes flicked over her figure; his mouth curved with humor. "It's nice to meet a woman who's confident in her appeal."

She waved a hand, hating that her cheeks flushed. A blushing redhead was a tower of clashing color. "I'm talking of cosmetics and lotions and perfumes, not myself. My father named the company for himself. As he built it, and our fortune, I came to know many of the men he knows. Knew." She shuddered away the gray sense of loss. "I was the only child of my parents. All the knowledge they had to impart, they tipped into my head."

"A beautiful vessel for Meredith Beauty."

"Stop that. You told me you'd be serious. I'm just trying to explain an answer to a question *you* asked."

Composing his features, he nodded. "I beg your pardon. It's rather a habit of mine."

"Mocking someone while appearing to give compliments? Yes, I know it's a habit, and it's an unsettling one."

"Is it really? And yet I am attempting to smooth along our conversation. Unfortunately, my dear make-believe widow, the course of conversation never does run smoothly with you."

"Maybe because we know a bit too much about one another for that sort of playacting."

"Maybe." He took a half step toward her, erasing the distance she had placed between them, and a strange expression crossed his face. Something wistful or weary or angry, but which, she couldn't tell. "Or maybe we don't know enough. And as we are just coming to know one another, every word carries a great deal of weight."

Unpredictable man—yet so far, with words alone, she had kept him at a safe distance. Now as he drew closer, she stepped back again, remembering the curious crowds around them. At an arm's length away, that odd expression of his tugged at her less deeply, and she could no longer distinguish his scent of sandalwood.

Which was good.

Not that sandalwood was anything to become bothered about, or eager or curious. It was nothing but an aromatic oil distilled from a tree. There was nothing to Joss's credit about choosing it. One might just as well compliment Augusta for possessing silk gowns, when the silkworms and dressmakers had done all the hard work of creating her clothing.

Yet she wondered why he had chosen sandalwood. How he had come by it. The heiress to Meredith Beauty couldn't help but notice such a scent.

He must have noticed her step backward or some play of emotions over her face in turn. "What is the matter, fidgeting woman? You do not say so, but I think I must owe you a list."

"A list?" She had no idea what he meant.

"A *list*, yes. A list of potential lovers in exchange for your list of sources. Four possibilities would be a fair exchange for the four names you provided, though it seems excessive, does it not? Even for a widow, I mean. Surely one name would do."

Another blush tainted her cheeks. "You told me you'd be serious. We just discussed this."

"I *am* being serious. I do seriously believe that you ought not to take four lovers."

"Speak more quietly, please." Myriad conversations filled the Pump Room, but one never knew whose ears would catch an enticing overheard snippet like *four lovers*. "And I was never considering such an action."

"It would be more than one action. It would be at least four."

A laugh and a gasp fought their way from her throat together, and the result was—alas—a splutter. Augusta pressed her lips together, as though that could undo the sound.

Joss grinned, lifting his hands in supplication. "All right, I wasn't being *entirely* serious. You must give me time to identify the perfect fellow for you, my dear fake widow. I haven't yet spoken to many people in Bath."

"Let us remedy that right now. I'll fetch Lady Tallant, so the three of us can go make our obeisance to the master of ceremonies. Then all of Bath society will see how much we adore your company."

"Oh? And how much is that, precisely?" she heard

him ask, but she was already flouncing away and pretended not to hear.

Because this was only a matter of business.

And because she could not reply when she did not know the answer herself.

Five

"I THINK," SAID EMILY, HANDING A CUP OF TEA TO Augusta, "that this morning's visit to the Pump Room went rather well."

"Hmm." Augusta set the saucer aside, pressing her fingertips to the heat of the fragile china cup. Though the yellow-papered drawing room of the Queen Square house was bright and compact, not even a leaping coal fire could banish the feeling of cold. The early March chill crept in through every seam in the house: prying at window frames and doorways, whistling down chimneys. This winter was much milder than last year, but the drizzle! My God. Augusta hadn't felt warm since 1815.

Except in the Upper Rooms the previous night.

"And sometime this afternoon," Emily continued as she poured out strong black tea for herself, "Mr. Everett has promised to pay a call on us. On you, I rather think."

"You are sounding much like your old self," Augusta observed. "Something is raising your spirits. Is it the mineral waters or the interference in my affairs?"

Emily adopted an expression of angelic innocence, and she sat straighter in her button-backed slipper chair. "I simply take an interest in what's going on in my house." She coughed with great dramatic force. "Though at the moment I am feeling a bit ill. I might have to leave you alone with him when he calls. As an invalid, I need my rest, you know."

"So much coughing. A new symptom? I was not aware you were suffering from a lung ailment."

Over the rim of her teacup, Emily shot Augusta a mischievous look. "It's whatever type of ailment I need it to be. If my health is going to render my life more difficult, it might as well render it more entertaining too."

Augusta smiled. "By making sport of me?"

"Of course. That's the main benefit of being an invalid. One may get away with all sorts of inconsiderate acts." A thump sounded from below, and Emily set down her teacup at once. "Now if you'll pardon me, I find myself exhausted."

"That wasn't the door knocker. It sounded like a servant tripping over furniture."

"Oh. In that case, I feel fine. For a little while longer." Emily settled against the tawny fabric of her chair, looking at Augusta expectantly across the tea table. "Meddling does improve my spirits, at that. It makes me feel as though there's a bit of the old me left."

"You are still you, Emily." The words tripped from Augusta's tongue easily; she must have heard them recently.

Oh. Yes. From Joss Everett.

At the time, she'd thought he was mocking her

for her false identity. But those same words, spoken to Emily, seemed to give comfort. The countess's lips curved. "Sometimes I almost feel that I am. I must work on freeing that old Emily and making her stronger."

"Shall you feed yourself beef tea? Beefsteak? Er… beef…pudding? Beef ice?"

"I see you attended to the doctor's instructions about nourishing foods. But if you ever present me with a beef ice, you will find yourself wearing it." Too quickly, Emily's smile faded.

Always, it seemed, the memory of loss lurked, ever ready to pounce, to claw at one's heart, to drain one of strength. One could hope to leash it for a short while with laughter and distraction, but not even these were infallible.

Augusta scooted to the edge of her armchair, setting her cup on the tea tray. "It's easier during the day, isn't it?"

"Pretending? Or forgetting?" Emily pulled in a shuddery breath. "Both, you mean. Both."

"Yes. Both." Without the teacup bleeding warmth, Augusta's fingers felt a little numb. "Maybe that's why people rise so early in Bath. Not because a morning bath is particularly healthful, but—"

"Because they want to make the night end," Emily finished. "Yes. I thought I could get away from the grief. I thought if I just left London, if I came somewhere new, I would leave it behind."

"*But you are still you,*" Augusta murmured again. The mouth she imagined speaking the words was creased with bitter humor; the dark eyes wry.

Everyone wanted to flee something. That was why

they ended up in Bath—a city for those who needed
to become stronger.

Emily had apparently taken Augusta's quiet words
as a reply. "What can we do about it, then?" A hint of
shadow flitted across her face.

"About being ourselves?" Augusta laughed, quick
and mirthless. "I've no idea. I have no advice to give."

"Rubbish. You advised Mr. Everett this morning,
did you not?"

This laugh came a little more naturally. "I did, so
that might be our answer. I shall throw myself into
the world of business, and you shall pry into my
private affairs."

Emily's lips twitched. "I am equal to that task."

"Our problems are solved, then. I am delighted to
hear it."

"But you'll have to make it worth my while to pry,
Augusta. Do something quite entertaining, now that
you're pretending to be a widow. Cause a scandal.
Become the talk of Bath."

"If I do that, no prying into my affairs will be
required," Augusta said lightly. "You would be very
bored if I became the talk of Bath. I must keep my
scandals quiet, so that you may have a challenge to
occupy you."

Surely taking a lover would serve the purpose.
Someone attractive but bland, whom she could make
use of and then drop. Someone no one would know
of except her.

And the man in question, of course.

And maybe Emily, if the countess's bloodhound-
like gift for sniffing out secrets did not fail her. But

Emily had forgiven Augusta's past trespasses; maybe she would also pardon those yet to come.

"So is Mr. Everett calling on you this afternoon for business or for scandal?" Emily asked. "I dearly hope it is the latter."

At the thought of seeing Joss again so soon, excitement pulsed, unexpected, in her veins. "I am sorry to disappoint any hope, especially a dear one. But this is only a call of business."

"But he is Lord Sutcliffe's man of business. How can he work for you too? No, he must be calling for some dark and delicious purpose. You cannot deceive me. Every time you try to keep a secret, you turn pink as a berry, or you avoid looking at me."

"Mr. Everett does not work *for* me." Augusta devoted careful scrutiny to a plate of assorted biscuits, then pushed it across the tea table in Emily's direction. "He is working *with* me. On something for Lord Sutcliffe. That he needs help with."

"How kind of you to be so helpful to an acquaintance. And you ask nothing in return?" Emily picked up a macaroon and crumbled the edge. "That is selfless indeed. Selfless to an unusual degree, or so it seems to me. But perhaps this is the sort of thing Mrs. Flowers enjoys."

Augusta's mouth opened, then decided simply to close again without speaking.

"Did I say pink? I ought to have said red, because you have turned the most lovely shade," Emily observed. "I am trying to decide if it is more like a ruby or a garnet."

"Eat your macaroon," Augusta managed.

Emily reached out her hand, and before Augusta realized what the countess was doing, she found the macaroon pressed into her own palm. "You eat it instead, Augusta. Sweeten your speech before your caller arrives."

With a shuddery sigh, Emily rose to her feet. When Augusta made to follow, she said, "No, no, don't stand, Mrs. Flowers. I really do need a bit of rest, but you must stay here to welcome our caller."

"I—you—but—"

The countess did not deign to respond to this incoherence. Instead, she made her way to the doorway of the room, her step a bit quicker than it had been this morning. The rest—and beefsteak, maybe—were improving her health, even if she had not yet recovered peace of mind.

At the doorway, Emily turned back. Her brow puckered, she asked, "Is this all right with you, to be alone when Mr. Everett calls? I could send a maid to keep you company. You mustn't do anything you don't like."

"I won't." Augusta was sure the ruby or possibly garnet shade of her cheeks had not ebbed. "No maid will be necessary, but thank you."

"All right." Emily relaxed, tossing a grin over her shoulder. "Then I expect a full report later, whether scandal or business. As selfless as you are, you cannot deny the request of an invalid, can you?"

❦

So many servants. This rented house in Queen Square was better staffed than Sutcliffe's country estate.

Fewer stairs than Joss expected, though. He had already grown used to climbing to the topmost story of the Trim Street house to reach his rented room; now it seemed odd to be shown up by a servant to a drawing room at the first turn of the staircase. The treads were still carpeted here, the newel an elaborately turned spiral. This was the public part of the house, and Joss was shown into the drawing room like an honored guest, instead of being shuttled away to the servants' quarters as he was at Sutcliffe Hall.

The first thing he noticed when the door opened was the warmth of the room; no skimping on coal in this household. Adding to the impression of cozy cheer was the furniture, all carved wood and soft, ruddy-colored upholstery. Between two slipper chairs, a burnished tea table bore a laden tray and a plate heaped with biscuits.

And behind that table stood Augusta Meredith, wearing a blush along with her russet-colored silk afternoon dress. Her every garment seemed the shade and shape of luxury, making her hair glow like new bronze.

Joss had polished his boots before walking the distance between their lodgings, but he realized now he ought also to have changed his neckcloth. Or his waistcoat. Being in the presence of effortless wealth made him ill at ease.

Then he realized something else, something that struck him as odd: Augusta was alone in the room.

As the drawing room door shut behind him, Joss looked around. "Is your friend Lady Tallant unwell? Come now, you cannot meet with me alone. It's not proper."

She shrugged, though her blush did not fade. "The countess is resting. And I'm a widow, am I not? What could you possibly do to me that hasn't been done before?"

"You don't really want me to answer that question, do you?" He held her eye until she smiled.

"Merely a figure of speech." Seating herself, she added, "What a strange sense of honor you have. You mock me quite frankly, yet you take nothing from me but my sense of control over our conversation."

"And a list of four names," he added, taking a seat in the chair facing hers. "I took those from you quite gladly."

Already he knew them by heart.

Ebenezer Paynter. Businessman. Hoards land in the southern portion of England.

George Duffy. Agent for Stothert and Pitt foundry. Would be interested in nearby coal as fuel.

Lord Whittingham. Viscount with a considerable fortune. Speculates wildly.

Lord Chatfield. Marquess. Knows things.

"And how," asked Augusta, "did your conversation with Paynter proceed this morning? I assume you called to discuss that?"

She and Lady Tallant had been present when Joss made his apologetic bow to the master of ceremonies. Augusta—no, Mrs. Flowers—had giggled through their introduction, employing flirtation enough to distract an army. The master of ceremonies had been no match for the combination of Lady Tallant's genial manners and Mrs. Flowers's dockyard. Within a few minutes, Joss's trespass was excused and an introduction to Paynter secured.

Then the women had slipped away before there was any chance Paynter could spot Mrs. Flowers. Probably for the best, because—"He's a canny man," Joss replied. "I think the conversation proceeded exactly as he wanted it to."

Which had not been to Joss's advantage, or to the benefit of his task for Sutcliffe.

In this warm, comfortable room, it was difficult to remember the price of honor—or the cost of it. Cost and price were of no concern to women whose rented drawing room had a marble chimneypiece and a coffered ceiling. Who provided a half-dozen types of biscuits to a lone afternoon caller. Who tossed more coal into a single fire than Joss permitted himself in a week.

Though it was much larger than his rented room, the bright walls of this drawing room pressed in upon him.

On impulse, Joss stood. "I can think better in the open air. Will you walk out with me so we might continue our conversation? If, that is, Mrs. Flowers is allowed to leave the house."

She rose to her feet at once. "Indeed she is. Mrs. Flowers is a widow, so she is prone to doing things even if she ought not. And her bonnet will shield her face well enough. Is it still raining?"

"It wasn't when I walked from Trim Street." Which was fortunate, as he didn't own an umbrella.

A few minutes was sufficient for Augusta to dash upstairs to inform the resting Lady Tallant of their outing, then to gather a bonnet, gloves, and pelisse. Once Joss retrieved his own gloves, hat, and cloak from a footman, they were off. Down the steps of the Queen Square house, where they paused.

"We have arrived outdoors, as you wished," said Augusta from behind the wall of a lace-trimmed poke bonnet. "Do tell me about the startling and profound thoughts that occur to you with this change of scenery."

Joss snorted, for the change of scenery was little to the city's advantage. Bath lay in a bowl of land footed by the River Avon, and every rain turned the city's sloping streets into slides of pale, chalky mud. After a morning of drizzle, the air hung cold and humid, each breath heavy.

Which suited Joss fine. He and Augusta would be equally uncomfortable, a welcome change from this morning's verbal trouncing by Paynter.

"Let us walk in the garden across the square," Joss suggested, "and I shall astonish you with my thoughts."

The brim of the bonnet wiggled back and forth. "I am not easy to astonish, but I should like to see you try." She took his arm, and they hurried through an interval of muck to the Queen Square garden. Surrounded by a low stone balustrade topped with elegant iron pickets, nothing so vulgar as mud or damp was welcome in its manicured confines. Neat, graveled pathways and symmetrical plantings provided clean places on which the feet might stride, peaceful shapes on which the eye could rest.

"Your old friend Paynter," Joss began as their feet crunched on still-damp gravel, "reminded me of an aged highwayman. That grizzled hair in a widow's peak, and that scar through one brow."

Augusta chuckled. "He apprenticed in a forge as a young man; I think the scar happened at that time. But he's very kind. Married, seven children, all that. I used to play with his youngest daughter."

"'All that' includes a talent for silence. You might have warned me that he hoards words as well as land."

They were passing beneath the stretching branches of a winter-bare tree, and Augusta stopped walking in its shadow. "Oh, dear. He got you talking, I expect. What did you say?"

"The usual pleasantries." Joss flicked at a spindly twig, sending a drop of dew flying. "But chat about the weather won nothing but a stern look. An allusion to my acquaintance with Miss Meredith, whom I hastened to mention I had not seen in some months, earned nothing but a grunt. It wasn't until I mentioned the nature of my business in Bath that he came to life."

Augusta tipped her face up, an expression of utter exasperation crossing her fine features. "Never tell me you mentioned that someone was being blackmailed."

The frustration in her tone was no more than Joss felt himself, yet her words stung a bit. "You give me too little credit. No, I only mentioned that I hoped to sell some land."

Tugging at his arm, Augusta began walking again. "You might as well have told a dog that you had a pocket full of meat, but that it wasn't for him. Now he'll try to sniff it out, and he'll snap it up if he can."

"A well-turned metaphor." Joss covered her fingers with his. Despite the thick leather of his gloves, his fingertips were being nipped; hers must be colder within their thin kid. "Believe me, I could tell at once

I had blundered. As soon as I mentioned land for sale, Paynter drawled something about how low land prices have fallen at the present, even though I hadn't offered to sell to him."

"That doesn't matter. If he knows you *need* to sell land, he will never offer you a good price."

She made a fair point. Prices were always bad for those who needed to sell land, because no one sold land except out of desperation. And Sutcliffe was desperate indeed.

"What ought I to have done differently, though?" Joss asked. "I merely tried to converse with him as one does a fellow human being."

"Of the *beau monde*, yes. But those methods won't work on Paynter. Nor on Duffy." For a few steps, there was only the sound of tiny stones being scattered by their boots, the distant bark of a dog, the terrified chitter of a bird fleeing a bush by which they walked. "I assumed a man of business would have frequent dealings with, well, men of business. But I suppose that's not necessarily true."

"Your veiled insults are enchanting." Would it be impolite to shake a branch over her head and soak her with cold raindrops? Probably.

"It is not an insult, but a statement of fact. You work for a baron, and you deal with men like him—or with simple tradesmen, whom you could likely intimidate with a lift of one brow. Yes, exactly like that."

With his free hand, Joss rubbed at his forehead until his brows relaxed.

"I would love to be a part of these negotiations," Augusta added. "It would be a pleasure to pit my wits against those of my father's old friends. But Paynter cannot meet with Mrs. Flowers or Mrs. Flowers will cease to exist."

The regret in her tone mollified Joss, and he stopped looking down the neat row of trees for branches against which he could accidentally brush. "What would you do differently from me?"

"You request my advice? What happened to the damnable pride you could not say enough about yesterday?"

Joss gave a dry laugh. "I can't afford so much of it as I could then. Sutcliffe is growing more worried by the hour. I owe him a success."

"Hmm."

"I can still afford honor," he added, "so don't you go making me another of your indecent propositions."

She sniffed. "I wouldn't dream of it."

A pity, for he would. Had. Did. Last night, he had dreamed of her awaiting him in a large bed, her bright hair long and unbound, her wicked mouth speaking delicious lewdness into his ear. They had stroked one another, taking pleasure, and it was all right because she wanted him just as he was, and there had never been any question of him wanting her, with her needle-sharp mind and siren's body. Kisses and embraces and words of passion, until his dream body had been wound hard and tight with passion. When he finally covered her, ready to thrust—

His body had jerked, snapping him awake. To the sight of the sloping ceiling of his rented room. To solitude, and a superfluous erection, and an awkward awareness that he had never had such a passionate dream about any of his few and cursory past lovers.

"You relieve my mind," he said, only because that sounded better than, *Are you sure? Not even one more proposition? Not even a little indecency?*

Better for them both to keep the gloves on, to remain at a safe distance.

If there was such a thing as *safe distance* when one person sought a blackmailer and the other a lover.

"I can't exactly tell you how to proceed with Paynter and Duffy," Augusta explained, heedless, "because you cannot do what I would do, using a breathy voice and batted eyelashes."

With an effort, Joss dismissed his heated dream and returned to the present. "Two weapons outside my armory, that is true. How are they best employed?"

"When interfering in my father's business affairs without seeming to do so. If I wore trousers and had my hair cropped short, I might be credited with knowledge. But since I am burdened with gowns and a *dockyard*"—Joss choked—"then Meredith Beauty's affairs are overseen by trustees."

"Men, I assume, who wear none of the company's lotions or cosmetics or perfumes."

"Not in public, no. They do not. Their private affairs might be quite different." Augusta paused at a turning in the path. "Which way ought we to go?"

"To the left," Joss said at random, and onward they walked. When he ventured a look back through the lacework of tree branches, he could just see the northern side of Queen Square. It appeared to be one giant mansion of pale stone, yet it was cleverly chopped into a series of houses behind the long pedimented facade. Nothing was quite what it seemed among the wealthy.

"How do you persuade the trustees around to your way of thinking?"

"I give them a bit of cooing on minor matters related to the company's products. The labeling that catches the eyes of flighty females. The pricing suited to a lady's pin money."

"Labeling and pricing? You advise them on important aspects of the business, then."

She tipped her face up to his, and a devious smile crossed her lips. "I don't know what you mean, sir. Those are only small affairs, far beneath the dignity of men. As my breathy voice and batted eyelashes make entirely clear."

With a low laugh, Joss said, "I see you were not exaggerating your persuasive abilities. Indeed, you persuaded me to take a list of four names, when I thought myself too proud to take anything at all."

"About that list, yes." Her voice returned from a coo to its usual timbre. "There's probably no purpose to speaking to Paynter again, since he won't give you a good price for your cousin's land. If you choose to meet with Whittingham or Duffy, take care not to... oh, I don't know what to call it. 'Man flirt,' maybe."

Joss stumbled. In righting himself, he shook her hand from his forearm. "Man flirt? *Man flirt?*"

"You know what I mean. All those sly smiles and jokes that may or may not be bawdy and chatter about sporting events."

"I know what you mean, and I would *not* call it 'man flirting.' It is *conversation.*"

She shrugged. "Call it that if you like. Whatever the name, that approach works for puffed-up dandies of the *beau monde*. To a man of high society, money is the means to buy things to impress others. Like curricles and...I don't know. I'm not a man with deep pockets."

"I am not either," Joss replied. "But I see your point. And to men of business, I suppose, money is not the means, but the end in itself."

"Precisely." Augusta's look of gratified surprise was rather lowering, as though she had not expected him to follow her reasoning. "When dealing with self-made men, one must persuade differently."

What was the means, or the end, for a man such as Joss? For years, he had been bound to Sutcliffe's employment by family ties and poverty. Long enough, it seemed, that he had lost the knack for doing business with anyone who responded with subtlety and sense. In Bath, he had won himself a little distance. He had traveled a step closer toward independence. But it was only a single step, and then—what next?

He would figure that out when the time came. Surely.

Impatience seized him. "I shouldn't have brought you out here. It's too cold for walking." He took up Augusta's hands, rubbing her gloved fingers between his. He had thought of his own escape, but not of her comfort.

"That doesn't matter," Augusta said. "I'm always cold." She caught his eye for a moment, then looked away. Not quickly enough to hide the truth: though she attempted a smile, her eyes looked lost. Deep and worried and afraid and still. Oh, so still. Hoping if she were just still enough, no one would notice.

Or maybe he only saw his own reflection.

They had made a circuit of the garden by now, and

the northern face of the square was visible again. Once they stepped outside the bounds of the garden's fence, she would become Mrs. Flowers again, and he—no one of significance. Best to remember that. "I should get you inside so you can warm up. Bath doesn't need another invalid to add to its ranks."

"I told you, I'm always cold. Even indoors. Yet I'm healthy enough." Pulling her fingers free, she walked forward. "It looks like a new lodger has taken the house next to Emily's. See the carriage? It must have just arrived."

When Joss reached her side, he shaded his eyes below the brim of his hat until he could pick out the lines of the carriage's crest. "Oh, for God's sake," he muttered. "Not four days, and he's followed me."

"What? Do you know whose carriage that is?"

"Yes," he replied. "I do. Lord Sutcliffe has decided to grace Bath with his presence."

Six

AFTER SEEING AUGUSTA BACK TO HER DOORSTEP WITH more speed than grace, Joss marched next door and rapped on it with a fist. He wished he had something larger to knock with—a cudgel, maybe, or a mace.

An unfamiliar manservant opened the door, all high-bridged nose and supercilious smirk.

Joss ignored both. "I need to see Lord Sutcliffe. Please tell him his man of business is here."

The cursed man began to swing the door closed in Joss's face, but thundering footsteps sounded on the staircase. Joss craned his neck to see over the shoulder of the servant. As he expected, within a few seconds Sutcliffe skidded across the marble-tiled entryway.

"Let him in! Let him in! Let Everett in!" Panting, Sutcliffe tugged at the door. The servant still seemed disinclined to grant Joss entry, but after a pause that was slightly too long, he bowed and stepped back.

"Everett," Sutcliffe said. "Thank God. I thought I'd have to search high and low for you. Where have you been? We arrived ten minutes ago at least."

Everything about the baron was quick, impulsive,

scattered. In his mid-thirties, he was blond and gray-eyed to Joss's dark coloring. Though too thin for handsomeness, his free-spending ways and boundless energy were enough to keep him at the center of any crowd.

"A red coat, my lord? How elegant you appear during your travel," Joss observed as he crossed the threshold, removing his hat. "It's new, is it not? And the boots too. Hoby, I assume?" The baron had overspent his budget for this quarter before the last quarter had even begun; now he must be running through the funds intended for the summer.

Sutcliffe extended a foot, his boot as glossy and black as the marble tile on which he stood. "Nothing else for me. They're the best. Your boots have lost their shine, Everett; you ought to see to them. But not now—no, not now." He caught Joss's arm, as though he thought Joss might head off in search of a cleaning cloth that instant. "Thank God you're here, Everett. I've written you so many letters and you didn't answer any of them."

Joss laid his hat on a stack of trunks against one wall, then snatched it up again as a pair of footmen entered with another trunk to heft atop the tower. "I did, in fact. My replies will probably reach the hall later today. Perhaps tomorrow."

His voice had fallen into a soothing timbre. Sometimes this worked. Sometimes it didn't.

"I couldn't wait for that. I got"—Sutcliffe lowered his voice to a carrying whisper—"another of those notes."

Ah. This explained the fit of nervous energy, excessive even for Sutcliffe.

A wave of fatigue crashed over Joss. It seemed

five hours ago rather than a few minutes that he had walked with Augusta in the bracing chill of the garden.

"I am sorry to hear it," he told his cousin—not that either of them, ever, referred to one another as such. "Did you bring it with you this time?"

"Yes. It's in my pocket." The baron patted at the breast of his red wool coat, then his pale eyes opened wide. "My pouch! Where's my pouch?" Frantic fingers scrabbled inside his coat; then with a sigh of relief that made his whole body sag, the baron pulled forth a small leather bag no bigger than a man's palm. Hundreds of times, Joss had seen this panicky reaction and the successive relief.

"Is there a room here where we might look at the letter?" Joss said as though nothing had interrupted them.

A twitch of Sutcliffe's head. "Not here; too many servants. Let's go to your house."

Joss shifted his feet. "We can, if you like. But it's only a room."

"Nonsense."

"No, it really is only a room," Joss said mildly. "Though now you've arrived, perhaps I can give it up and lodge with you. Did you take this whole house?"

"Ah. I—" The baron cut himself off, striding to the doorway and calling some instructions to the footmen. When he returned to Joss, his eyes sought out the chandelier in the center of the entry ceiling. "So many servants about! The place is crawling. No, you know I'd like nothing better than to have you stay with here. But I'm not sure how long I'll need to remain in Bath. I'm taking the house a week at a time, so it's easier for you if you stay where you are. Eh?"

"Of course. That seems perfectly logical." Joss hadn't expected a different answer, yet Sutcliffe's expression of relief still made his throat stick with dull disappointment.

"Let's be off, then," said the older man. "How far is your lodging from here? We can take my carriage."

Joss shook his head. "It is still being unloaded, as you just saw. We can walk. It'll take only a few minutes."

"But there might be rain!"

"Let us bring your umbrella."

Sutcliffe chewed at his lower lip. "Do you have brandy? I need something to settle my stomach."

To another man, Joss might say, *Surely it's a bit early. You haven't even dined yet.* To Sutcliffe, he only said, "Surely there's a decanter somewhere in the house."

"Quite right. Quite right." Off darted the baron through a side doorway; he returned even before the door had managed to close behind him. "Right, indeed. That was some sort of drawing room. Last tenants must have left this. What luck!" He brandished a glass bottle in which an inch of sediment and syrupy liquid sloshed.

"Excellent." Joss feigned a smile. "Off we go, then."

After he located an umbrella, the two men began their short walk. In the few minutes it took to pass from the crisp facade of Queen Square to the older houses of Trim Street, Sutcliffe kept up a constant stream of talk about the way Lady Sutcliffe had plagued him about wanting to accompany him, but that would have meant bringing their three children, and they would take up the best bits of the carriage seat and never cease talking, and then they *would* want to take the waters, which he hadn't ruled out himself, not that he needed it because he was in fine form except for these cursed letters, which surely he had done nothing to deserve.

So quick and determined was his flow of talk that at one point Joss had to tug him back from the path of a Bath chair. Twice did a wild gesture smack a passerby; Joss hastily apologized as his employer strode on, oblivious.

When they reached the Trim Street house, Sutcliffe asked to see the landlady. A pleasant-natured, stoutish woman met them in the cozy, cluttered entryway. Somehow Joss was shunted backward, laden with the foul-looking decanter and Sutcliffe's umbrella, as his cousin stepped forward with a bright grin to request an introduction.

Mrs. Jeffries, a widow of late middle age, professed herself honored to meet "a real lord." Her curtsy to Sutcliffe was all the baron could desire; his kiss on her hand, all she could wish.

"My good woman," said the baron with another flash of straight teeth, "I wonder if you might arrange for a teapot of hot water to be sent to the drawing room? Mr. Everett and I will be talking in there."

"Not boiling one another," Joss added. Not that either of them were listening to him.

"Mr. Everett's lodging doesn't cover use of the drawing room, my lord." The woman's cheeks went red, and she looked uncertainly from Sutcliffe to Joss. "But if it's not in use right now, I'm sure I wouldn't mind just this once."

Sutcliffe held up a hand. "Not necessary, Mrs.

Jeffries. It was my error entirely. Mr. Everett and I shall speak in his room, if we might just have that hot water. Extremely hot, I mean. Just off the boil."

"Of course." Looking relieved, she curtsied again. "And I'll have some tea things put together too, my lord."

Joss's stomach expressed interest. He had not, after all, partaken of any biscuits or tea with Augusta before escaping to the chilly outdoors.

"No need, no need. Just the water—and a cup, of course. Wouldn't want you to go to any extra trouble." With a smile that left the landlady dithering, Sutcliffe caught Joss's arm. "Show me up, Everett."

"I wouldn't mind tea," Joss murmured.

"Eh? What's that?" Sutcliffe looked confused, as though the unexpected words were a fly buzzing around his head. His free hand wandered to his coat pocket.

"Never mind. Follow me." Up the stairs they went, three flights in all. Each one narrower, until they reached the top of the house.

"Good God," Sutcliffe wheezed. "We must have climbed all the way to heaven."

"Let us see if you still say that when you see the room." Joss unlocked the chamber and showed his cousin inside, setting the umbrella and decanter on the floor by the door.

He could scarcely imagine what the room looked like through Sutcliffe's eyes. Had the baron ever entered servants' quarters? Had it occurred to him that a floor could be other than carpeted or marble, or that some ceilings sloped under the line of a roof instead of soaring high?

Yet the plain wood was clean, the plaster of the

unpapered walls neatly whitewashed. Mrs. Jeffries kept no slatternly servants here. True, there was a small leak in the roof above the room, but Joss had put a basin on the floor until such time as the leak was repaired. The patchwork quilt spread across the bed had been pieced together from velvet and satin scraps. Jewel-bright and supple despite its age, it had probably been created from snipped-up gowns by some long-ago lady's maid or daughter of a wealthy house. A little taste of luxury in this small room.

"How interesting this room is!" Sutcliffe seated himself on the narrow bed, bouncing to test the tension of the ropes. "Why, it's like living in medieval times, isn't it? Only you've no fire. There ought to be a great fire with a sheep on a spit. And a servant bringing tankards of mead."

"I'll keep that in mind," Joss said drily, seating himself in the wooden chair at the writing desk. He moved aside a stack of correspondence. "Now. Show me the letter."

Sutcliffe pulled forth a single sheet and stretched it out to Joss. Unfolding it, Joss read the spiky, ink-clotted capitals aloud. "'One thousand is not enough. Make it five. Delivered by the end of the month or your wife knows all.'"

He caught Sutcliffe's eye. "It's succinct, if nothing else."

"Lady Sutcliffe *can't* know, Everett. She'd leave me and take all her money. The marriage settlements—ah, her father knew what he was doing. Her fortune is all held in trust for the children, not for me."

As Joss held the crackling paper in his fingertips, several replies came to mind.

The first, that if Sutcliffe cared so much about having money, he could spend it less freely and hold fast to what he had.

The second, that Joss's grandmother or mother ought to have been so lucky as Lady Sutcliffe, to have money tied to them irrevocably by legal strings even after marriage.

The third was yet more pointless, but Joss said it all the same. "I think you ought to tell your wife the truth, Sutcliffe. The law does not permit her to leave you or take her children from you. Not even if you recognize the maid's child."

For that was the crux of the matter: after decades of flirting with servants and doing God only knew what else with them, Sutcliffe had impregnated a housemaid. The woman had been sent away, and with Joss's influence, given a stipend to ensure her comfort and health. Sutcliffe was indignant that the woman had been so foolish as to fall pregnant.

Joss was not of the opinion that blame lay with the younger, weaker, poorer person.

Sutcliffe shook his head. "Lady Sutcliffe can tie up her money, though. She and her father have already put me on a spending allowance. Why—"

Tap tap. The door swung open to reveal a young maid holding a tray that Joss recognized as his landlady's finest. A pewter affair with blocky handles, it bore a white porcelain teapot with rows of tiny hand-painted flowers. Also the finest in the house. There were two cups on the tray, bless Mrs. Jeffries, but Joss knew Sutcliffe intended the pot of hot water for his exclusive use.

"Thank you, my dear," said the baron, setting the tray atop Joss's desk. As Joss tugged his papers from beneath the shining surface, Sutcliffe spoke again to the maid. "What a pretty little thing you are. Do you like magic?"

"Thank you, sir. I mean, my lord. Yes, my lord." A pale slip in her late teens, she nodded and curtsied again. Her mobcap slipped down her forehead. As she pushed it back into place, Sutcliffe tapped her nose, then ran a forefinger around her ear.

"Aha!" He pulled back his hand, open-palmed, to reveal a shilling. "For you, my dear. It was inside your head all along."

The maid covered her mouth, giggling.

"Add another coin to pay for the hot water," Joss said drily.

As Sutcliffe took out another coin, he asked, "Do you have a special fellow, my dear girl?"

Before the maid could answer, Joss rose to his feet. "That will do. Thank you, miss."

The maid looked from Joss to Sutcliffe, then bobbed another curtsy and departed. Joss turned on his cousin. "Sutcliffe. Good *Lord*. What were we *just* talking about?"

"My allowance?" Sutcliffe poured out some of the steaming water into a cup, then pulled forth the leather pouch from his breast pocket. Untying its cord, he shook out a quantity of small green blades into the cup. *Somalata*, as always. After a pause, the baron popped a few dry blades into his mouth before stowing the pouch again.

"We were talking," Joss continued after this ritual

was complete, "of your financial difficulties at present, the greatest of which comes from your unwillingness to leave the female servants alone. That being the case, I would appreciate it if you would not harass the maids in my lodging house."

"It was only a magic trick," Sutcliffe said carelessly, sipping at his brew. Joss knew from experience that further conversation would be pointless until the cup was drained.

In the meantime, Joss took another look at the new blackmail letter. Unfolding it before the window's light, he saw no watermark. No identifying information on the paper itself, and the letter had been stuck closed with a plain wafer rather than a seal.

However, the postal stamp was interesting. Rather than being sent from London as the first two letters had been… "This letter was posted in Bath," Joss observed.

"Exactly. That's why I've come." Sutcliffe swallowed the last of his beloved swill, chewing at the sodden blades. He then retrieved the decanter from his Queen Square house and splashed its contents into the cup, sediment and all. Tossing this back in one quick gulp, a tremor shook his thin frame. "Not bad, not bad."

"Sutcliffe, do you still regard these letters as credible? Five thousand pounds is an ungodly sum of money. Perhaps a creditor is taunting you." It was possible, for Sutcliffe owed money to half of London. Though as the baron was on good terms with nearly everyone who knew him, his debts hadn't caused him difficulty in the past.

"I must take them seriously," the baron said. "The

first letter knew the direction of that silly maid who got into trouble. Jenny."

"Jessie," Joss corrected.

"And, you'll recall, that letter was addressed to Lady Sutcliffe rather than to me. If I didn't open all her ladyship's mail, I'd have been in the soup for sure."

Yes, that had been the first letter: simple information, designed to poison the baroness's mind against her husband. *Libel*, Sutcliffe fumed to Joss. But of course it wasn't. His adultery with the maid—whether he had forced her or not, Joss had no idea—was not libel at all, but a fact. As was the child now growing in Jessie's belly.

The second letter, sent to Sutcliffe himself, had demanded money for silence. Sutcliffe's reaction had been to send Joss to Bath, to seek money in secret. The baron had also seized all of his wife's correspondence, in case the blackmailer should go back on his word and contact the baroness again.

Joss refolded the letter. "There's no way you can sell enough of your land to raise this money. Almost everything you possess is entailed or part of Lady Sutcliffe's dowry. I did try"—*rather clumsily*, he did not add—"to find someone interested in purchasing your available coal lands, but you must know that selling land in haste does not fetch the highest price."

Sutcliffe sighed, shaking the empty decanter. "You're right." He sank back onto the narrow bed, the ropes creaking as his weight shifted. "Are there any more gems we can sell?"

Joss could not abide the plural pronoun. "*You* sold all of the Sutcliffe jewels as soon as you reached majority. Everything you have is paste, except for what Lady Sutcliffe brought to the marriage."

"I could replace those with paste too." The baron brightened.

"No. You could not. Her ladyship would certainly notice the difference in their appearance." Joss rose, pacing the breadth of the room and back. His boots thumped dully on the bare planks, echoing the disappointed sound of his heart. "Sutcliffe, you promised me ten percent of anything I sold for you. A hundred pounds for selling your thousand pounds' worth of land."

At Joss's stern request, the baron wrote, signed, and sealed this promise before dispatching Joss to Bath. A paltry sum for his freedom, but it would do. He wasn't afraid to work for his bread; he just wanted it to be honest work. Sane work. Work that did not include an employer's constant ingestion of alarming substances, or that employer's even more alarming requests.

"What," Joss added, "do you intend to do now?"

Joss did not really expect a sensible reply. This expectation was fulfilled.

"I don't know, I don't know." Sutcliffe's booted feet drummed against the wooden baseboard of the bed. "That's why I came to you. I need your advice, Everett."

It had been years since Joss felt gratified by such a statement. Probably not since the year after he entered Sutcliffe's employment at the age of twenty-one—a full decade ago—and realized that all advice, like all good intentions, would soon be abandoned.

He could but try, though. "As you say, there is no putting one's trust in a blackmailer. I believe we must find and stop this person."

Joss thought of Augusta's list of names, of the final name in particular. *Lord Chatfield. Knows things.* A convenient talent, considering the blackmailer seemed now to be in Bath.

"You must take care of it," Sutcliffe said. "I can't be involved. Had to put it about that I wanted to visit Bath for my health. I moaned so much about my foot, Lady Sutcliffe really thought I had a touch of the gout. Excellent performance. It was excellent. I say, do they have a theater in Bath? There must be one."

"You are not going on the stage pretending to have gout." Joss pressed at his temples.

The baron laughed, a shrill arpeggio like the honk of a clarinet. "What an idea, Everett. You really are too much! No, no, I only want to get out and experience a bit of Bath society."

"Fine. Only see that you leave the maids alone." Joss toyed with the idea of asking Sutcliffe whether he was acquainted with Lord Chatfield. But as the reclining Sutcliffe's jaw worked at a new spear of *somalata*, Joss thought better of the matter.

He wondered dimly if a man who *knew things* was aware of Mrs. Flowers's true identity. Not that it mattered at the moment. At any moment.

"I shall see what I can do about the matter," Joss decided. "I'll send word to your lodging when I have more information."

"Good, good. Knew you would handle it." Sutcliffe stretched, cracking his fists against the sloped ceiling, and looked up with some surprise. "I'll be off, then. Have my carriage called, will you?"

"You didn't bring it. We walked from Queen Square."

"Well, have it sent for, then." Sutcliffe laughed. "Everett, honestly. With only a few days' absence, did you forget how gentlemen travel?"

No, he hadn't forgotten that. But he *had* forgotten the strain of maintaining constant courtesy. Of soothing Sutcliffe and diverting the man's whims.

Family was family, and that loyalty had carried Joss long beyond the point he would have stayed in service to a stranger. But this sojourn in Bath was a matter of business, not family. Not with Joss remaining in his own meager lodging instead of joining the baron's household, treated with less respect than a servant not of the master's blood.

Business it had probably always been. Sutcliffe had always regarded Joss as capable and convenient, but he had never been encouraged to regard Joss as family. Not with Joss's mixed birth—his wastrel of a father and his mother who had become little more than a servant in the house she had once graced as a daughter.

"I place one condition on my assistance," Joss said, opening the chamber's door for his cousin. "At the end of this month, whether or not you or your blackmailer has prevailed, I shall expect the greater of one hundred pounds or ten percent of land sale proceeds. I will draw up the paper tonight and bring it for your signature the next time I call."

"There's that maid again!" Sutcliffe preceded Joss down the stairs. "Look, she's tidying in that bedchamber. Would she like another shilling, d'you think?"

"I will take your response as agreement," Joss said. "Thank you very much."

"Eh? Dash it, I'm going to give her another shilling. I'll be right back."

"*No.*" Before Sutcliffe could pursue the blond maid again, Joss caught his elbow and dragged him down the remaining stairs, telling him all the while of the novelty of a ride in a Bath chair.

Within a few minutes, the baron was off, being trundled away to Queen Square by a grinning youth who had just had a shilling pulled from his ear.

Shaking his head, Joss remounted the stairs to his attic room. A tiny pleasure awaited: a pot of still-hot water and a clean china cup. He could use some of his own tea leaves to brew a bracing cup or two.

Nothing exotic. Nothing on which he relied, panicked, like his cousin depended on that small leather pouch. Just normal tea, like normal Englishmen drank.

It sounded fiendishly delicious.

But business first. Quickly—before the water could cool much more—he penned a few notes to the remaining names on Augusta's list requesting an appointment.

Seven

IN THE DAYS FOLLOWING THE WALK IN THE GARDEN, little occurred to mar Augusta's new routine in Bath. To the Pump Room each morning with Emily, where as they made their slow promenade, their new acquaintances smiled at ever-cheerful Mrs. Flowers as London never had at Augusta Meredith. Each smile felt like a victory; each tiny flirtation blossomed within her breast.

After a glass of the detestable mineral water, then came another outing if Emily felt up to it: perhaps to a bun shop, a coffeehouse, or the winding delights of elegant Sydney Gardens. Here they met the women of Bath, a less credulous bunch than the men, but quite willing to be plied with costly dainties and polite conversation.

After these interludes came church. St. Mary's Chapel, a small classical building of golden Bath stone, occupied one corner of Queen Square, and Emily had rented a pew therein at an exorbitant rate. "All the better to encourage regular attendance," she guessed, and indeed, she went to services each day they were performed. Augusta usually accompanied her, letting the familiar rites and ancient words of comfort wash around her. She did not like the raw reminder of the inscrutable hand of the divine, of love enduring beyond death; still, she went to hold Emily's hand. The countess always wore a veiled hat so no one would notice the tears that sometimes tracked down her cheeks.

Augusta noticed nonetheless, though she pretended not to.

Before dinner there was time for a rest; after dinner, another. Then came the lengthy preparations for the evening's outing: an assembly, the theater, a musical entertainment. Mrs. Flowers always wore pastels and was bright and blithe. She danced, she laughed, she flirted—but not *too* much. No one seemed quite right as a potential lover; for no one could she imagine dispensing with her candied, mannered shell and succumbing to raw passion.

For several days she did not see Joss Everett. Why should she, though? He was in Bath for business, and she had given him the means of conducting it.

Perhaps she would have been less helpful had she known her aid would take him from her presence.

Five days passed like this: days of quiet ease broken by sudden tides of loneliness that dragged at Augusta at unexpected times. She had come to think of these fits of melancholy as an object: a boulder balanced at the top of a steep hill. If she let it tumble, it would roll over and crush her. After she lost her parents and Colin Hawford within the span of a week, her shoulders had been bowed and the boulder had fallen.

Wrenching it back into place had taken agonizing months, and its equilibrium had felt precarious ever since. She knew now how easily knocked away were the chocks of love, of everyday life, of expectations.

And so when the boulder tipped, she smiled more brightly, added more flowers to her hair, laughed at every little joke. Day by day, the number of callers for Mrs. Flowers increased. Everyone liked to be with her, sunny and cheerful as she was.

Well. Not everyone, but enough people. At least… it ought to feel like enough.

On the sixth morning, Augusta flipped idly through *The Times* in the drawing room, looking for the new advertisements for Meredith Beauty's translucent soap. The soap was a marvel, hard and pure as a topaz. The advertisements should be much larger; she would write a fawning letter of persuasion to the trustees later.

The butler interrupted her perusal by entering with a letter delivered by "a grimy boy dragging about a Bath chair."

Augusta's stomach gave a curious flutter. Could this be Joss's erstwhile messenger? "How grimy was the boy?"

"Extremely grimy." The butler's nose wrinkled as he handed Augusta the salver bearing her note, then departed.

She folded the newspaper and left it on the drawing room's window seat, then pounced upon her letter. Indeed it was from Joss; already she knew his writing, strong and deeply slanted.

I flipped a penny to decide whom to approach next, and Whittington won. If you would like to take part

*in the negotiations, meet us in Sydney Gardens at
midday. Be Mrs. Flowers at her Mrs. Flowers-est.
I should like to see what she is capable of.*

She toyed with the idea of declining the summons;
it would be unwise to allow Whittington to see her.
But the frisson that shimmered through her body was
more excitement than nervousness. Joss wanted to see
what she was capable of.

Or he wanted to see her?

The thought seemed to lighten the air in the
swaddled, textured drawing room.

Mrs. Flowers was meant as an escape, was she not?
So, this would be an escape.

❧

Augusta thought of Sydney Gardens as the still grander
stepsister of the elegant arrangement at the center of
Queen Square. Tacked onto the eastern side of Bath,
one entered not through a mere gate, but through an
imposing hotel of stone. After paying admission to the
gardens, one was granted access to acres of elaborate
glee: smooth paths for walking, a labyrinth for losing
oneself, a green for springing one's horses, a canal to
cross over or boat along.

As soon as Augusta had deposited her fee with a
servant and stepped onto the winter-dry grass, Joss was
at her side. Dressed plainly as usual, he would have
blended into the shadow of the hotel had he not been
so cursedly handsome.

"You are early, Mrs. Flowers. The clock reads only
half past eleven."

"Yet you were waiting for me."

"A man can but hope, and hope that hope is rewarded." He looked her up and down, and a smile lit his features. "My heaven, Mrs. Flowers, you have outdone yourself. 'But soft, what light through yonder window breaks?'"

"Naught but the blinding print of my gown." She did a little twirl, sharing his smile. She had dressed according to her name, just as Joss had requested. Beneath her frilled parasol, far too frail for the March wind, her bonnet was a frenzy of silk blossoms and curling feathers. The accompanying gown had been purchased ready-made from an unassuming Bath dressmaker; it looked as though a garden had sneezed on it, all covered in blooms of riotous color and form. To complete the effect, Augusta had bought a handful of early-blooming phlox in a vivid, showy pink, and pinned it to her spencer.

When she looked in the glass before leaving Emily's house, she had laughed.

"You asked for Mrs. Flowers. Sir, she is at your service. Though might I ask why she is needed?"

"Indeed you may. I shall even answer you." He guided her to a scrolled wooden bench, then seated himself next to her. "I did not actually flip a coin to decide with whom I would attempt to speak next. Rather, I sent letters requesting appointments—all without *man flirting*, I assure you."

"Applause and felicitations."

"Thank you. There was one exception; before writing to Mr. Duffy of the foundry, I decided to visit it."

She lifted a hand—gloved in fussy ruffled lace,

naturally. "Hold one moment. Are you admitting that you engaged in a hen-witted espionage caper?"

Beneath the brim of his hat, Joss shot her a dark look. "No. Nothing of the sort. I merely took a walk through a part of Bath I had never yet visited."

"Hmm."

He ignored this. "The smell was like nothing I've ever encountered. Tar and burning things. Acrid and dreadful. I know we must have metal, and foundries must have coal to make it. But if Sutcliffe could sell his land whole rather than stripping the coal from it— well, it seems to me that would be better."

"It wouldn't be better for you, as his man of business. You could almost certainly see the coal sold at a decent price."

He looked away, in the direction of the canal just visible through winter-bare branches. A few brave souls were punting along the chill ribbon, their voices floating on the breeze with occasional snippets of song. When the punt passed beneath a delicate ironwork footbridge, the sound vanished.

"It wouldn't be better for the tenants," he said. "They are farmers, not miners. Nor would it be better for the land itself, which would become barren. Yet I know that to sell off the land outright would be worse for the estate. Perhaps we could buy it back one day, though, whole and unharmed."

"*We* could buy it back?"

"We. Sutcliffe and me. Or more likely, his son, if Ted proves less of a—" He pressed his lips together. "Proves inclined to careful stewardship of his holdings."

"And what do you need of me?"

He shaded his eyes and looked up at the sky, where sparrows or starlings or some sort of small bird arrowed, joyous and quick through the air. "I thought you might enjoy the amusement of an outing outside the stifling comforts of your rented house. Have you noticed how many men have tipped their hats at you, my dear fake widow? Perhaps this was my true motive: I wanted the smug satisfaction of being the man who sat at your side."

Did he mean it? Of course he did not; the odious expression of amusement was spreading over his features again. "Enjoy it while you can," she said primly, "for when Lord Whittingham presents himself, I shall have to leave you behind."

"Must you? I have no doubt that his lordship would be as delighted to see you as is every other man of your acquaintance."

"Every man?"

"Oh, well—perhaps half. As I said on the occasion of our first meeting in Bath, I haven't spoken to everyone."

"Nor have I, so you needn't make me sound like a hussy." She said this without heat, turning over the idea in her mind. Meeting Lord Whittingham would be a delight, a reminder of the years before she lost her parents. And it would knit her, in some small way, to Joss's side. It would be a place to fit, to belong, for a sliver of time.

He offered to open that window between her and others—or no, he asked her to open it herself.

"I shall think about it," she added. "We still have a bit of time before he arrives."

"If you stay for our meeting, say whatever you like, as long as you somehow discuss Whittingham giving money to Sutcliffe. I don't even care for what reason, honestly. If he wants to pay Sutcliffe to strip naked and dance through the streets of Bath, that's quite all right with me. I don't know who would want to see it, but Sutcliffe would certainly be willing to do it."

Augusta grinned. "I simply *must* meet your employer again." She recalled the baron as cheerful and impulsive, but then, she'd only met him and his baroness once at a ball. At which no one, to her knowledge, had stripped naked.

"You might be required to meet him eventually, but let us hope not."

Another passing man—vaguely familiar as a recent caller in Queen Square—tipped his hat to Augusta. She waved and smiled with her fluffy glove and friendly smile.

"Would he do as a lover, do you think?" some imp made her nudge Joss in the ribs and ask in a low voice.

There was no unsettling the man; he only leaned back against the bench and stuck out his boots, the picture of comfort. "I think not. Though I cannot judge male beauty with anything like the proper eye, he appears too languid for you. See how slowly he walks?"

"That could be because he wants to hang back and look at me more."

He arched a brow. "If he's that fascinated, then he ought to have the stones to turn around and speak to you. Unless you wish for a lover with no stones? That would seem to defeat the purpose, though."

This was what the imp had wished for: Joss Everett,

shaping words like *lover* and *stones* with his beautifully cut mouth. Warm and liquid, desire swirled within her. "I am quite sure that you ought not to be speaking this way to me," she managed.

"I am quite sure," he countered, "that you are right. But I am also quite sure that you like it. There is no need for you to play Mrs. Flowers with me."

Odd indeed, that the widowed part she played was far more innocent than her unwed true self. Yet Mrs. Flowers had to be bright as sunlight, where Augusta burned low and hot as fire.

Figuratively speaking. She shivered; within her dainty gloves, her fingers were cold.

"Perhaps you might satisfy my curiosity on one point, Augusta. If Mrs. Flowers is not meant to be wealthy nor wellborn, what is it about her that appeals to so many men?"

"Her lack of wealth and birth is to keep them from entertaining notions of marriage. Aside from those dreadful flaws, she is everything a man should wish."

"Which is?"

Twirling the flimsy handle of her parasol, she considered. "Pleasant, soft-spoken. Cheerful. So feminine—observe the gown, if you will—that she is a creature entirely without threat. Generous with laughter and with flaunts of the bosom."

He gave her a sidelong glance so quick she almost missed it. "I have observed no such behavior. Are you depriving me of bosom-flaunting?"

"Yes, but you are a special case. As you just informed me, there's no purpose to being Mrs. Flowers with you because you know she doesn't exist."

"And what of the other poor fellows of Bath?" Joss nodded toward the smoothly paved path, along which yet more individuals and couples promenaded. "With this figment, you shall spoil them for all other women. Then they shall be left with nothing."

"Exactly right. Nothing but a beautiful memory." The words were unexpectedly piquant on her tongue. She savored the taste.

"You sound a bit bloodthirsty," Joss observed. "But I'm sure that cannot be your intention, since you have just told me that you mean to be both soft-spoken and cheerful."

"I would find it easier to be so if you were a bit more soft-spoken and cheerful yourself."

"Rot," he said in a voice of perfect cheer. "Though I *can* be agreeable. Do look at the path: several gentle-men are walking in this direction. Perhaps I might identify one who will do as your lover."

She should have paid the extra sixpence for tea; her mouth felt dry. Moistening her lips, she offered a honeyed smile. "How industrious you are. Which one would you suggest?"

Joss indicated a bewigged elderly man the shape of a kettledrum, hitching himself along with the aid of two canes. "What of him? With that expres-sion of good cheer, he would doubtless treat you with great solicitude."

"You are terrible. That man is as fluffy-haired and fat as a pregnant sheep."

"Good heavens, you are particular," Joss chided. "I thought you wished only for someone to perform a service for you. Must he be as good-looking as all that?"

"I would prefer he not be painful to look upon."

"You underestimate the importance of an expression of good cheer," Joss said. "But let us pass on. What about the light-haired fellow swinging his cane about with such spirit?"

The object of Joss's comment was clearly a dandy, and something in his appearance set her on edge at once. Maybe it was the man's ringlets or his wasp-waisted coat or the smug expression on his indolent features.

Augusta pretended not to notice as her parasol knocked against Joss's hat. "What an excellent suggestion," she cooed. "He *is* handsome. And well-dressed, too. Should I speak to him? No, I suppose you'd best introduce us."

"Please cease beating me with your parasol." With a determined gesture, Joss tugged the parasol from Augusta's grasp and folded it shut. "Your bonnet is large enough to shield you and several other individuals from the sun. You've no need of this. And I am devastated to learn that Mrs. Flowers does not number an understanding of satire among her virtues."

"Of course she doesn't. She's too cheerful for satire." Augusta snatched back her parasol and held it sideways in her lap, a feminine bayonet. "To what do you refer?"

"I was *not* serious when I suggested the light-haired fellow. Well-dressed, indeed. His coat shoulders are as padded as his calves. Only imagine bringing him to your bedchamber, then gaping in dismay as his fine figure is left on the floor for a valet to pick up."

"You're saying things you ought not to say again."

Her cheeks felt as pink as one of the blown roses scattered over her gown. Saying what he ought not to say, yes—because the man she pictured in her bedchamber was Joss, and the form about which she wondered was his. No padding filled out the shoulders of his black coat, well cut but not tailored for his form. The thin knit of his trousers, snug over muscular thighs; the worn leather of his boots—he was unpretentious, unconcerned, and unimpressed.

And she was beginning to fear he would spoil her for other men.

He spoke again. "Here's a promising prospect. Do look at that fellow with his hair tugged back into a queue. Like a pirate, wouldn't you say? He could drag you off to the docks and ravish—"

"Stop." She cut him off. "You are no help at all. Keep silent until I identify someone whose appearance is acceptable to me, and then you may tell me if you know anything to his discredit."

Joss folded his arms.

"What? Nothing sarcastic to say by way of reply?"

He lifted one shoulder, a Gallic-looking gesture of complete nonchalance.

"*Now* he becomes obedient," Augusta muttered. "Very well. That man. Do you know anything of him?" Her gesture was broad and almost random, like a tired swimmer pulling for a faraway shore.

Fortunately, there was a man in her path to intercept it. A somewhat handsome, somewhat well-dressed man with somewhat dark hair, promenading along the path with a somewhat languorous air. And a great rose pinned to his lapel.

There. He was perfect for Mrs. Flowers, who had only somewhat of a personality.

"He'll never do for Mrs. Flowers." Lips unsealed by her question, Joss spoke with certainty. "That man is a cheat. I saw him outside the White Hart yesterday, trying to swindle a Bath chair carrier by arguing the distance. He was wearing a hothouse flower then too."

This last was spoken in a tone of scorn.

"There is nothing wrong with roses," Augusta said. "Or with looking out for one's own interests."

"Indeed there is not. But there is a difference between asserting oneself and flying into a temper, and this man did the latter. You would not wish for an argumentative lover, would you?"

"I do not see that it would be much of a problem, as speech is not the principal purpose of encounters with a lover." *Ruby or garnet*. Were Emily here, she would surely make a pronouncement on the color of Augusta's cheeks.

"Even so, I think it shows a certain lack of attention to the finer feelings of others. Only imagine: 'No, Mrs. Flowers, we shall do it my way.' Or, 'That will do for today, Mrs. Flowers. I've taken my pleasure. Stop pestering me.'"

My way. Pleasure. Her nipples went tight and hard. "You *must* stop telling me to imagine such things."

"Must I? Ah, well. If you insist."

How could he sound so bland? How could he remain so unaffected?

And why did she let him tease her, unsettling her so? She had let the rose-lapelled man—had let a dozen men—pass by without so much as trying to catch their eyes. Either she truly put her trust in Joss's opinion, or…

No. There was no reason to trust him so much, nor to change her plans now. But her dithering emotions proved that it was past time to retake control of the conversation.

Deliberately, she drew the folded parasol across her lap, then set it aside on the bench. "Mr. Everett. Joss. Have you ever taken a lover?"

Eight

AHA. AT LAST SHE WON A VICTORY OVER HIS CALM:
Joss twitched, a small but unmistakable fidget of
gloved hands. "I am quite sure, my dear fake widow,
that *you* ought not to be speaking this way to *me*."

Augusta remembered how effective Paynter's
silence had been on Joss. She simply waited for a
further reply, and at last he let out a breath that seemed
to draw from the worn toes of his Hessians. "I suppose
you might call them lovers, yes."

"Them?" The word made her want to throw something. Maybe him.

He removed his hat, letting the breeze ruffle his
black hair. "More than one. Not many more. It matters not. I meant little to them and they meant little
to me."

"How *could* you?" What she did not add—but
wanted to with a deep, jealous yearning—was, *And
how could you deny me?*

Joss shut his eyes, tilting his face to the chill sun.
When he spoke, his voice had gone brittle and
sharp. "I could because there was always the hope of

meaning. Of love grown from pleasure. But it never grew. I was not what they wanted, and vice versa." He leveled a stern look at her. "Never did I dally with a maiden. Never would I, never will I. And you have made quite clear to me, Madame All in a Huff of a Sudden, that you do not wish for any meaning in your chosen encounter."

"I am not in a huff," Augusta said. "At least, not all of a sudden. I simply wondered."

And just like that, his calm was back. With the languid indifference of a cat, he stretched out his arms, then crammed his hat atop his head. "It's all right; you only caught me by surprise. But you may wonder whatever you like. I know quite well you don't want me; you just want *someone*. What about that fellow?"

The fellow in question—a passing gentleman she had never seen before—had shining Hessians and a beautifully tailored coat. He also had bandy legs, nothing like the sleek line of muscled thigh that filled Joss's pantaloons.

"Not handsome enough," she said, not daring to look at Joss.

"Ah, yes. Your unwonted particularity. With the lights out, would his appearance really matter?" He sighed. "I do hope you will make your lover wear a French letter."

"A—what?"

When she glanced at him, curious, color stained his cheekbones. "It's a sort of sheath. For your protection against…well. I am, as you said, quite sure I ought not to be speaking this way to you."

"No," she said faintly. Somehow, as she went

colder and colder at her extremities, her core burned hotter, as though Joss drew all the heat from her and worked it into a tight, pulsing ball at her center. She squirmed on her seat, wanting to study him, to learn the ingredients that made him so…so *Joss*.

This was only natural, wasn't it? For how many lotions and skin creams had she studied the formulas? Yes, that was it. His presence was just another unguent, something she could wash her hands of if it grew too overpowering.

"So we pass along to the third name on your list. Lord Whittingham." He spoke as though they had parsed no passersby as suitable lovers; as though they'd discussed nothing at all improper and had only just seated themselves on this bench to enjoy the rare clear weather. "I believe our quarry—I mean, honored guest—draws near. He told me I might know him by his height."

This was a kind way of putting the matter, for Lord Whittingham stood no more than five feet tall. Augusta had not seen the viscount for nearly a decade, but little about his appearance had changed. His skin was more tanned, his thin face more lined, but he was as impeccable as always in bottle-green wool and a gilt-striped waistcoat. His clothing tended to be beautifully tailored and of a startling pattern, as though fabric that caught the eye would make sure his small form was not overlooked.

As Augusta and Joss stood to greet him, Whittingham's face creased into a smile of such glee that one could not help but share in it. "If it isn't Augusta Meredith, as I live and breathe," he said, shaking her hand warmly. "Mr. Everett told me an old acquaintance of mine might be accompanying him, but I never imagined it would be you. I haven't seen you since you were a girl. My, my, how pretty you've turned out."

He looked up at her, chucking her under the chin, and Augusta had to laugh as she returned his greeting.

"But what's this I hear?" He pulled a frown. "My dear young friend has got married and saved me none of the cake?"

"Oh, I'm not married." Augusta had thought over this inevitable question and her planned answer during the Bath chair ride to the gardens. The risk-mad Whittingham traveled a great deal now that Waterloo and peace had flung open the barred doors of the Continent. He might not know whether his old compatriot's friend was wed or widowed, neither or both. Though the dodge had not worked with Joss, it was worth a try with Whittingham. Though she would not lie, she would allow him to fill in the gaps.

And indeed he did. "A widow! How dreadful, my dear; you have my condolences. Out of mourning, though, I see. I'm glad you've found such a handsome fellow to console you." He bowed to Joss, who had fallen back a step. "Rather dark, aren't you, Everett? Have you Spanish blood? I was in Spain not long ago."

"Ah—no, I haven't any Spanish ancestry, my lord," Joss said. "And I am desolated to admit that you mistake the nature of my escort. I serve only as our lovely friend's chaperone."

Whittingham laughed, a silvery sound of consummate elegance, as he turned away. "Indeed? She's safe enough from me, but I suppose there are plenty of men in Bath who would like to hang upon her skirts." He tucked his Malacca cane under one arm and offered the other to Augusta. "Suppose we walk about a bit, Augusta, and you tell me what's on your mind." Raising a hand to his lips in theatrical surprise, he added, "*Mea culpa*; I'm meant to hear what's on Mr. Everett's mind, am I not? Well, Augusta, you must join me in listening."

"I'm not much good at that," Augusta laughed.

"Quite true." Joss cleared his throat, then offered Augusta his arm as well. She stood between them— peacock and raven—in a welter of flowers. What a trio they must make.

The principal walkway through the gardens sloped gently uphill to a pavilion, and they followed the path with slow strides. Despite his promise to listen, Whittingham bubbled with conversation. His recent travels had led him across France, into bits of Spain and Portugal, and then, "Home, alas. I mean, 'at last,' of course. Dear me, I ought to sound more pleased about being on my home shores, ought I not?"

"Not if they do not truly feel like home," Joss said.

Whittingham leaned forward to peer at Joss as they walked. "Well put, Mr. Everett. You almost sound as if you've found yourself in the same predicament."

Beneath Augusta's fingertips, the corded muscles of Joss's arm tensed.

"And how is Lady Whittingham?" Augusta asked brightly.

The viscount accepted the turn of subject. "More than fair. She's been amusing herself in my absence.

Sauce for the goose, you know. Or is my wife the gander? I never can recall."

In comparison to her diminutive husband, Lady Whittingham was a positive Amazon. She and her husband lived separate lives, which suited them both quite well. The fact of their marriage was enough to silence those who had wondered whether his lordship was perhaps spending too much time with the attractive eldest son of the Earl of Mowbray.

"You are the gander, of course." Augusta gave his arm a quick squeeze. "Though I hope you are not sauced at this hour."

"If I am—which I'm not, for drunkenness doesn't match this waistcoat—it would be only too just. I am, alas, completely ruined."

"You already said 'alas' once." Joss released Augusta's arm, dropping back again as they crunched down the neatly laid path.

The viscount swung his cane in a wide arc. "It's a marvelous word. Alas, alas. It gives all the flavor of genuine sorrow without requiring a bit of real feeling."

Augusta smiled. "I should stuff the two of you into a cage and let you battle."

"Stuffed in a cage with your handsome so-called chaperone? You tempt me grievously, young Augusta."

From a step behind them, there issued a sound that bore a strong resemblance to a snort.

Augusta picked up the dropped thread of conversation that accompanied the last *alas*. "But what's this about being ruined, my lord? If you are truly out of pocket, London's tailors will be weeping their eyes out." *And you will never be able to help Joss—that is, Sutcliffe.*

"Not to mention the boot makers," added the viscount. "I would be in tears myself if my new wardrobe hadn't been delivered just before I left France. But that's the tragedy: I've tied up a fortune in France, and my ship has not come in. Quite literally. The *Barbacoa* was laden with silks and expected in Nice a month ago. If she's sunk, so am I."

"You seem untroubled by the fact," Joss observed.

"What is there to trouble me? Where one fortune vanishes, another shall appear. Quite soon, I hope, or a marvelous tailor on the *Rue de la Crème* shall have me strung up for debt." Over his shoulder, Whittingham wiggled his cane. "Enough of such talk, now. 'Tis a beautiful day. You, Mr. Everett, seem untroubled—or undelighted, ought I to say—to be walking right behind a lovely woman whose backside you can watch. Or perhaps I ought not to have said that."

"Oh, you definitely ought to have said it," Joss replied. "Is Mrs. Flowers turning red? I do so love it when she turns red."

Whittingham peered up at Augusta from under the brim of his swooping plumed hat. "A ripe shade," he said. "Like a cranberry."

She pulled her arm free. "I'm going to push you both into the canal."

"I haven't swum in ages! It would be delightful." Whittingham beamed at Augusta.

"Very bracing," Joss agreed.

Thus meandered their conversation along with their steps. It was impossible not to be carried along by the viscount's flighty cheer.

As they walked, Whittingham inevitably drew a

crowd about him. Beautiful clothes, an unusual stature, and a carrying voice were an irresistible combination, and several jovial acquaintances of the viscount located the walking party and fell into step with them. As one after another joined them, worry began to curl up Augusta's spine. With a crowd around, with Whittingham knowing who she was—somewhat— the chance seemed too great that she would slip, that everyone would learn who she was, that she should not have come.

And the risk was all to no purpose. If Whittingham was ruined, their errand had failed.

There was nothing to do but smile more brightly and talk less and less. Just agree; just smile, pleasant and bland, and nod at each introduction. A young married couple who finished one another's sentences with nauseating delight. A woman with dyed hair and far too much rouge who was probably a Cyprian. A trio of blue-coated dandies.

After greeting Whittingham, these last shuttled around Augusta, separating her from the viscount as they argued over who would take her arm.

"Any friend of Whittingham's and whatnot. She shall be mine," quoth one in a tremulous tone. "A bloom on her lips, an ornament on my arm. Mr. Pettigrew at your service, dear lady."

"How nice to make your acquain—"

"Dash it." The second, the tallest of the three, speared the first with a scornful glance. "The blooms are on her gown, not her lips. If you haven't eyes in your head, you shouldn't escort such a pretty woman." With set jaw, this second snapped her hand from the first's grasp and tucked it into his. "And judging from the way you've tied your cravat, you *haven't* eyes in your head, Mr. Pettigrew. Madam, permit me to introduce myself. Mr. Protheroe."

"It's a pleasure to meet—"

"Fine talk from someone who pads the shoulders of his coat." The third took Augusta's other hand, dragging their progress to a halt. "Mr. Petersham, ma'am. I assure you—"

"Nothing!" Pettigrew yanked at Augusta's elbow. "Your assurances are worth nothing, you…you… poacher of manservants!"

"Lies!" Petersham went white about the nostrils as he yanked Augusta toward him. "Your manservant begged me to leave your service for mine. At last he has an employer capable of keeping the gloss on his boots for more than a half hour!"

A shocked intake of breath all around and then a clamor. Yanking hands and raised voices, the cultured tones ringing with disgust as the dandies glared at one another. At the center, polite phrases withered on Augusta's lips—phrases that would surely have gone unheard.

Had this happened on the stage, she would have chuckled. Had it happened in a crowded ballroom, she would have felt triumphant. But to be at the center of a clamor in a sedate public garden? No. Mrs. Flowers could not afford to become a spectacle.

Her heart began to thud, heavy and incoherent, beneath the flowered wall of her gown. Whittingham had walked ahead, in conversation with the Cyprian, and—where was Joss? She was penned in by a wall of strangers. The phlox at her breast seemed cloying in their sweet honey scent, and the voices around her filled the leaden sky.

"I feel faint," she blurted into the middle of a harshly worded criticism of Protheroe's pomade. "I think—perhaps I ought to return home."

She had never fainted in her life. But these men didn't know that, and their chorus of commiseration came swiftly. The tugging hands made gestures of sympathy; the cutting tones became polite. Somehow the effect was to force her to the outside of their knot.

Ahead on the path, the others walked on. The viscount's Malacca cane waved back over his diminutive shoulder, all but hidden within the cluster of promenaders. "Good day, you lovely creature! What a pleasure it was to see you!"

Like dogs summoned by a whistle, the argumentative dandies raced after Whittingham.

And onward the unlikely assortment trundled, like a ball of bright sweets rolling uphill to the pavilion.

Their receding voices made the silence around Augusta vibrate. "Well, if that doesn't beat all. They left me."

"Not all of them."

She started, heels scraping in the gravel as she twisted. "Joss. I thought you left too."

"Of course not. I'm your chaperone." He held out a gloved hand—and her folded parasol, which she only now realized she had left behind. "Shall I really see you home, or were you merely making an excuse?"

"Both." She clasped his hand for a moment before he drew hers into the crook of his elbow. "I confess,

I am not impressed with Mrs. Flowers. She must be so careful not to say or do the wrong thing that she is hardly more than an ornament." The dandies had found her worthy of notice because there was only one of her, and the others must not be permitted to possess her. Rather like a bespoke pocket watch or a particularly fine cockade for a hat.

"Mrs. Flowers did fine," Joss said as they began retracing their steps in the direction of the garden's entrance. "Not as well as Miss Meredith, but well enough."

"Miss Meredith would never have threatened to faint."

"No, she would probably have made good on her threat of tossing men into the canal, which would end in all the fashionable men of Bath dying of a lung fever. In addition, Miss Meredith would never have laughed so much at so little, which, considering the company, is exactly what the occasion called for."

His honesty was like a diamond, bright and cleaving. It cleared the cobwebs from her head and made the sky a little lighter. "It was effective enough in the end," she granted. "But we only learned Whittingham cannot invest in Lord Sutcliffe's…"

"Difficulties."

"Precisely. So there was no real benefit to the meeting at all."

"No benefit? You are quite wrong, my dear fake widow. We have learned the location of Lord Whittingham's favored tailor in France. Surely that is worth a few hours of our mortal lives."

"I really should have thrown you into the canal."

He pressed a hand to his heart. "It would be my honor to take a tumble for you."

Tumble. Did he mean it in the bawdy sense? She was unsure, and so her cheeks—of course—flushed. "Are you sure you ought to be speaking to me in that way?" she said lightly. "I have asked you so many times."

"I have begun to think," he said, "that there is precious little I *ought* to say to you, and precious little that I won't."

She liked this reply, but she did not know what sort to return. To freeze off this sally was unthinkable, but what would be the purpose of flirting back?

Or was he flirting at all? It was so difficult to tell when a man, by his own admission, would say almost anything.

As he walked at her side, legs striding long and certain, shoulders square, it was impossible not to think of a tumble. Of being stripped bare. Of…trusting.

How had those women of his past persuaded him out of his clothing? How had they won his hope? What had they offered; what had they promised?

Augusta had given him honesty, and it had not been enough. Or perhaps it was too much. It was hard to tell the difference sometimes.

A few people greeted Mrs. Flowers as they walked, and Augusta felt more and more as though she were wearing a costume. And as one at a masquerade, the compliments and praise were good only while the farce lasted. They had no reflection on her real self.

Joss accompanied her to the door of Emily's house. At the top step, he took her hands in his. Bending his head to hers, he kissed her on the forehead—a swift, warm press of lips that sent a sweet pulse of shock through her.

"Thank you for your company, Mrs. Flowers. Miss Meredith." His eyes were shadowed and deep, his mouth a firm curve. So long had they walked in silence that she almost forgot speech was allowed. Still, she could manage none; she only nodded a farewell before stepping inside.

She caught sight of herself in the foyer glass, bonnet wind-tumbled and cheeks pink with confusion and desire; lips that had spoken foolish words, then been silent at the wrong time. What should she have said, though? What did he mean; what did he want?

Atop her shoulders, the invisible boulder threatened to roll. Her chest gave a warning hitch.

"That won't do," she told her reflection. "You're Mrs. Flowers." She glared until the mirror woman began to correct her expression. Feature by feature, she changed herself: closing her eyes until they agreed not to make tears; breathing slowly through her nose until it resumed working with her lungs, collecting air without that terrible heavy hitch pressing on her.

When she opened her eyes again, she managed to smile. "Emily," she called upstairs. "How do you feel? Shall we go to an assembly tonight?"

Sometimes one was far too lonely to be left alone.

Nine

"Why," Augusta asked with some suspicion the following day, "are there four places laid for dinner? I thought we were to dine alone before attending the theater tonight."

From the doorway of the dining room, Emily replied, "A slight change of plans. As of a few days ago, we've a new neighbor to the west."

"Lord Sutcliffe, you mean?"

"Yes, I have invited him to dine with us. Poor fellow, his servants have hardly unpacked, and there's no telling what his cook may be feeding him. A dinner with friends is much more pleasant than a meat pie from a public house, wouldn't you say?"

"Certainly." Augusta regarded her clothing with some doubt. "Though I ought to change my gown."

She had planned to don an evening frock after dinner, before she and Emily ventured out to the theater. At the moment, then, she still wore her tawny cotton day dress. Earlier today, it had traveled on a carriage ride to Claverton Downs with a man named Prewitt, and it had entertained Hiccuper—whose real name proved to be Harris—and a few friends for tea. It had clothed Mrs. Flowers for a long day of smiles and coos and pleasant chatter.

Augusta had looked forward to being Miss Meredith for a while this evening.

"You haven't time to change. They'll be here any minute, as they have only to walk from next door." Emily shook her perfectly coiffed auburn head. She had changed for dinner, and despite her pallor, she looked elegant in buttery silk with puffed sleeves and sweeping swags of lace about the skirt.

Augusta indicated the fourth place setting. "Who will accompany Lord Sutcliffe?"

"Mr. Everett, of course." Emily beamed at Augusta. "Do you hear the door knocker? I think they've arrived. Come, we'll meet them in the drawing room."

Augusta's heart thumped harder than was necessary for a healthy young woman climbing a single flight of stairs. Foolish organ.

The men reached the drawing room only a minute after Emily and Augusta had settled themselves. Lord Sutcliffe entered first, thin yet resplendent in a plum-colored velvet coat, and Joss trailing behind wearing his usual black. The women greeted them warmly, Augusta trying to smooth the wrinkles from her day dress as she stood.

"Thank you for joining us," Emily said. "I am so glad we have two such amiable neighbors next door."

"Oh, Everett doesn't stay at my lodging." Lord Sutcliffe carried a bottle of something spirituous, which he handed to Joss as he made his bows to the women.

Augusta tilted her head, surprised, but before she

could comment, Joss replied. "Of course not. Lord Sutcliffe is a sedate married man. I cannot have him circumscribing my pleasures."

"How wicked, Mr. Everett! You must tell us more." Emily twinkled, and Sutcliffe beamed at her. Joss's own smile looked odd, merely an ill-fitting shape on his face. When Augusta caught his eye, he looked away, fingers gripping the bottle's neck tightly.

"Lord Sutcliffe," Emily added, "I believe you have met my friend, Mrs.—" Emily cut herself off, eyes opening wide. Augusta's fingers went cold. *Of course.* She had met Sutcliffe before in London. He would know her true name. *Oh, damn.*

"Mrs. Flowers," Joss spoke up from behind the baron, directing a tiny shake of his head to the women. "No, Sutcliffe, I don't think you have yet made her acquaintance."

"Then the honor is mine." The baron bowed over Augusta's right hand as her left still tried to bring order to her worn day dress. "Sure we haven't been introduced before, ma'am? You do look familiar. I never forget a pretty face."

"Well, if we *had* met, I'm sure I should never forget a baron. So therefore we must not have met, my lord." As though this made perfect sense, Augusta mustered Mrs. Flowers's smile, a simper with a dash of syrup. "I am so glad we have the chance to make one another's acquaintance. For the first time."

"The honor is mine. And what a pleasure to dine in this lovely house!" Sutcliffe spread his arms wide. "Lovely, lovely. I ought to have you come look around mine, Lady Tallant, to lend it your magic touch. The furniture is in a sad state compared to this house. Why, some of the velvet on the drawing room settee is worn to the nap."

"Dear me," Emily said. "That sounds most uncomfortable. Have you taken a long lease?"

"A week at a time. But I'm here for as long as need be." Sutcliffe winked. "There's so much in Bath I haven't seen yet. Did you know a man can hire a private bath, and no one would even know who would come and go? We could have an assembly in a bath!"

"I take a private bath daily, but I never thought of hosting an assembly in a bathhouse." Only the slight tilt of Emily's head betrayed her bemusement.

"Lord Sutcliffe is a fount of ideas," murmured Joss.

The blond-haired man beamed. "Truer words were never spoken, and all that. When I'm next in London, I shall see whether I can have a bath constructed for my house. In the ballroom, maybe? It would be simple to have an assembly in a bath if the bath were in a ballroom. Everett, hold tight to that bottle. I had it sent all the way from Switzerland."

They all blinked into this whirlwind of conversation for an instant.

Augusta filled the succeeding pause. "Ah—Lady Tallant, I believe you mentioned that dinner was likely ready?"

"Indeed, yes!" Emily jumped on this excuse. "Lord Sutcliffe, please do see me down. Mr. Everett, you will accompany Mrs. Flowers?"

With more spirit than grace, Emily seized the baron's arm and dragged him from the room. As soon as they crossed the threshold, Augusta whispered,

"Thank you, Joss. I had not realized in time that your cousin had met me before. I just learned the pair of you were to dine tonight, which is why I'm still wearing—" She cut herself off, fisting a wad of cotton skirts. The state of her clothing mattered far less than the state of her reputation. "Well. Thank you again for covering my uncertainty. But surely he'll remember at any time, won't he? Best that I pretend to be ill and bow out of the dinner."

"No need, I assure you." A pinched smile marred Joss's handsome features. "Lord Sutcliffe has a poor memory for names, and as the meal goes on, it shall only become poorer." He brandished the tinted glass bottle, which contained a pale liquid.

He held out his other arm, and once Augusta tucked her hand into the crook of his elbow, he added, "Only act as though all is well, and all shall be well. I've known him my whole life, and I can promise you you're quite safe. Lord Sutcliffe is ready to be pleased."

"And you?" Beneath his coat sleeve, she could feel the strong line of his forearm. "What are you ready for?"

His eyes were dark as smoke as he caught her gaze. "My dear fake widow, I am ready for whatever lies ahead."

❦

An hour later, Joss was relieved that his comforting words to Augusta had been proved accurate. Between Lady Tallant's gracious manners, Lord Sutcliffe's chatter, and Augusta's relentless smiles, there was scarcely a pause in the flow of conversation. The dining room itself was cheerful as a garden, its pale green wallpaper overgrown with vines and fat pink flowers. Silver and china beamed up from the glossy table, and an extravagant fire snapped impishly from the grate. Even the portrait over the chimneypiece, a fat old bewigged gentleman, looked pleased with itself.

Good. For now, everything was good. And where Sutcliffe was concerned, *for now* was the only thing on which he could rely.

Joss forked up a bite of capon, savoring the tender richness of the roasted meat. Along with this delicacy, their hostess had provided puffy little Yorkshire puddings, savory from drippings. Also arrayed about the table were creamed turnips, sweetbreads, a ham, walnuts, and several sorts of boiled vegetables. And wine, of course—a deep red wine as well as a sherry.

Just a small dinner at one's home. Nothing fancy.

As usual, Sutcliffe had allowed himself to be served a full plate of food, then messed about with it so industriously that no one suspected he hardly ate a thing. His glass had been refilled several times, though, and Joss had noticed the baron's fingers wandering toward the breast pocket in which his pouch of *soma-lata* always waited. He had shared out the mysterious beverage from Switzerland, too.

"Absinthe," he explained as a footman poured the pale green beverage into glasses. "It's made from wormwood and fennel. Medicinal! Some people mix it with water, but I don't believe there's any need for that bother."

He raised his glass in a toast to his hostess and "her lovely companion," then tossed back his drink as though it were lemonade. Joss sipped at the unfamiliar beverage slowly. It smelled of anise, and it bit sharply at the tongue and the back of his throat. One taste was enough; he set it aside in favor of wine.

Lady Tallant and Augusta seemed to have thought the same; after a dutiful sip, they too set their glasses aside.

"Thank you for allowing us to sample the absinthe," Augusta said. As Mrs. Flowers, her voice was sweeter and higher than the usual. "I do love trying something new."

"Here now, you're not going to finish it? It *does* have that strong flavor. Medicinal, as I said. Good for the health! But if you prefer wine, that never did anyone harm either." Sutcliffe tilted his own empty glass, squinting at the dregs. "Pass me your glasses, dear ladies; I shall tidy up every hint of the offending liquor."

True to his word, the second and third glasses joined the first in quick succession. "To keep my health in fine form, I do love to try remedies from around the world," the baron confided. "It's my way of traveling, since family responsibilities keep me at home so much."

Joss gulped his wine to help him swallow the *ha* of protest that threatened to burst forth. If by *family responsibilities* Sutcliffe meant *overspending the allowance from my wife through gambling and extravagance*, then indeed, family responsibilities curtailed the baron's dreams of traveling the world and imbibing absinthe in its homeland.

"I understand completely," said Lady Tallant. In the dim light of the fire and overhead chandelier, she looked shadow-eyed, though her expression was as

"Teddy," Joss muttered. "A toddy is a drink."

"A drink?" Sutcliffe glanced his way. "You think we ought to have a drink, Everett? Not a bad idea. Not at all." Motioning for the footman, he had his glass refilled with the last of the absinthe. "How about you, Mrs. Flowers? Any children?"

Joss watched with some amusement as Augusta looked around for a reply, then finally recollected that she was Mrs. Flowers. "Me? Oh, goodness, no." Her giggle rang like a sleigh bell. "I wasn't married long at all."

Her gaze dropped to her plate—demurely, it seemed. Wise woman. If she met Joss's eye, he was likely to betray them both with laughter.

"Any brothers and sisters? I have five sisters." Sutcliffe paused, his glass halfway to his lips. "That can't be right. Five? Five is far too many. Everett, how many sisters have I?"

"Six."

"Six, right," Sutcliffe said cheerfully. "I knew I had to frank a cursed lot of letters for them. Everett is like my own brain walking about in a different body. Saves me the trouble of remembering things."

Now it was Joss's turn to regard his china plate with great interest. Were he to catch Augusta's gaze, he would either snort with laughter or roll his eyes until they popped from their sockets. An extended amount of time in his cousin's company inspired both reactions, sometimes at once.

"You are fortunate to hail from a large family, my lord." The sugary voice of Mrs. Flowers dissolved into Augusta's own lower tones. "I was the only child of my parents, though they always hoped for more."

"Nonsense! They must have been delighted with you. How could anyone hope for more?"

Rare was the individual who could remain immune to Sutcliffe long when he set out to charm. Augusta returned the baron's dazzling smile, but Joss noticed that Lady Tallant had begun to droop. Under the table, he kicked Sutcliffe and shot him a fierce unspoken message: *Turn the subject.*

"Besides which," the baron added smoothly, "sometimes children turn out in the oddest ways. They were lucky with you, but another son or daughter could have turned out rotten. Why, Everett was his mother's only child, and a good thing, too. Not because he was rotten, but because—well, it was for the best."

Did he refer to the poverty of Joss's mother, or the bad blood of his drunken, absent father? Joss cleared his throat. "A child's temperament does not always reflect his upbringing."

"Of course it doesn't," Sutcliffe agreed. "If it did, you'd have finished your absinthe. Eh?"

This was evidently meant as a hilarious jest—though if parsed, it reflected as much on Sutcliffe's drinking as it did on Joss's heritage.

Sutcliffe never seemed to realize that the joke could be on him. Life was, in itself, joke enough.

Joss forced a smile. He always made himself smile when Sutcliffe poked at the bruises of his birth, heedless of their shared ancestry. There was no chance Sutcliffe would ever stop; it wasn't in his upbringing to think Joss could be offended, especially by the truth. So Joss had long ago decided to act as though he wasn't bothered a bit.

Sometimes it worked. Tonight, with Lady Tallant putting on a brave face and Augusta wearing a puzzled one, the heedlessness rankled.

So he drank his wine under Sutcliffe's approving eye, and looked forward to the date when his eternal penance would end.

Ten

When the dinner guests bade the women farewell, Augusta watched them descend the steps of Emily's Queen Square house. Ducking into the shadow of the stone-trimmed doorway, she peered after them as the two tall figures made their way down the pavement to the west.

The afternoon had grown late, and the sun was hanging low in the blue-gray sky. Lord Sutcliffe's velvet coat caught the light in burnished flicks of purple each time he gesticulated broadly. At his side, Joss's back was stern and broad, his strides measured. Once, he drew his cousin away from the muddy street. At the foot of the steps to the next house, he doffed his hat, then the men parted.

As Joss turned back the way he had come, Augusta pressed herself against the black front door. With a single step, a single press of the door handle, she could be back in the house. Resting or changing her gown for the theater or chatting with Emily, who had been quiet for the remainder of the meal.

She could do any of those things. She *should* do all of them.

But instead, she stepped forward. "Mr. Everett."

Joss squinted below the brim of his hat, then again tipped it. "Mrs. Flowers. Did we leave something behind?"

"No." She descended the stone steps, hugging herself tightly. Her thin cotton gown was no barrier to the breeze—not that furs and cloaks and gloves seemed ever to warm her. "May I be quite frank with you?"

"Of course you may. Though perhaps you should employ your frankness indoors on such a chilly day."

"It doesn't matter; I'm always cold. Let us go to the mews to talk." Behind the long row of houses, Bath's wealthy kept their carriages and horses. Augusta enjoyed walking the mews, out from under the eyes of household servants. If one took a few carrots or apples, the horses would stretch out their beautiful heads for a treat, soft muzzles like velvet as they lipped the food from her hand.

Today she had nothing with her. She hadn't even worn sturdy boots, and her slippers were sure to be ruined—if not by mud, by coarse straw and droppings. Not that it mattered. The heiress to Meredith Beauty could always buy more.

Joss regarded her with some skepticism, then fell into step beside her. Once more he turned his steps westward, passing the doorway to Lord Sutcliffe's house without a sideways glance. "Even so. By now, you must be even colder than usual," he said. "Here."

Before she could stop him, he shrugged free of his coat and dropped the heavy garment on her shoulders. Jaw set, he tugged at the lapels until they met just below her chin. "Hold fast, now."

So quickly and efficiently did he disrobe, enfold her, and stride on that Augusta could only trot after him, her mouth struggling to shape some appropriate reply.

You shouldn't have was perfectly true, for a gentleman ought never to appear in his shirtsleeves in public. As he had drawn a few steps ahead, she could see Joss's sleeves rippling in the breeze, the thin cotton outlining the hard planes of his forearm. His black waistcoat, dark breeches, and tall boots framed his figure, capable and swift, stark against the silvery sky.

Augusta clutched tightly at the lapels of the coat, letting the rough fabric scratch at the bare skin of her hands and arms. Despite the breeze, she caught the scent of sandalwood from the fabric, and she breathed in deeply. "Thank you."

His steps slowed, though he did not turn. "You're quite welcome" was tossed over his shoulder, though the tone of it sounded more like *I had to, because if you freeze out here and expire, I will probably be blamed.*

Joss paused at the end of the square's long facade. Turning toward Augusta, he said, "Will this spot do for whatever you would like to tell me? You need not ruin your slippers along with your health."

"The latter is fine, and the former is of no concern to me." And she led him through a gap to the mews serving the houses.

Compared to the aggressive grandeur of the facade, the mews seemed almost tumbledown. The first stables had been built of sturdy stone with tile roofs, but offshoots and lean-tos and alcoves had been added over time, a mixture of brick and wood. Rain barrels caught the constant drip from drizzle-damp eaves.

Hay lay in great piles under shelter, and the smell of mucked-out stalls and the earthy scent of horses over-laid the sandalwood Augusta had just been breathing. Most of Bath society rested at this hour, and the streets were quieter than usual. In the mews, animal whick-ers and the occasional voice of a groom made a low counterpoint to the breath of the wind.

"What is this all about, then?" Joss looked down at Augusta. "You *did* once promise me not to engage in hen-witted espionage capers. Now I am forced to strip to my shirtsleeves to keep you from catching a dreadful chill. Your manner indicated some urgency, and your level of dress—or undress—even more so."

"I can always tell," Augusta replied, "when you are getting ready to say something clever and cutting to me, because one of your brows shoots up. And though I do thank you for the loan of your coat, you offered it; I did not request it. *And* I would greatly appreciate you waiting until I say something horrid before you are horrid to me."

He poked at his wayward brow, frowning. "Ah, but then you'd always have the advantage."

She settled deeper into the warm wool of his coat. "Must someone always have the advantage?"

"Only someone who has always had the advantage would ask that question."

"I'll be brief, then, so as not to offend your ears with excessive privilege. Here is what I wanted to say. Thank you for dining with us today. Thank you even more for taking trouble to keep the secret of Mrs. Flowers. And I'm sorry your cousin isn't more cordial to you."

She tugged the coat off and held it out to him. "That's all. Good day to you."

He didn't reach out his hand; instead, he tilted down his chin and fixed her with his dark eyes. "Why do you say such a thing about Lord Sutcliffe? All the world finds him pleasant."

Her arm tiring, she pulled it back and folded the coat into a bundle. The sharp, smoke-sweet hint of sandalwood caught her again, scattering her thoughts for a moment before she managed a reply. "He was pleasant, yes. Although he asked so many questions about family, he never referred to you as his cousin. It surprised me, especially since you work with him daily."

"Ah. Well. A bit of distance can sometimes do as much good as a medicinal drink." His mouth twisted.

"Or medicinal grasses?"

"Or those, yes. Lord Sutcliffe is concerned with his health," Joss said.

"But not with yours?"

Joss pulled off his hat and worked the brim with his gloved fingers. Short-cropped and slightly curling, his hair ruffled in the breeze. "It's not his job to worry about me. It's my job to worry about him."

As an orphan and only child, the idea of a family member who worried over her was appealing. "You must be important to him, then."

"Oh, probably. But in a way no more meaningful than a child thinking it needs a sweet or a boat. I'm the person who helps him achieve his whims. Anyone else could become as efficient in time; I simply have the advantage of long practice."

He spoke with a flat precision that seemed to press

Augusta down. More than once, he had hinted at a fraught relationship with his cousin and employer, though his words had danced by, glanced off whatever mirrored surface Augusta had sought to become that day. "I'm sorry, Joss. I did not realize that was the case."

"I did not want you to realize. Damnable pride, you know. Though I wouldn't have minded if you asked." He looked up at the sharp line of the house roofs looming behind the mews. "You never asked."

"I was trying to be kind. I didn't want to ask anything more of you than you wanted to give."

"Then why, when we first met in the assembly rooms, did you not simply believe I would keep your secrets and walk away?"

The main reason, of course, was that she couldn't bring herself to. She had not dared trust him, but she also hadn't wanted to leave him. His familiarity was a relief, an escape into the honesty she had begun to crave.

Yet Mrs. Flowers was supposed to be the escape. Augusta was farther than ever from slaking her grief, from finding the peace she sought.

She clutched his coat closer, a wall of masculine cloth and scent that made her throat dry, her nipples as tight from eagerness as from cold. "I would have walked away if I could."

"I see," he said quietly. And she wondered just how much he saw.

"Just—just for tonight," she stammered, "you could leave Lord Sutcliffe behind. Come to the theater with Lady Tallant and me."

He lifted both brows. Was he about to let fly *two*

cutting and clever remarks? Augusta parried. "Only for business, of course. The countess has taken a box with no view of the stage at all, but one can spy on the entire audience without being seen. Perhaps you might even spot another person from your list."

"*Your* list," Joss corrected, donning his hat again. "Naturally I assumed the invitation was for business, my dear fake widow. Alas, I cannot accept for other reasons of business. This evening I am to meet with your Lord Chatfield. Of a sudden, I require the aid of a man who knows things more than the commerce of a man who buys things."

"He's not *my* Lord Chatfield." In a slide of disappointment, Augusta fumbled for words. "That is—he buys things, too. And he knows things. So you might be able to sell things and learn things."

Surely no one had ever babbled out the word *things* so often in a single sentence. Again, she held out his coat, hoping she would feel less muddled without the distraction of the sandalwood scent, the dark wool rubbing at her arms.

This time he accepted the coat from her, though he only held it in a folded bundle as she had. "If you've no great desire to attend the theater, would you care to come with me this evening when I call upon Lord Chatfield? It might do you good to speak to someone else who knows Miss Meredith."

"No. I couldn't." She shook her head, folding her bare arms tightly under her breasts. Let him make a joke about her *dockyard*. Let him.

But he did not; his eyes looked tired. "Why could you not? What would be so terrible if a man who *knows things* learns you are going under a false name? People who *know things* are generally discreet." He paused. "Or they are blackmailers. One or the other."

"No, I'm sure he's not a blackmailer. I—he—" Augusta pressed her lips together. "I don't know. I think—he would be disappointed to know I had set aside my parents' name. He knew them quite well, you see."

These last words brought the press of tears to her eyes, but she held them back. After the grinding smiling, dinner conversation—too much worry over Emily, too many secrets to keep—the boulder of grief was unsteady. She could not let it rock anymore; she could not bear the idea of another fall, another grueling tug upward.

But a few images flitted into her mind, summoned by the mention of her family. Her mother's hair, just as red as Augusta's, though in the last year of her life, it had become threaded with gray strands. Her father— not quite as tall as her mother—had the sort of laugh that made everyone around him happier. His hair was thin, his middle thick, his eyes wistful. How they had wanted a large family.

If they'd had one, Augusta would never have been left alone.

And maybe she would have been wiser, too. With more people to love her, surely she would have been less desperate to dive into the arms of a liar like Colin Hawford.

Joss shook out his coat, holding it up as though fitting it to an invisible companion. "What do you fear? That Chatfield will fault you for lying about your name? Or that he would divine the scandalous reason why?"

"Yes," she said numbly. "Yes, all of it."

His hands sank, the coat brushing the muddy straw beneath their feet. "I already know those things, yet I can tolerate your presence."

For the first time all day, her smile felt real. Instead of folding her face into false lines, it slipped cleanly over her features. A little frisson ran through her body, but it didn't feel cold. "That was rather kind. Did you mean it to be so?"

"Did you think it was? Dear me. It wasn't even that kind. I ought to be more aggressive with my polite comments." The smile he returned to her looked a little…shy.

Shy? Truly? But so it appeared; his fine mouth curved gently, his deep, black-lashed eyes caught her gaze, then flicked away. He picked up his coat to a safe height and brushed at its hem, then folded it up again. It seemed he would not wear it if she would not.

"I'm not going to make you another indecent proposition," Augusta said. "I've too much pride for that."

She had to say it, hoping to convince herself— because more and more often, she thought of touching his skin, tracing the hard lines of his features, clutching him close—close enough to make her forget, close enough to chase away everything dark.

But he could not do so, she knew, for he was too much like her. He had lost his parents; he had tried to win the heart of a cold lover. He kept his cousin's secrets, and a man who kept secrets knew how hard it was to force them down.

"I am glad you have too much pride," Joss said. "Because I've too much pride to take anything from you." He drew closer, no more than a hairbreadth away, and added, "I should like to give you something, though."

He didn't ask if she would permit that, or she might have forced herself to skitter away before he could bend his head to hers. Flirtation was about control, and lust about its loss—and oh, this was lust; she practically shivered with it, with wanting to close the distance between them. When her lips parted, her breath turned to frost in the air.

He didn't kiss her right away. Instead, he brushed back a fallen lock of her hair, and she realized she had run outside with no bonnet as well as no cloak. Then he wrapped the coat around her, almost holding her in an embrace as he caught up its edges.

"My dear fake widow," he murmured, and brushed her lips with his. Just a sweet flutter, almost like a chance encounter between mouths. Light and lovely and over in an instant.

It was little enough; it was far too much. All the hesitancy in her crumbled, and she grabbed for him, clutching at his shoulders, stretching up to her toes to crush her mouth against his with a graceless clash. With such force did she fling herself that he stumbled back, almost losing his balance and his grip on the coat. When he caught his footing, she was pressed heavily against his chest before stumbling back. His fists, still gripping the coat around her, settled between her breasts, and she choked to hold back a little moan.

"My dear *God*," he murmured against her lips.

"I require more arms." His hands held her tight within the coat. Up and down, he rolled his balled fists gently, seeking the curve of her breasts through the heavy fabric. "Have I truly never been kind to you? Are you quite sure I have never complimented your appearance?"

"I don't know," Augusta said, letting her eyes fall shut. "I don't remember anything right now."

Thank God—it was the oblivion she had hoped for, though she knew it would be fleeting. Again, he brushed her mouth with his, gently, yet she could feel the coiled tension in his hands. He was hungry, he was eager, he was fighting with himself for control.

She began to thaw at the edges; her fingers and toes, though ungloved and shod in thin slippers, were the first freed from ice. Nothing could warm her enough to reach her heart—but to have her hands back, her feet back, was more than she had felt in almost two years. With her hands no longer frozen, she could reach out for him; with her feet no longer numb, she could step toward him.

And then there was no distance between them, nothing at all, as her hands fought free from the cloaking coat and encircled his hard waist. He moaned and opened his mouth to hers, brushing her tongue with his own, breathing her in. She breathed him in too, drinking and tasting him. He was wine-sweet and strong, and so determined to make her warm. If they had enough time, he could melt more of her with the heat of his hands. His lips. The whole breadth and length of his body. Already, her core was damp with desire.

A shrill whistle rang high through the mews, followed by applause.

Augusta's eyes snapped open. Not ten yards away in the shelter of a lean-to, a stable boy in rough work clothing grinned fit to bust his young face. "Don't let me stop ye, govs!"

Joss stepped back, chuckling. "Sorry, lad. Go to the theater if you want a show."

He slid an arm around Augusta's shoulders in a gesture that felt more like politeness than passion, turning her in the direction from which they'd come. "That was not quite what I meant to do, my dear fake widow, though I shan't apologize."

"Nor shall I." Augusta could feel the blush rising in her cheeks, not from embarrassment but from shock at how quickly she had forgotten herself. Where was the control she sought? What was the point of taking a lover if she ended worse off than she already was?

Joss was not a safe choice. She had known this at once. With all his pride, he would never stand for the limits she would set on a lover, nor the speed with which she intended to discard one. He was not at all what she wanted.

Yet she could not bring herself to leave the cradle of his arm. To walk away from him. She could not rely on herself to obey her own edicts, and the realization was like falling: a leap, a flight, and the inevitability of a crash.

Although as they walked back from the mews toward respectability, and he never removed his arm or his coat from around her shoulders, she felt as though she was still in flight. It was hard to remember that the crash was inevitable, or how much it had hurt each time in the past.

She wondered whether she was right about that *not what she wanted* business.

Probably they passed other people who thought their appearance odd, but Augusta noticed nothing. Possibly some people even spoke to them, but she heard nothing either. She only felt, and wondered... what the devil was she doing?

When they reached the steps of Emily's house, Joss walked her up, then faced her in front of the door. Slowly, he drew his coat off her shoulders, and she felt as though he were undressing her completely. She shivered.

"Augusta," he said quietly, "you are a worthy person. The man who made you doubt that did a terrible thing."

She stared at him, doubting, but his eyebrows remained straight over his fixed gaze. "Oh," she said.

"What about a 'Thank you, Joss'?" Then he shook his head. "My dear fake widow, you still have difficulty trusting me? Another sin to lay at that fellow's feet."

He reached past her, and for an instant she thought he was going to embrace her. Maybe kiss her again.

Rap rap. No, he only tapped with the brass door knocker, then stood back again. Within a few seconds, a servant had opened the door. "Mrs. Flowers, you must be frozen!"

"She won't admit to it," Joss said. "But I think she wouldn't mind a bit of hot punch." He caught Augusta's eye. "Medicinal, you know."

With a wink and a tip of his hat, he turned and

descended the steps, then strode—still holding his coat in his shirtsleeved arms—in the direction of his lodgings.

Huh.

Augusta let herself be tugged inside, her feet slid into clean slippers, her shoulders wrapped in a shawl. A cup of hot tea was pressed into her hand. Then she was sent upstairs to rest, the fire built up high in her bedchamber. A maid promised to return in an hour to help her dress and arrange her hair for the theater.

And still, as another door closed behind her, all she could think was: *huh.*

She sat on the carpet before the fireplace and watched the flames flicker and dance.

Though Joss had kissed her as though they were ready to tumble into a bed, though he had held his coat about her shoulders with gentleness, he hadn't really flirted with her. No sweet words to entice her further. The closest he had veered to praise was to ask whether he had ever complimented her appearance—and then, contrary man, he never *had* said anything kind.

Until they parted. *You are a worthy person.*

Maybe she had an incomplete idea of what constituted flirtation. Or maybe he was simply being... well...decent.

You are worthy ought to be such a truism that to state it openly was foolish. Like *You are female* or *Your hair is red.* But through years of grief and foolish choices, it had stopped feeling true. And somehow, he had seen that, and he'd told her what she wanted most in the world to believe again.

Maybe she would one day. For today, it was good to know someone else in the world thought so.

◆

And *that*, more than any compliment he might have given her on her appearance—and almost more than his kiss—made her feel a bit warmer inside as she stretched her hands out before the fire.

Eleven

JOSS HAD BEEN IN BATH FOR LESS THAN A FORTNIGHT, so it was no great wonder he had not yet visited one of the hot springs that gave the city its name. But that would change today: Lord Chatfield had expressed his willingness to meet with Joss on the evening of his choice, provided that the meeting was held in a private bath. His lordship, it seemed, had a strict therapeutic regimen.

Though Joss placed little faith in the healing powers of Bath's sulfurous springs, they would certainly do the marquess no harm. Unlike some of Sutcliffe's favorite *medicinal* concoctions.

He had spent the few hours since dinner trying not to think of the incendiary kisses of Augusta Meredith. Instead, with dogged persistence, he had sifted through Sutcliffe's correspondence, attempting to plot a means of identifying the baron's blackmailer, though coming up with little. All for Sutcliffe, always.

Soon enough, Joss would be able to live for himself. And he hoped such a life would include more of Augusta Meredith, in any and many forms.

But not tonight. Tonight she was at the theater, probably dressed in silk cut to the latest fashion. And she was not even Miss Meredith: she was Mrs. Flowers when out in public, flirting and laughing to convince the men of Bath that she was all dockyard and no sense.

With a grimace, he scraped his muddy boots at the doorway to the building to which Chatfield had directed him.

It was a blocky structure of Bath stone, stretching up three stories. Wrapping around one side, Joss noticed a wooden veranda with a swooping roof. The spindly, organic shape of it looked oddly foreign, especially connected to a solidly English structure.

He liked it. It reminded him of himself, a bit foreign on an English foundation. With a wry smile lingering on his lips, he knocked on the door.

It was opened by a dark-skinned attendant in simple white robes, who bowed. "Mr. Everett? The marquess awaits you," he said in lightly accented tones, taking Joss's hat and gloves.

Looking around the vestibule, Joss had scarcely time to collect an impression of Oriental luxury—lacy-carved wood, glossy tile, painted murals of reclining moguls—before he was shown down an equally elaborate short corridor, then into a side chamber.

Luxury, unfamiliar yet unmistakable, framed his gaze. Lamps lined the edges of the room, their flames gentle. The floor was marble, with a great stone tub to one side. In the shadowed edges of the room, Joss made out the lines of pipes. They ran vertically, feeding the tub and a smaller tank, within which lay an unfamiliar apparatus that looked like a great cloth funnel. In the humid air, the familiar scent of sandalwood overlaid the sulfurous scent of piped-in mineral water.

And in the tub, wearing a capacious bathing outfit of dark wool, reclined a man Joss presumed to be Lord Chatfield. The marquess was a robust-looking man of perhaps fifty years. His damp hair was receding at the forehead; a stern jaw and cleft chin saved his round face from softness. His eyes were closed, arms resting at the edge of the tub to balance his weight. A glossy skim of perfumed oil reflecting atop the water was, Joss guessed, the source of the sandalwood scent in the room.

"My lord, it is I. Josiah Everett." Joss waited at a courteous distance.

"Everett." Lord Chatfield's eyes blinked open. "Quite pleased to make your acquaintance. Are you prepared to enter into discussion at once, or do you wish to bathe first?"

"I most certainly do not wish to bathe," Joss confirmed. Private baths often cost nearly four shillings, and in a therapeutic palace such as this, a bath was surely even farther beyond his means.

"A turn in the vaporizer, then?" The marquess indicated the odd funnel-looking device. "It does something clever with steam and Indian oils. Excellent for the circulation of the blood."

"No." Joss forced a polite smile. "Thank you."

Behind Joss, the door opened. Another servant in pristine robes brought in a chair, and Joss nodded thanks before the dark-skinned man bowed his way out.

"For you, Everett," Chatfield confirmed. "I suspected you'd wish to get on with our chat. The best time to work, after all, is while others are playing. You'll forgive me if I remain seated."

His voice was low and resonant, calm and certain. When he spoke these words, Joss found it impossible not to sit in the chair, impossible to take offense at the odd circumstances of the meeting. "Of course. Thank you for your time, my lord."

The elder man nodded. "So. I presume you're here because your employer, Sutcliffe, is in trouble. What is it? Gambling? Women? Unnatural lusts?"

Joss hesitated. "I do not mean to offend, my lord, but I must request your word of honor that this matter will remain discreet."

The marquess's brows shot up; his weight shifted, sending ripples across the scented surface of the water. "You sought an appointment with me, but you do not trust me with your confidence?"

"My lord, your help was recommended by…a friend. But I'm not certain whether it is seemly to request this type of help from an acquaintance so new."

"By your friend, you mean Augusta Meredith." One hand rubbed at his chin. "Well. Just because she's lying about who *she* is doesn't mean she's lying about who *I* am."

"You believe she is lying about who she is?" Lord Chatfield had said the words in such an offhand fashion. And Augusta had been so afraid of his reaction.

"I don't believe it. I know it. But you must decide how to proceed for yourself. A fellow like you is surely used to doing that."

Joss drew his head back, trying not to bristle. "What do you mean, 'a fellow like me'? My lord."

The marquess leaned his head back, resting it against the marble wall behind the tub. "Grandson of a baron. Cousin to a baron. Treated like a servant, probably because of your Indian blood. It's all in Debrett's, Everett. You may think your birth a secret, but not all the world is as thick-witted as your cousin Sutcliffe." Hooded eyes studied Joss. "You've done well for yourself."

Grateful for the steadiness of the chair beneath him, Joss could only make an odd noise that he hoped sounded like agreement. So used was he to being overlooked, a shadow at the edge of a room, that he had forgotten his existence was easily investigated— should anyone care to.

There was no sense in regretting the inheritance laws that favored men over women, the laws that had taken the barony from his mother's line and handed it to Sutcliffe's. And truly, Joss had never wished to be a baron any more than he aspired to be king. He only wanted to be…well, he didn't know what. Not part of the *ton*; he hadn't the resources or desire for that life. But not rejected, either. Not a servant, shunted from the family lodging.

Above all, not forgotten.

"I see." His throat felt raw. "Our mutual acquaintance was quite correct when she stated that you know things."

"Knowing things is my preferred pastime," said the marquess. "And the greatest part of knowing things is learning how to find information. People carry it about with them. For example, when the servant brought the chair, you acknowledged his presence. A nobleman would never do this, yet you have noble ancestry. Why, then? Is it because you recognize his blood in you, or because you believe you share his status?" He lifted a hand. "You need not answer, for the answers aren't important. Only the questions."

Joss looked aslant at the wide tub, at the older man within it, mostly hidden beneath the lamp-glossed surface of the water. Though Chatfield was wet and seated and not fully dressed, Joss had no illusion that the marquess was at a disadvantage.

What, after all, did Joss have to lose by requesting the man's help? The secrets he held were Sutcliffe's. Maybe Lord Chatfield would help them both, but if not, at least his intercession would help Joss break free.

"As a matter of fact, my lord, there is an answer that is *very* important to me at present." And briefly, he sketched out the baron's indiscretion, the pregnant maid. The financial strings held by the long-suffering baroness. The blackmail demands Sutcliffe could not meet without telling his wife.

"Unless, that is, I can sell off his coal to raise the money—or, even better, find the blackmailer," Joss finished. "I've only one clue, though. As one letter was sent from London and the most recent from Bath, the person has probably arrived here recently."

"But no seal, you say; only a gummed wafer and plain printed writing." The marquess had sat up straighter as Joss recounted the matter. His straight brows had lifted; again, a hand rubbed at his chin. "An interesting little problem, to be sure. And we must solve it by?"

"The end of the month."

"Twelve days, then. So be it. And how shall you pay for my services?"

Joss blinked. He hadn't considered this, though he realized he had been naïf to presume a nobleman would help a stranger out of the goodness of his heart. "If you seek information, I doubt I have any you don't already possess. But if it's a matter of mere coin, Lord Sutcliffe will pay you whatever you require, as long as it is within his means."

Chatfield tilted his head on its thick neck. "Are you sure of that? Who wants the answer more, him or you?"

"He—if—" Words stumbled, half-formed, as Joss felt off-balance again. The answer seemed obvious—but was it? To Sutcliffe, a blackmailer was an inconvenience to be handled so his wife wouldn't restrict his financial freedom. To Joss, it *was* financial freedom, or the promise of it.

The marquess pursed his lips. "Hmm. Yes. Well, we shall sort that matter out when I have found out what you wish to know." He turned the subject. "So, you have been spending a lot of time with Mrs. Flowers, as our young friend is calling herself these days."

"Hmm," Joss echoed, folding his arms.

Chatfield grinned, a flash of straight teeth in the lamplight. "A diplomatic silence. I like that. Though as it is a fact, there is nothing about which you need to be diplomatic. She *is* calling herself Mrs. Flowers, and you *have* been spending a great deal of time with her. Why?"

Joss thought of asking to which part of the statement the "why" referred, but the answers were intertwined.

He picked his way carefully through a few sentences. "I have been spending time with her largely *because* she calls herself Mrs. Flowers. I was previously acquainted with her. She did not intend to be recognized, and in exchange for my reticence, she offered me help."

"You intended to reveal her true identity, then?"

"No, I did not intend that." The suggestion of being judged wrongly made him bristle again; the humid, warm air was causing his neck to perspire under its tight-fitting cravat. "But the blasted woman wouldn't trust me, and so she inflicted all this unrequested...*help* on me. Including the suggestion that I meet with you."

"Hmm."

"For which, by the way, I thank you," Joss added gruffly.

"Hmm."

"But the fact remains that I did not ask for it, and that she helped me because she did not trust me."

"Hmm."

God. Joss shoved himself to his feet. "Thank you for your time. I won't take any more of it."

The marquess's dark-clad figure moved like a seal: a quick splash and flop, and he was up at the front of the huge tub, elbows supporting his weight on the side. "No, no, don't leave yet. We still haven't got to the right question. Which is: *why* is she posing as a widow?"

If their conversation had been rocky before, now it was slippery as a glacier. Joss remained standing, his feet planted where he was sure of his footing. "I believe she is playing a game with herself. Because of some ill treatment by a man in the past."

"Ah, I wondered whether that was still bothering her. A nasty business right around the time of her parents' deaths, and she's had no one to rely on since." He spoke as blandly as though he were reading an advertisement out of *The Times*. "The Merediths were on their way to Portsmouth for business, the first time they had left London in years. Our girl took the chance to meet with that lover of hers."

Joss's knees requested that he take a seat at once. "She had a lover?" His voice cracked like an adolescent's on the final word. Clearing his throat, he amended, "Ah. I mean—of course. Her lover. Yes." It was a surprise to hear, but it shouldn't be. For her to seek a lover now—out of revenge, it seemed—she must have had one in the past. Augusta Meredith was too bright to play the Mrs. Flowers game for no reason at all.

And she was too lovely, too passionate, to be resisted by a man she truly wanted.

Or so Joss presumed. From tooth-gritting experience, he knew it was difficult enough to resist her when she tossed a bland *You would do* in his direction.

"He was the younger son of a baronet," Chatfield continued. "No money of his own, and no chance at a title. Likely her fortune was what he wanted, though he played the adoring suitor well enough. He dropped her after her parents died."

Joss shook his head. "Why? If he liked her, and she was wealthy, why not propose marriage?"

The marquess shifted in the tub, shaking out his arms. "Mr. Meredith was a crafty fellow. His will stated that the trustees of his daughter's fortune had to approve her marriage should she wish to wed before the age of twenty-five."

"And they didn't approve him?"

"I think they might have, given time. But he didn't bother trying to win them over. He dropped our young friend instead."

Why? Joss wanted to ask. Just...*why?* What would make a man be so foolish or so selfish?

Or—what would make a woman so eager that she was so completely wrong about a man's true feelings?

All he could do was shake his head again. As Chatfield had said earlier, the answers weren't important; only the questions. These things had happened. It was enough to wonder why, for the *why* meant that these things were wrong, that they should not have taken place. There would likely never be an answering *because.*

"Tell me, what do you think of her?" the marquess asked.

Joss arched a brow. "My answer doesn't matter, does it?"

"Indulge me. Abandon diplomacy."

The resonant voice was impossible to gainsay a second time, and a great bitterness rose up in Joss: a bitterness scraped together from tiny fires and hoarded pence and tea leaves used twice, thrice, until there was no flavor left. And of a woman who owned furs and silks and walked out with no cloak, so certain was she that someone would take care of her, that the world would not let her be cold.

And she was right. He wouldn't; he couldn't.

How could she wish to be someone else?

Though she had sworn she was still cold. Always cold. Maybe she wasn't testing the world's regard; maybe she simply didn't care what became of her.

"I think she is unappreciative." Joss paused. "But intelligent. And, of course, pretty."

"You are right on all counts." The marquess smiled, a quick flash of approval. "Is it fair to fault her for being unable to count her blessings? She has lived among them too long to see them as abnormal. She is far too occupied with counting coin or counting the steps in a dance."

"Or counting the callers who fawn over Mrs. Flowers."

"Yes, though I can't imagine she feels much triumph in that. Since, as you say, they are really Mrs. Flowers's men."

The way Chatfield *knew things* was beginning to seem a little terrifying. Still, Joss insisted, "Mrs. Flowers and Miss Meredith are the same person."

"Not quite. But I'm not sure where the difference lies. What do you think?"

A few days ago, an aeon ago, she had described her false self to Joss. *She has more possibilities open to her than I do.*

But that wasn't enough of an explanation. It didn't capture the difference in her voice, her laugh; the quick, darting way she looked at people, then pretended she hadn't. It was all done by the same person, though, one person making decisions as though she were two beings.

Joss shook his head. "I can't answer that."

"The answer doesn't matter as much as the question. And I think you won't forget the question."

"As you wish, my lord." Joss bit the words off crisply. Too many questions; not enough answers. "Excuse me, please. If we've concluded our business, I must go."

"No, you mustn't," Chatfield said. "You're staying alone in an attic room, and every minute you remain with me is a minute less of coal you must scrounge. Stay a bit longer. Hear me out. Or let me hear you out, if you prefer."

This was how the marquess knew things, Joss thought. He learned enough about a person's wishes and dreams to make himself dangerous, to insinuate himself wherever he wanted to be. And right now, he knew that the promise of savings—of another brief while that Joss didn't have to be in a chilly dark room alone—was dreadfully tempting against the late winter night.

Before he could profess his agreement or withhold it, Chatfield observed, "You are unappreciative too."

Joss's head snapped back, and he glared at the older man. A complacent wide oval of a face, a damnably calm expression. And why was he in the bath for so long?

This meeting had been a foolish idea. "I do not think you are correct, my lord," Joss shot back. "I support myself, and it is done with some difficulty."

"Hmm." Chatfield leaned forward, stirring the water with one hand, and the scent of sandalwood grew stronger. "Do you work in a mine or somewhere that places you in daily peril? Did you hunger for education but had no opportunity to gain it?" He paused. "Are you an unmarried female who must be accompanied everywhere by a servant, lest her reputation—her future—be destroyed?"

Joss narrowed his eyes until Chatfield was nothing but blurs.

"You dislike what I say," said the marquess. "You think your birth and straitened upbringing has given you a right to feel wronged. I can't say as it hasn't, but I also can't see what good the resentment does you."

"I beg your pardon, my lord." Joss set his teeth. "But I cannot imagine what someone in your position would know about feeling wronged. Or about wishing for anything that cannot be gained."

"You cannot," the older man said mildly. "I suppose that makes sense. Well, before you leave, help me to rise, Everett. There are towels against the wall, if you wouldn't mind fetching one."

Still cross, Joss picked up one of the soft cloths and approached the tub for the first time. He caught the marquess's wool-clad forearms, but the man didn't rise in one smooth motion. Instead, he shifted, a low sound of a heavy body dragging against stone as he got his legs under him.

Pulling heavily against Joss's weight, he hoisted himself out of the water. And at once, Joss recognized his error, and the reason for Chatfield's great effort: his right leg was missing below the knee.

Oh.

Oh.

Chagrin locked his tongue for a few dreadful seconds, then he managed, "I'm so sorry, my lord. I didn't realize."

"What, that a horse fell on my leg when I was

a reckless-riding boy? That a surgeon set the break incorrectly? That I traded the leg for my life?" The marquess's voice came with effort as he struggled to stand and balance. "Of course you didn't realize. But if you had, I presume you'd have acted no differently just now. Surely you wouldn't have left a marquess to flounder in his own filth."

"Scented by sandalwood?" Joss braced the older man around his shoulders, helping him seat himself on the broad edge of the tub. He then sat at the marquess's side, facing away from the water. "You and I have a different idea of filth, my lord."

"I'm not sure we *do* have a different idea of it." Chatfield's left leg and foot dabbled in the hot mineral water. "And it's no bad thing to be underestimated, Everett. No bad thing at all. Keep that in mind when you start to feel wronged again."

"No bad thing," Joss replied, "as long as the underestimation doesn't limit one."

They sat side by side in silence, while Joss's thoughts rippled and heated like the water at his back. Everyone had something to grieve, did they not? A leg, a parent, an inconstant lover. There was always something more that could be lost.

Which meant there was always something for which to be grateful.

Chatfield was the first to break the silence. "Here is my fee for helping you. If I find Sutcliffe's blackmailer and you get what you want, you must come and work for me."

For the second time in a few minutes, words escaped Joss. "I must—what? Why?"

The heavy body breathed a great sigh. "A man cannot live on the interest of a few hundred pounds, or whatever you hope to extract from Lord Sutcliffe as his penance. You must plan to seek a new position. I shall provide it, at double your present salary."

"Why?" Joss asked again.

The marquess turned to look Joss in the face. Seated side by side as they were, the direct gaze was uncomfortably close. In the low glow of the lamps, his eyes glinted as dark as Joss's own. "Because," he answered, "you didn't trust me at once. And because to find me, you accepted help from a woman. In the business of collecting information, there is no budget for foolishness and there is no time for senseless pride."

"I'll think on it." This might be a lie. It might be true. Joss shook his head, then sprung to his feet. "Truly, I must leave now, my lord. Can I assist you in any other way before I depart?"

Chatfield smiled again, an indulgent twist of lips. "Just think on it. That's all I ask right now."

❧

Taking the long way back to Trim Street, through steeply inclined city streets and around the pie-shaped road of the Circus, Joss thought about it. Step after step, he thought about money and pride, and which was worth more.

He took a break from this musing only to think about another idea Chatfield had planted. *Here I am, walking alone at night without fear.* It had never occurred to him to be grateful for the simple state of being male. Healthy. Sufficiently tall and fit—and insufficiently wealthy-looking—to be a target for thieves. Even on a night such as this, when the moon was nothing but a sliver and the sky was like spilled ink.

So long, he had been pinched and lonely and impatient, but he had never really been afraid. Instead, he had assumed there was nothing worthwhile that could be taken from him. But perhaps he was not correct about that.

Hmm, as Chatfield would have said. Hmm.

Yet there was no denying he had never fit into the polite world. Though his blood was too blue and his speech too crisp to place him among servants, his dark skin marked him indelibly as *not one of you*. But he knew little of India beyond the plants once cultivated in the Sutcliffe Hall conservatory, or the black-bound book left behind by his grandmother. All that was left now was *somalata,* the moon plant, which ruled Sutcliffe's every waking hour.

Maybe it was for this reason that he wanted Augusta's secrets. Her trust. Her kisses too, if he were honest.

Neither of them fit tidily into society; neither was quite what the *ton* expected. Not that this meant they had anything in common.

And yet.

A version of himself *with more possibilities open.* Wasn't that everything he wanted too?

Twelve

Augusta hoped a noisy, luxurious evening at the theater would distract her. She needed distraction badly—not only from the memory of a private conversation with Joss that probably shouldn't have happened, but also from a kiss that *certainly* shouldn't have happened.

And from the realization that she dwelled on both without ever quite getting around to regretting either.

Her gown of blush-colored silk trimmed with glass beads and blond lace had once seemed the height of elegance, yet tonight she recalled how Joss had kissed her when she wore wrinkled cotton. And unfortunately, the performance they attended was *She Stoops to Conquer*. Augusta was not quite in the mood to enjoy a comedy in which the heroine took on a false identity and pretended to be poor, all to win over the heart of the skittish hero.

Not that such a story had anything to do with Augusta. First, because she didn't want to win any-one's heart. And second, because Joss Everett was no more skittish than Augusta was...well, than she was content to sit in a plush seat in Emily's theater box, exchanging whispered inanities with a Mr. Hereford, who had now called twice and who seemed enamored with Mrs. Flowers.

Oh. And third, because Joss was not her hero.

Though he had called her *worthy*. As she lay sleepless that night, balled up under her heavy coverlet, the word echoed within her so often, so long, that she realized how hollow she had let herself become.

∽

Having fallen into a restless sleep at an aggravatingly late hour, Augusta pled for a quiet morning at home, and Emily's lady's maid again accompanied the countess to the Pump Room. Augusta preferred to remain alone in the drawing room of their rented house, curled on a settee and idly flipping the pages of one of Emily's fashion periodicals, until she could remove the haggard shadows from beneath her eyes and expunge her most troublesome thoughts.

Mrs. Flowers could not be seen without a smile, for she could not afford even the most solicitous of questions. This was another way Mrs. Flowers failed to serve as the escape Augusta desired: never before had she been unable to afford what she wished.

And as long as she was thinking of questions—what might Joss and Chatfield have said to one another? What would each of them have asked and told?

She snapped the illustrated pages shut, and Emily's plans for a spring wardrobe tumbled to the thick carpet of the drawing room.

Joss and Chatfield had not met for the purpose of

discussing Augusta, but surely her name would have come up. Neither man was the type to shy from a subject, especially not one so obvious as *who helped us communicate with one another?*

Somehow, she did not like the idea of two men who knew her—the *real* her—talking about her. It took away the control she coveted, that she wanted so desperately to retain.

That afternoon, then, Augusta decided to learn what had happened. If Chatfield and Joss could, as she had put it, *know things*, surely she could too.

While Emily rested, Augusta sneaked a plain wool cloak from one of the servants, then escaped through the kitchen and darted through the rain-dampened streets. Drizzle was turning to sleet, and though she stayed on the pavement whenever she could, her boots soon became mud-caked and her wool cloak clammy. She clutched the hood tightly beneath her chin, hurrying.

The Bath chair–dragging urchin who had once carried messages to and from Joss had told Augusta where "the dark gov'nuh" kept a room. Trim Street soon stretched before her, narrow and walled in by rows of neat houses. Scraping her boots before she knocked at the one where Joss lodged, she appeared reasonably presentable when the door opened. She handed coins to every servant who spoke to her, and within a few minutes, she was permitted up the stairs.

When she reached the door of the attic room, she hesitated. *Coward.* Her hand rapped at the door.

Footsteps creaked on bare boards, and a familiar low voice called, "A moment, please." Some thirty seconds later, Joss opened the door, patting his face with a small towel.

"Mmm." Augusta couldn't hold in her surprised hum—because the Joss before her was stripped down and informal, unlike any man she had ever seen.

With his coat removed, his shirtsleeves were rolled back, exposing corded forearms. His hair was damp, and the short black locks had sprung into an unruly wave. Cravat undone, a bead of water slid down the line of his throat to rest in the hollow of his collarbone.

The towel fell from his hands. "Augusta. Good lord." He stared at her, then fumbled for the ends of his cravat. "I'm—sorry about this. I thought you must be Sutcliffe."

"I hear that all the time." Her voice sounded too high. Awkward. She cleared her throat, then tried again. "You were expecting Sutcliffe?"

"Where Sutcliffe is concerned, I expect anything and everything." He took hold of her shoulder with his free hand, pressing her back; then he shook his head and tugged her forward instead. "Come in, come in. Only give me a moment to put myself to rights before we speak."

"That's not necessary." *Damn*. She hoped her cloak would hide her blush. "I mean, it's not necessary that we speak in private."

"Are you sure that's what you meant?"

His knowing smile made her want to shake him. Oh, how she could imagine it: grabbing those barely clad shoulders in her fingers and tugging at him as hard as she could. Yanking him roughly close, forceful enough that he knew how in earnest she was, and pressing him against the full length of her body...

Damn again. That wasn't shaking she was thinking of. Clearly the night of poor sleep and the chilly walk had addled her wits.

"Never mind," she replied. "If it means so much to you, I'll come inside."

His lips still in a wicked twist, he stood back to give her room to enter the chamber. Before she did, she stalled for a moment, swooping to pick up the fallen towel. *You shouldn't have come,* snarled the weeds of her darkest thoughts. *What could you possibly gain? You'll only make things worse for everyone.*

Maybe so. But at least she would do so as herself, not Mrs. Flowers.

Joss paused once inside the room. "Have a seat at— ah, the desk, I suppose."

Against the room's west wall, a writing desk sat beneath the window. Joss pulled forth a plain wooden chair, the only seat in the chamber. Augusta sat, then averted her eyes from the flurry of movement at the other side of the room—Joss, tying his cravat and shrugging back into his coat. Atop the desk, a stack of letters and thin old ledgers, a blotter, and writing implements had been shoved to one side to make room for a stoneware basin and shaving kit. This explained the damp hair, the towel to his face. The rolled-up sleeves and the forbidden sight of olive skin.

Sleet tapped at the small glass panes of the window. Outside, the sky was a silvery gray. Pushing back the hood of her cloak, Augusta breathed in deeply, settling herself.

Sandalwood. The scent caught her unawares, making her fingers tingle. "Earlier today, I wrote to the

Meredith Beauty trustees about a new scented oil taking hold in fashionable circles," she babbled. "The idea was inspired by you. By the—your—I noticed that—well. If one of our translucent soaps was imbued with sandalwood, surely men would use it. Not all soaps need smell like flowers."

"So says Mrs. Flowers?" Joss spoke up from behind her. "I do agree about the raw masculinity of sandalwood oil. It is an irresistible scent. Whenever I wear a bit of it on my person, people of all classes flock to do my bidding."

His voice leaped lightly over the words—yet when he said *do my bidding*, heat squeezed Augusta's belly.

"I had just finished shaving when you called," Joss explained. "If Sutcliffe did not call upon me this afternoon, I planned to visit him after dinner."

"Most of the men I know take pride in having a manservant shave them."

"Well, now you know a different sort of man. I neither take nor give pride, but keep it all for myself."

"Yes," she said. "Your damnable pride; so you've told me. I meant it only as an observation, not a criticism." Of course he kept no manservant. Not if he stayed in quarters like this. Which meant he was alone, daily and nightly.

The idea of such solitude was startling. She turned it over, savoring it as one might a boiled sweet. Would it become lonely? Or was it a relief to drop all pretense?

Both, she thought. Almost certainly both.

"Is it too much to hope you meant it as praise?" he asked. "Remember, I possess sandalwood oil, which makes me a paragon of masculinity. And certainly a paragon can shave his own jaw."

"A paragon can do whatever he likes, can he not?"

"Can he?" His sardonic brow lifted. *Whatever he likes.* Did his thoughts turn, as did hers, to their desperate kiss? To what might come next, should they kiss again?

Her breasts felt sensitive, full and eager for touch within her frail pink bodice. She drew in a deep breath which did nothing to calm her, then turned away. Eyes alighting on the basin atop the desk, she asked, "Have you finished with this water?"

When he answered in the affirmative, she stretched forward to tip the basin's contents out the window, imagining that her fluttering uncertainty sluiced down to earth with the water. She then handed Joss the broad stoneware bowl. Eyeing the ceiling, he carried the basin to a particular spot and set it on the floor.

"The ceiling sometimes drips at this spot," he explained. "The basin will catch it." When he faced her again, he added, "I do apologize for my unruly appearance when I greeted you."

"It was an unexpected eyeful, but you carried it off well. As you and I both know, you are a paragon of masculinity." She paused but could not suppress her smile. "You have now apologized twice for your state at the time of my unexpected arrival, which is more my fault than yours. I am beginning to wonder, Joss, if a guilty conscience plagues you."

"Many things plague me, my dear fake widow. But a guilty conscience is not generally one of them."

She had just spoken his name, and suddenly she

wanted him to call her by nothing but her own. "Please don't call me that anymore."

"What? 'My dear fake widow'?"

"Yes. If you say it again, I shall throw you out the window after your shaving water."

Drawing close to her, he looked down at her with a smile. Oh, she had kissed those incorrigible lips, had kissed them as though he held all the air she needed, all the warmth she craved. "You don't believe me?" she said, a bit breathless. "I will. I'm horribly strong."

"Oh, I know you are. You've grabbed at me more than once, you wicked woman. I was just getting a look at the dimensions of the window. It's rather small; I don't think you'll be able to stuff me through the frame. So sorry."

He remained near her, fingertips resting lightly on the edge of the desk. His nails were short and blunt, his hands darkly tanned. When he stood this close, she could breathe in his sandalwood again; just a hint of it made her skin tingle, wanting more of his kisses. Anywhere. Everywhere.

Which made her heart pound with fear. *You are so close to losing yourself.*

Augusta wasn't sure where to look. Her eyes fastened on the window muntins, but then she didn't want to seem as though she was self-consciously avoiding the sight of Joss, so she looked at the grate of the fireplace tucked near one corner. Coals had fallen low, casting little warmth and light. Across the room, a large trunk had been shoved against the wall. Joss had left the shaving kit atop it, a hint of unexpected intimacy. Above the trunk, a glass in a tarnished silver frame hung on the wall. No doubt it had once been lovely, but it was now cracked horizontally, fragmenting anything reflected in its depths.

Besides this, there was only a bed stretched against the wall opposite the door. And near her stood Joss, his head almost touching the sloping ceiling. Looking down at her as though waiting for a verdict.

"Do sit," she said.

One of his black brows arched. "I presume you do not intend for me to drop into your lap. Will you be scandalized if I sit on the bed?" When she shook her head, he seated himself on the jewel-blue quilt. Boots braced on the floor, he leaned forward, resting his elbows on the hard line of his thighs. "I realize this room is not as lovely as your lodgings in Queen Square. I will do you the credit of assuming you realize that too."

"It's not the same sort of space. But—I like it. Everything in this room serves a purpose."

Coffee-dark eyes studied her. "If you say so. To what do I owe the honor of your visit?"

"I wondered how your meeting with Lord Chatfield went. I came to see if all was well."

"We talked about you a great deal, if that's what you want to know."

This surprised a laugh from her. "Yes. That's what I was wondering."

Does he blame me or think me foolish or wrong? Do you? What do you think of me? Her lips parted, but the questions died unspoken. Good or bad, she was not ready for the answers.

It's not the answer that matters, only the question. Sitting in the corner of her father's study with a bit of

pencil and paper and ears open for knowledge, she had
so often heard the marquess speak those words. Her
father always laughed his big laugh and told Chatfield
the answer mattered plenty if it could be turned to
a profit. And often it could: a sweet-scented profit
in rose extracts and spices and the smooth oil from
sheep's wool.

In this case, Chatfield was right. The questions
mattered very much, for they proved that she faulted
herself even if others did not.

"He knows a terrifying amount," Joss said. "About
everything going on around him, and many things
that are now. I believe, one way or another, he will
solve Sutcliffe's problem. Which will, of course,
solve mine."

With an effort, she set aside her troubled thoughts.
"That is good news, then."

"Probably so, yes. I must thank you for giving me
the name of someone so capable. Only you must tell
me what would make you feel properly thanked. You
greet your callers with capons and biscuits; I greet
mine with old shaving water."

"A bit of novelty is never amiss." She propped one
of her elbows on the desk, then rested her temple on
her upraised hand. Her free hand explored the items
on the desk: the quills he used to write in that strong
black script; an ink bottle capped and uncapped by
his careful fingers. A stub of a candle, a stick of red
sealing wax. Everyday items, all touched by Joss. Now
touched by Augusta.

A small thing to notice or to care about. But she
had meant what she said: everything here was so *real*.

Joss had a purpose. He knew, always, what he need do next.

"I don't need to be thanked," she said low. "But if it's all right with you, I would like to stay here for a short while and be Augusta."

"Were you concerned that you might become someone else?"

"Yes. Or—maybe concerned that I would not. I'm not sure how to tell." She lifted her head, then traced an ancient scar in the wood of the desk. "Every caller for Mrs. Flowers requires me to lie more and say less. I can't say anything that's true of my real self; I have to be so *careful*. And so I wind up saying nothing and smiling like a doll."

"Dear me. It sounds as though you are telling me that adopting a false identity has constrained you. But that cannot be true, because Mrs. Flowers was to free you for sin and scandal."

"Even sinners must take an occasional break for conversation." Her retort lacked heat. Just as Mrs. Flowers's conversation lacked interest, or the spice of sin or scandal. "I admit you were right. Does that gratify you? Mrs. Flowers is not the solution to…well, to anything."

"Ah, but I wasn't right."

Augusta's eyes opened wide, only to see Joss shake his head. "I once informed you that Mrs. Flowers was still you. But now I don't think she is. She's you with all the most interesting parts stripped away."

Augusta picked up the stick of sealing wax, digging her thumbnail into the soft, red surface. "I disagree."

Mrs. Flowers was the best parts of Augusta. The

untroubled parts. That was the problem, though: there wasn't enough of her to make a whole person.

She flicked a bit of wax free to the floor and scooted it aside with her boot.

"You are certainly free to disagree," Joss replied. "But it doesn't change my mind. Here, stop spoiling my wax." Leaning forward, he plucked the stick of wax from her fingers and tossed it back onto the desk, where it rolled against a small brown glass bottle. "What I mean is, Miss Meredith is the one who talks about business and admits to having scandalous urges."

"I most certainly did not admit—"

"*And*," Joss added, "Miss Meredith is the one who offered me the names of four men who might help me. She did so out of a sense of obligation, I grant you, but still, the result will be positive. By contrast, Mrs. Flowers can do nothing but make herself invisible and act as though her ears are full of cotton wool."

The brown glass bottle on the desk was pretty, and she turned it with gentle fingers. "The men of Bath must like that sort of thing. I've never been so popular in my life, though as they don't know me, it's no real compliment at all."

"I'm not from Bath."

She looked up sharply, expecting to see the mocking look on his face again.

But instead he looked wistful. The way she had always felt standing at the edge of a London ballroom, her hair too bright and her clothing too ornate. As though there were a plate-glass window between them and what they wanted. Close enough to touch, yet impossible to lay hands on.

"I'm not from Bath," he said again. "Perhaps that is why I greatly prefer Miss Meredith. The men of Bath are sheep, and they like a woman as gentle as they."

"But I am not gentle."

"No, you are not, Augusta Meredith. Nor am I. So." He lifted his hands, ticking off points on his fingers. "You don't want to be recognized as Miss Meredith, and you don't want to be courted as Mrs. Flowers. But you created her so that you might be free of—what bothered you in London."

"Right." She pressed at her temple with the heel of her hand, as though the pressure might crush her dark thoughts. "I did. I did want that."

But it had not worked. It could not. She should have known that as soon as she caught herself blurting her secrets to Josiah Everett, desperate for someone to know what she had done—desperate to shed any secret, even the smallest one she kept.

Instead, she was more trapped than ever, cautious around old acquaintances, or chary of them. Bound within bonnets and simpering smiles, behind more and more and more glass. And the one man who knew the truth was the one with whom she could not, *not* take the chance of greater vulnerability. For Joss was not gentle, and he knew her well enough to break her to splinters.

"You are still you," he said. "Change does not come from without, does it? I suppose it would be ungracious to say 'I told you so.'"

"It would, because I have already admitted that you were right."

"True." Joss rose from his seat on the bed. For a

moment, Augusta thought he was reaching out for her; but no, he only lit a twisted paper spill from the low fire, then transferred the tiny flame to a lamp on the mantel. "So. You did not wish to entertain callers this afternoon. Why not plead a sick headache and stay in your chamber with a good fire and a laden tea tray?"

She shook her head. She couldn't explain that staying in her room, knowing a drawing room full of callers awaited below, was more lonely than being in true solitude.

Instead, she snatched up a paper from the desk and fanned herself with it. "I feel a bit faint."

"Take off your cloak, then." His tone was piqued, but when he stepped closer, the hands that teased free the knot at her neck were kind. "Wearing a wool cloak in a room this size. Honestly, woman. You must be broiling."

"I'm fine." Without lifting her head, she raised her eyes to his face. The lamplight burnished his skin, throwing the angle of his cheekbone into sharper relief. The rest of him, like the room at the corners, fell into shadow. As Augusta shook free of the cloak, feeling hazy air brush at her arms and throat, the world grew a bit smaller. "I'm fine," she repeated.

"So you said. But I would believe you more if you said it less." With one forefinger, he traced the line of her jaw, forcing her to look into his mahogany eyes.

So deep, so clear. For a moment his gaze held hers, a moment that reminded her of his coat, their kiss, the way she had flung away control to settle into his arms. Lust tumbled hot in her belly; fear thumped in her chest. She wanted him, and she was very much afraid she would do anything to have him.

"I shouldn't have come," she gasped, shoving back the chair. "I'm sorry. Please forgive me. I ought to go at once."

Rising to her feet, she snapped up the cloak. She bumped the leg of the chair with one of her boots and stumbled toward the door. Her vision was dim, or maybe it was only the ever-gray light outside. There was no sun. There was never a sun.

"Wait," came a voice that sounded distant. "Please, wait."

A hand caught her shoulder, gently but too firmly for her to shake free. "Augusta. Wait."

Before his door, her arms full of damp, wadded-up wool, she let her shoulders sag. She wanted him to let her run; she wanted him to turn her around and kiss her until she forgot herself again.

He did neither, only rested his hand upon her. Not pulling or pushing, just…holding. "It's nearly three o'clock, Augusta. Will you have dinner with me?"

She dropped the cloak.

He laughed. "It seems to be our fate today to drop whatever cloth we may be holding. But please, do me the honor. Something still weighs on your mind, does it not? I have found that such burdens seem lighter when one is well fed."

She turned to face him, and he stepped back, dousing the lamp and banking the coals in the fire. Through none of that did he look at her, but she felt he saw her all the same. *Her*, wanton and proud and afraid and ruthless. Fractured like the reflection in his cracked looking glass. He granted her time to decide on a reply.

How sharp was his sincerity, as precise and unyielding as the cut of a diamond. Yet it was clear and beautiful, too. Could she confine their encounters to words, each meeting would be valuable. Precious. It was so strange and lovely to be told, and to tell, the truth.

"Yes," she said. "Yes, I will go with you."

Thirteen

"SADLY, CAPON IS NOT AVAILABLE HERE," JOSS couldn't resist teasing Augusta as they made their way to a corner table. "After becoming used to the fine dishes put forth by Lady Tallant's cook, I do hope you will be able to find something acceptable to eat."

"I've no doubt I will," she replied. "I am so tired of capon. And truffles and roe and potatoes and rosewater ice. Give me coarse brown bread and pigs' trotters."

Joss laughed, ducking his head to avoid the low ceiling beam in the corner, and drew forth a chair for his dinner companion.

The sleet had transformed again into drizzle by the time they reached the door of his lodging house, and the pair of them splashed through the sodden streets to the White Hart Inn, a stone cube of a public house across the road from the Pump Room. The White Hart was, as usual, swarming with foot traffic and new arrivals by carriage. It served as both a destination for travelers to Bath and a haven for those in search of a hearty meal. The crowded room steamed with wet cloaks and sodden boots, the smell of people and coal and the odd wet dog—and above all, of roasted meat and yeasty-sweet spilled ale.

Sturdy and old and comfortable, the public room's floor was made of wide planks, the once-rough wood tables smoothed over time by thousands of palms and plates. A wall of windows flanked the front entrance, allowing gray daylight to filter in. The low ceiling of the room caused voices to bounce and echo; the only way to be heard was to lean in close, to speak low.

As Joss drew his chair closer to Augusta's, facing out into the large room, he decided this was an enjoyable arrangement. "Do you have a preferred meal or beverage? The menu is limited, I do warn you."

"Whatever you think Mrs. Flowers would like." She looked about with some curiosity.

"As Mrs. Flowers would never gainsay any gentleman, I shall order whatever seizes my fancy."

She shrugged free from her long wool cloak, then drew off her gloves. "How I yearn to discover what seizes your fancy, Mr. Everett."

"Careful, careful. That sounds as though you're pondering a spot of indecent talk. At least wait until you have the excuse of a bellyful of spirits." He raised his hand and a barmaid wandered over.

"Small beer for the lady," Joss said. "Ale for me. And two mutton dinners."

The thin young barmaid had a rushed, worn look, as though she had been working for so many hours that fatigue had sunk into her bones. When she looked at Augusta, though, her shoulders straightened and her tiredness seemed to drop away. "My lands." Her light eyes wide, she dropped a curtsy. "Shall I get ye the private dining room, my lady?"

Augusta's brows knit with surprise; before she could reply, Joss spoke up. "This is quite all right. Thank you, miss."

Still staring at Augusta, the barmaid dropped another curtsy, then tucked a strand of dark hair under her mobcap and hurried off to fill the order.

Augusta leaned toward Joss, her voice low in his ear, "'My lady'? Why in heaven's name would she call me that, and stare at me as though I had two heads?"

"Not two heads, but probably the loveliest gown she's ever seen." Thus given permission to look her over, Joss studied the bits of Augusta he could see over the tabletop. Though her pale pink gown was of a simple design, its exquisite tailoring marked it as costly—short sleeves trimmed with a fold of satin, and more satin piping the low vee of her bodice above a red sash. With her bright hair and lily skin, she looked like a garden brought indoors. A startling, lovely picture at any season, but especially on a cold March day in the middle of a muddy city.

At some point while he studied her, Augusta had picked up her gloves and, one finger at a time, began turning them inside out. "I didn't realize it was anything special. My gown, I mean."

"That's all right. The barmaid *did* think so."

This simple statement seemed to trouble her. She frowned at her gloves, worrying at their well-made seams and turning them right way out again, until the barmaid returned with two tankards. One for Joss, one for Augusta. She cast another longing look at the gown as she set down the beverages.

"Miss," Augusta faltered. She blushed, looking as ill at ease as Joss had ever seen her, then held out her ivory kid gloves. "These would look so pretty against your fair skin and dark hair. Would you care to have them?"

"I, my lady?" The barmaid took a step back.

"Not 'my lady.' Just 'miss,'" Augusta corrected. "That is—'Mrs.' Yes, I should like you to have them. If—if you want them."

"Oh. *Oh*, thank you, my lady—I mean, Mrs. Yes. Thank you." With a hesitant hand, the young woman reached for the gloves. For a moment, she only stroked the soft kid, looking as though she did not dare to draw them from Augusta's grasp into her own. Augusta rose from her chair, just enough to lean over the table, and she pressed the gloves into the barmaid's hand.

"Enjoy them," she said. "I hope your fellow shall notice how lovely you look with them on. But really, he should notice your loveliness all the time."

The two women shared a smile: one plain and one vivid, one tired and one cosseted. Somehow, they both looked prettier in their moment of shared delight in a simple pair of gloves.

But it was not so simple, was it? The gloves she gave away with scarcely a thought were forever beyond the means of the barmaid. Of men like Joss, should they wish to give her a gift.

He had thought to draw her closer by bringing her to a place where he belonged. It was so easy for the truth to find them, though; to remind him of the chasm between them.

As the delighted barmaid swanned away to fetch

their dinners, Joss folded his arms against a crawling frustration. "Why flaunt your wealth by giving such a gift to the barmaid? You do not even know her."

"I know something about her." Her gaze followed the thin figure between the tables; the woman now seemed to have a spring in her step. "She likes pretty things. And she probably doesn't have as many as she deserves."

"How are you to know what she deserves?" What if she turned her attention to him next? If she gave him charity, he could not abide it—but the alternative was to think he deserved nothing.

"I don't. I don't know anything about what she deserves, or you, or anyone else in the world. All I know is what I deserve, and I know that I have far more than that. So someone else in the world probably has less." She ran her hand over the wood of the table; to her bare fingers, it must feel smooth and faintly sticky from spilled ale. "A pair of gloves won't make a difference to the barmaid. Not really. But it made her smile for a few minutes. Isn't that better than if she never smiled at all?"

Maybe. But when the smile disappeared, it was all the more difficult to bear. Like a promise broken. "It's not your responsibility to make anyone smile."

Her brows lifted. "Josiah Everett. I have little responsibility in the world, but I have a great many gloves. Please stop your caterwauling." A tremulous smile touched her lips. "You said I was worthy. I want to be, even just in small ways."

With such gifts, she wanted to help herself along with others. Charity he could not stand, but generosity with a dash of self-interest—well, that he could bear quite well. "You are worthy no matter how you treat others. And I am sorry I was harsh. You were kind to her. You showed her that a fellow human noticed her." He gave his tankard a half turn but did not lift it. "These are not the small things you might think them."

Her brows had practically reached her hairline by the time Joss finished speaking. "You are giving me quite a bouquet of kind words. I must take care not to let them go to my head. This beer, however…" Putting the tankard to her lips, she took a long drink of the small beer. Joss had tasted it before: yeasty sweet and amber colored, with a thick, sudsy head.

Her throat worked. As she lowered the tankard again, a bit of foam was left on her top lip.

He had no right to reach out a thumb, to brush it feather-lightly over the curve of her mouth. No right, yet he wanted to so much he had to clench his fist. *You would do*, Joss reminded himself against a groaning throb of lust. *That's all she said. You would do.*

Until she could say more than that—with words, not only with a stolen, fiery kiss—he must keep his hands to himself.

Pink tongue darting out, she licked her lip clean, then spoke. "I like this place, Joss. It's…alive."

"Alive? In what sense?"

"Interesting. Busy. Loud."

"It certainly is those things. But there's nothing particularly romantic or elegant about taking mutton in a public room."

"There's nothing shameful or improper about it either. Just as there's nothing admirable about having a cook prepare far more food than anyone could ever eat, then wasting it with a languid appetite." Her brandy-brown eyes drank in the room as eagerly as she had drunk the small beer. "I've never eaten in a public house before. Can you credit that? My parents always wanted the best for me, and when I traveled, that meant taking my meals in the carriage with a lady's maid. In truth, I didn't even travel much. Life was in London. Business was in London."

"Life was business?"

"Yes," she said quietly. "I suppose it was."

He had never wondered whether a life of *only the best* could limit one's choices. With wealth, how could a person not pursue whatever he or she wanted? But each class had its own expectations. Its own proper sphere, outside of which one was not to stray.

It was a relief when the barmaid returned with their dinner, for Joss wasn't sure how to reply.

"We've a fine cheddar," said the young woman. "I brought you a wedge of that, plus the mutton and potatoes. Will there be anything else, my lady—Mrs.?"

Joss had become invisible, it seemed. This was often the case when he ventured into public in London. His plain clothing and dark complexion suited him for shadowy corners, to be overlooked until needed.

Just now, he didn't mind a bit. All the better to look at Augusta's sunshine face, at the smile with which the barmaid's long day was brightened.

"Thank you," said Augusta. "That will be all." After the barmaid had bobbed another curtsy and turned away, Augusta leaned forward. Her eyes closed as she inhaled the aroma of the meat. "This smells wonderful."

Joss sawed at his mutton, then speared a bite. It was tough, but well seasoned and rich. Satisfying after a long, cold morning and a short, cold walk.

"I had curried mutton once in London," Augusta said, cutting at her own dish. "At an odd little restaurant in George Street. My father wanted to meet the owner, and I begged him to take me along. The man was a Hindu Indian who had once worked for the British East India Company."

Joss had just taken a deep pull of ale. Dark and sweet upon first taste, yet bitter as it rolled through his mouth. *Clunk.* He set down his tankard harder than he intended to. "What did you think of the place?"

She freed a bite of mutton and speared it on her fork. "As I remember, the meat was tender and had a lovely flavor of spices. Clove, I think? It was unexpected, and I liked it."

"I imagine it was delicious." During Joss's childhood, his grandmother's Calcutta-born cook still worked at Sutcliffe Hall. Though the aged man usually prepared English fare, he was permitted to cook Indian food when the Sutcliffe family was absent from the estate. Not for decades had Joss tasted a sauce laced with clove and cardamom, with earthy cumin and bright turmeric, or torn into flat bread so chewy it resisted one's bite. But he would always remember the feeling of warm, floury dough dusty on his fingertips, of spice popping on the tongue.

"Since I was just a girl, my father didn't allow me to speak to the owner myself," Augusta added, "but he seemed to like the man a great deal. My father loved to speak with anyone who had a notion and turned it into a business. People with dreams turned real." She chewed thoughtfully. "I don't think the restaurant is open anymore."

"Oh." Joss cut more of his mutton into rough-sawed pieces. "I wonder what happened to the man. If he stayed in England."

"I don't know, but I was glad to get the chance to go along. I always liked learning things. Seeing places most women didn't get to see, not merely the back room of a dressmaker's shop or the corners of a London ballroom." Her jaw was set as she hacked at the wedge of cheddar they had not yet touched. "Do you want some of this?"

"Certainly." He took a ragged chunk of cheese from her and bit it, letting the curds squeak in his teeth, salty and sharp. Before Augusta could do further damage with her knife, he pulled the board toward himself and began chopping off small slices. "I assume what your parents thought of as the best was not always what you wanted the most."

She shrugged. "What parents and offspring are always in perfect accord?"

"A good question, and the answer is probably *none*." She didn't return his smile; her expression had not shed the worried pucker he had hoped to chase away. "Augusta. You called on me today—very scandalous of you, I might add—because your mind was burdened with many weighty thoughts. I have tried feeding you into a contented stupor, but you won't have it. So instead I shall sit here and eat cheese. If you wish to unburden yourself, my ears are at your disposal."

She traced the metal hoops that gave shape to her

wooden tankard. "I don't really want to talk at the moment. I would rather listen."

Joss dropped the knife in a parody of shock. "Surely not."

"Indeed, it's true. A paragon of masculinity once told me I ought to tell less and ask more."

"He was being far too harsh. Indeed, he sounds like the sort of fellow who is often more harsh than he ought to be."

"He is honest," Augusta said. "Which I have come to…to value."

A smile touched his lips; he felt as though she had touched him far more deeply. "What would you like, then? A story? Perhaps one about a kind fairy who gives kid gloves to everyone, at least until fairyland's supply of kidskin is exhausted."

"No, no fairy stories. I want an answer. An honest answer to just one question."

The answer doesn't matter as much as the question. Chatfield's calm words rang in his ears. In this corner, hidden behind a wall of sound and bustle, they were nearly as alone as if the room were empty. "One answer, then." What her question might be, he could not imagine.

She scooted her chair nearer until she could whisper below the din. Breathing deeply, she shut her eyes. "Why do you wear sandalwood oil?"

When her eyes opened, she was so close—close enough, almost, to capture.

He did not know the name of his favorite flower. He did not even know if it was a real fragrance or something concocted by a gifted perfumer. He only knew that its scent lay sweetly in the hollow of her throat, and that he wanted to lean closer. Breathe her in, take her in his arms, make her some part of him and himself a part of her.

But it was impossible. Not only because of honor—an efficient summation of thirty-one years of difficult decisions—but because he belonged nowhere but alone. Always alone, outside the clique of society or the camaraderie of the servants. Part English and part alien; part respectable and part scandal.

He did not want to be alone.

He traced a crack in the tabletop, where the old, time-rubbed wood had long ago split apart.

"I choose sandalwood," he said, "because it reminds me of my birth. You see, my grandmother was born in India, and my mother was half-Indian."

Fourteen

HER ELBOW SLID ON THE TABLE; HER SLEEPY-LOOKING eyes flew open. "You're of Indian descent?"

As he had expected, she sounded surprised—though somehow, he had hoped the truth wouldn't matter. "In part. Yes." Joss leaned away from her in his chair.

"I had no idea."

"What would you have me do? Write 'Josiah Everett, possesses Indian blood' in the Pump Room guest book?"

"That would be intriguing."

"Please note," he said loftily, "that I am glaring at you. Because I am not amused."

"All right, all right." She picked at the edge of her cloak, wadded over a chair, then let it fall again. "It just seems unfair that your secret is hidden and mine is obvious."

"It's not obvious that you're not a widow. And how could it be hidden that I have mixed blood? I wear it all over my skin. Figuratively," he added when her nose wrinkled.

"I didn't think about it, honestly. I've seen

Welshmen as dark as you, so your coloring does not seem unusual. Have you ever been thought Welsh?"

Joss snorted, folding his arms tight about himself for what seemed like the thousandth time since this odd dinner began.

Augusta arched a brow. "Don't fly into a rage. I'm merely interested. You've given me new information, much like if you told me you had a twin. I just need to add it to my mental list of things that I know about you."

Despite his wariness, this piqued his curiosity. "Indeed? What else is on the list?"

She considered. "Sharp tongue. Two eyes, nose, mouth. Shoulders, arms—"

"Ah. So your list is concerned with my body."

She turned red, a deep brick shade that argued with the color of her hair. "Ah—never mind. I wish I had bargained for more than one question. Because right now, I really want to know whether this is why you don't lodge with your cousin in Queen Square."

"What, the fact that my grandmother was born on a different continent?" He spoke the words lightly, as though the question was ludicrous.

But the truth was: he didn't know.

His fraction of noble blood opened the narrow corners of the *ton* to him, but he was far too angular and sharp to slot neatly into them. What caused him not to fit? Was it his relative poverty? The scandal surrounding his parents' almost-too-late marriage? Or was it his Indian blood? His conception represented so many sins against society that he could never be completely absolved.

Did that matter, though? He had a seat in Lady

Tallant's drawing room when he wanted it. Once, he had even had been invited by the countess's dear friend—now the Duchess of Wyverne—to visit the Duke of Wyverne's estate in Lancashire.

Surely it was not necessary to win over all of society as long as one could rely on a few friendly faces. Surely it was not even necessary to be treated as family by a man like Sutcliffe, who had little feeling for anyone other than himself. A man so shallow ought not to be able to inflict a deep wound.

Ought not. And yet. "My Indian blood doesn't affect who I am," he said. "It doesn't matter to me."

This was not true, of course. As he had just admitted to Augusta, he thought of it every time he opened his last vial of sandalwood oil and breathed its faraway scent. Every time he looked at his grandmother's worn botanical ledger and wondered when *somalata* had first grown in the Sutcliffe Hall conservatory.

Every time Sutcliffe spoke to him as a servant rather than a relative.

Still. He meant to be reassuring, so Augusta would once again see him as a proper English gentleman.

Well. Semiproper. Somewhat gentlemanly.

But as he had once observed, the course of conversation never ran smoothly around Augusta. Far from appearing reassured, she looked appalled. "I hope you don't mean that. Or even *think* you mean that."

"Why? What possible argument could you make with my determination to be English?"

"That is not the part that bothers me. It's the fact that you just said you would cut away one of your grandparents. As if she doesn't matter to you."

Guilt tugged at him. "I never knew her," he excused. "She died before I was born."

"But you would never have been born at all if she hadn't given birth to your mother. Your grandmother is *part* of you."

He stared at her, surprised by this vehemence. Fiddling with one of her hairpins, she added, "Do you suppose I was never embarrassed by my parents? My father had the broadest Portsmouth accent you could imagine. Every word was clipped off, every vowel an 'ay.' My mother always thought more lace, more trim, more bugles were better on every gown. They'd been born poor and became wealthy. They wanted better for me, and they didn't always pursue it the right way. But don't you see? They *made* me. If they had been a lord and lady, they'd have been ashamed of my unfashionable red hair. If I had been raised the daughter of an earl, I would never have been allowed to learn so much about business."

At some point in this speech, Joss realized that Augusta's outpouring of feeling was directed less toward him than to some wound in her own heart. Something at which she had hinted, some loss that still lanced her.

He toyed with the idea of making some serious reply. *Tell me something else you remember about your parents.* Augusta had had more than two decades with her parents. Long enough to hoard memories by the hundreds—the thousands. Happy, everyday memories. The sort other people seemed to take for granted. The sort of which Joss possessed far too few.

But no, that reply would be too dangerous. It would

wrap them in an intimacy even deeper than when they had kissed: the intimacy of memory revealed.

So he settled upon flippancy instead. "I thought you wanted to listen, not speak."

She grimaced at him. "I did, yes. But I needed to say that. And maybe you needed to hear it."

Blunt-spoken woman, wasn't she? Yet her carrying speech about family creating one—personality as well as body, behavior along with soul—made sense. So long, he had taken for granted that the mixing of races had made him different from everyone else he met. This was true, but she was right: it had made *him*. And rarity alone was no cause for shame. There was only one king, after all. One prime minister. One yearly winner of the Epsom Derby.

Such comparisons made him smile with their unlikeliness. "Thank you." He stroked back a strand of Augusta's hair that had tumbled free from her pins. "I suppose I did need to hear it. You give me a new way to think about the matter."

For a moment, she leaned into his touch, catlike, shutting her eyes. Then she was all clipped energy again. "Think of this, too, Joss: the prime minister has Indian blood. Lord Liverpool. He is welcomed everywhere in society. He's powerful."

Joss drew his hand away, then picked up the knife and stabbed at their remaining cheddar. "Lord Liverpool is also wealthy and titled. He could speak to Parliament dressed in petticoats and a bonnet, and no one would think the less of him. I do not set my sights at the level of the prime minister. Tutored commoners of indifferent birth, such as I am, are thick on the ground."

"Maybe so, but you are the only Joss Everett." She tilted her head, setting the loose curl free again. "Are you doing what you wish?"

Doing what he wished? No, of course he wasn't. Right now he wished he could make her smile as she had when giving away her gloves. He wished he could dispense with his conscience and plead for her to take him as a lover. He wished he could pluck the pins from her sunset hair and send it tumbling over her naked skin, wished he could stop kissing her only to make her cry out in pleasure.

But always, in the face of a wish, came prosaic reality. A scarred wooden table, a plate of mutton and potatoes, a wedge of cheese. An adequate fire and a roof over one's head. Such a reality was perfectly acceptable, even if it didn't hold the luster of a gemlike fantasy.

"I try to wish," he said in a calm voice, "for what I know I might attain. For respectable employment for a reasonable wage. For a reasonable employer."

This brought a faint smile to her features, but the expression fell away in another instant. "That seems a very small dream."

"What on *earth* do you mean by that? It's a very suitable dream."

"But it's not really a dream, is it? It's what you have now, just shuffled about a bit."

Again, he folded his arms. She lifted her hands, placating. "As you say, it's perfectly suitable. And if you insist that it's exactly what you want, then I suppose it is a dream, after all."

Of *course* it wasn't a dream. It was good sense. It was practicality. "I don't know what else I ought to wish for. This is my life. I am a man of business for a noble-man." Remembering Chatfield's words, he added, "I am not in bodily danger, nor in mortal peril. It could be far worse."

"It could be. But if you want it to be better…"

"Not everyone is fortunate enough to be able to buy happiness."

"No one is fortunate enough for that." She turned over her fork and scratched the tines into the surface of the table. "That's not what I meant. I know happiness can't be bought, or I would have bought it."

Whatever clouded her mind, here was the muddy base of it. He seized the chance to turn the conversation from himself. "Are you recalling the loss of your lover?"

The fork in her hand skidded; four tiny notches were gouged in the wood.

He expected a heated retort, the sort of fiery response that got them both a bit too flustered for sense. Instead, though, her auburn brows knit. "We probably should not refer to him with that word. There wasn't any love involved, as I eventually learned. Lord Chatfield told you something of him, I suppose."

As she did not present this as a question, Joss thought he was safe from having to provide an answer.

Her lips tightened. "I thought he might. Chatfield loves to know things, and to him, much of the fun of knowing is telling what he knows." With a harsh laugh, she added, "That's how I knew he could not be a blackmailer. He doesn't hoard secrets for money, only for other types of gain."

You must come and work for me. Chatfield wished to

turn Joss into an extension of himself. But that was what a man of business always became, if he had any sort of competence.

Against his silence, Augusta gave a faint sigh. "The man you called lover, for lack of a better word, always assumed he could find someone better than me. I must have been his insurance against a life of poverty. But people hope never to need their insurance, isn't that so?"

"Do forgive me if I am being dull-witted." *Slice. Slice.* Joss made a neat tower of Cheddar cheese. "But you have told me you seek a lover. It seems as though you want to replace someone who, when you felt terrible, made you feel worse."

"Exactly." The fervor in her voice made him look up, puzzled. "I shall *replace* him. If someone else is in that role—someone of my choosing, whom I control—then he will be gone from my thoughts."

Such a vain hope on which to toss away one's heart and body. Joss's insides twisted at the thought. "That is not the only possible outcome."

Tipping back her tankard, she drained it. A hard look was on her face when she set the mug down. "Very well, *not* replace. I don't want someone to pretend he wants anything more from me than sex. I know now that love and sex and marriage have nothing to do with one another."

"I wish you did not."

"Why? Because I'm too fragile?"

He hesitated. "Because I wish no one had ever treated you badly."

Her brows drew together. "You are serious?"

"Rarely."

She rolled her eyes. "Right now, I mean. You—mean that?"

"It would be unkind of me to wish the opposite."

"True." She pursed her lips and studied him; the sinking light from the windows painted her face in rosy tints. "I am coming to think of you as quite a good man."

"I am nothing of the sort." Somehow, he managed to feign a haughty tone, though warmth shot through his chest. *Good.* He had never been called that before. *Clever,* maybe. *Amusing. Damned useful,* even. But never *good.* It was an old word, and a simple one, and a very deep one.

"Well, Joss, here's what I want. Here is my dream." She spoke the words delicately, as though testing their sound in a foreign tongue. "When my parents died, there was no one left who loved me just as I was. I want to have that again someday. Though I know it's impossible, I want to be listened to without having to play any games or tricks. I want people to know my mind without being distracted by my—"

"Dockyard?" He could not resist.

"Yes. Right." Setting down the fork, she traced her forefinger over the holes left behind in the table. "Or my money. Or this pestilential femininity that makes most men assume there's nothing on my mind but a bonnet. I certainly *like* bonnets, but I should hate to have my entire person reduced to what I was wearing."

"Is that why you gave away your gloves to the barmaid who admired your appearance?"

She frowned. "Maybe. Damnation, that would make it a selfish act instead of a kind one, wouldn't it?"

He had thought exactly this, but he liked her all the better for it. "No matter why you did it, the gift made her smile."

It was very tempting to offer to admire her appearance in the hope she would shed more clothing. Instead, he pointed out, "If you do not wish to play any tricks in order to gain attention, it might have been a poor strategy to pretend to be a widow named Mrs. Flowers."

Folding her arms on the table, she groaned and rested her chin upon them. "If I tell you again that you are right, will you promise that this is the last time you will bring up the matter?"

"No."

She chuckled. "Fair enough. I wouldn't make such a promise either. I will simply admit that I thought Mrs. Flowers would free me, but she has restricted me to the silly bits of life that I grow tired of. Yet she's better liked than I ever was. Discouraging, to say the least."

"I wonder," Joss said slowly, even as the beat of his heart sped up, "if it has occurred to you that I am listening to you right now, Augusta, and that you are not playing any tricks to get me to do so."

In an instant, she was sitting up straight again. Seizing the fork as though she'd be rewarded for the amount of damage that she caused, she dug its tines into the holes she had created.

Gratified by this reaction, Joss pressed on. "Also, at the moment I am thinking less of your dockyard than of the fact that if the proprietor sees you carving up his furniture with his cutlery, we shall be thrown out on our ears."

She drove the fork so deeply into the wood that it swayed, upright, before toppling with a clatter.

"Impressive strength." His heart was pounding now: too eager to lie, too wary for the truth. In the end, those amber-gold eyes were too much to resist. "I wonder, too, if it has occurred to you that the things you say are *not you*—your admirable dockyard, for one, or the fact of your femininity—are indeed you. You should not be the magnificent Augusta Meredith if you were a scrubby little creature. Or a man."

"I can never tell if you are mocking me or not."

"Usually it is best to assume I am mocking someone, but I do not seem to be able to mock you. And if I cannot deny my Indian blood, you cannot deny the fact of…*you*. Certainly being raised by loving parents at the edge of the polite world, growing up beautiful and wealthy, has shaped you more than I was shaped by the chance inheritance of foreign blood from an ancestress I cannot even remember."

Blithe words, blithely spoken. They were not entirely true, of course; his blood was half his mother's, and he had known her well indeed. Poor woman, there was no one who had loved Kitty Sutcliffe Everett *just as she was*, as Augusta had put the matter, except for her young son, Josiah. And a child was helpless to act in any significant way.

"Maybe you are right," Augusta said at last. Again raising her tankard, she eyed its empty depths with some disappointment until Joss shoved his own ale in her direction. "Oh. Thank you." Her deep draught seemed to wash free some hesitation. "I didn't have imagination enough to choose a sensible name for my widowed alter ego, and I certainly don't have enough to imagine myself as poor as my parents grew up. And...I think they would have wanted it that way. They wanted me to belong. They wanted better for me." She paused. "Mainly because they thought it would make me happy to step up in the world. I suppose that's what they really wanted: for me to be happy."

Yes. Probably so. And what a dream that would be, wouldn't it? If only happiness really *could* be bought. So long he had hoped one hundred pounds might be sufficient for this—but as Augusta had trenchantly pointed out, this would merely permit him to continue his old life in a new place.

"As long as we are asking one another difficult questions," he said, "what do you think might ensure your happiness?"

Stretching her arms before her, she looked at the short puffs of her sleeves. "I lack the imagination for that too. I've no inkling what would ensure my happiness, as you put it, for the rest of my life. Nor even for a year."

"What about for a day? Or even an hour?"

"An hour? I don't know. But a minute, maybe." She traced the pits she'd dug in the table, then stretched out her hand to him. "Just for a minute, will you hold my hand?"

"A man would have to be a monster to refuse such a request." His fingers laced with hers, warming them.

She was right: she really was dreadfully cold. "Must I refrain from making improper comments?"

A smile touched her lips. "No. You may say whatever you like. It's only fair for you to be happy too."

Ha. It would take more than a bit of hand holding to accomplish the feat.

Though for a minute, this was pleasant. Sitting at a table in the White Hart, with people eating and drinking and coming and going in a swirl of color and conversation. With the earthy scent of the coal fire, the savory remains of their dinners, a hint of sweet flowers at Augusta's throat, no more than a tantalizing trace. Joss had grown used to life at the edges of rooms, and he liked this comfortable space. With his hand in Augusta's, his blunt fingers around her slim ones…he liked it even more.

And he wanted it to last for far longer than a minute.

"You asked me what I wished for," he said. "I wish for things that would make you gasp to learn of them, things that would make you blush should I speak them in your ear. Things that would make you look on me with pity, or maybe with surprise. Passionate things and everyday things and, most of all, quite simple things."

Sometime while he spoke, her lashes had become wet. With his free hand, he pulled forth his handkerchief and skated the cotton square over her cheekbones. "Like the right to dry your tears. Or to hold your hand when it's cold."

"My hands are always cold," she said.

"Then I always want to hold them."

He had thought it might be difficult to admit these things, but actually it was quite easy.

No, what was difficult was watching the expression on her face change. Second by second, it hardened; he could almost watch her donning her armor—hard and polished and bright on the surface. He had no idea what lay behind it. "That is impossible," she said.

The silence that followed was practically alive: a thrashing, vermillion thing full of words barely swallowed.

"Of course it's impossible." He managed to sound calm, logical. "For one thing, we should have the devil of a time changing our clothing. It was only a wish. It has nothing to do with what's real."

Her amber eyes went liquid again. "No. It does not. But I can't—I can't." Now she looked stricken, which was even worse than her armor.

Only now did she pull her hand free, and he stood, stumbling as her chair shoved back. Joss had no choice but to stand, too. He pulled a few coins from his coat pocket, leaving them on the table.

"Thank you for joining me for dinner." The smile across his features fit smoothly—a perfect mockery of joy. "It was a most enlightening meal. Do let me walk you back to Queen Square, Mrs. Flowers."

⸎

Though all the streets leading back to Queen Square were familiar, for the first time since arriving in Bath, Augusta felt she was venturing somewhere new.

The city's Assembly Rooms, beautiful though they were, held the same nervous young women and hopeful mothers as any London ballroom. The Queen

Square garden had her walking in pointless circles through its well-tended order.

Then Joss's rooms startled her, made her feel raw and different. Next, the White Hart—so busy, so bustling, that there was room for everyone within its walls.

Never had she heard anything more seductive than when Joss said he always wanted to hold her hand.

Never could she remember being more afraid. She could not lose control again, and there was no one so likely to strip it from her as Joss Everett. And she would let him; she wanted to surrender so badly.

She must be very careful.

They walked in silence, and the sound of Joss's footsteps was almost lost in the afternoon bustle of the streets. Bath chairs being tugged through mud, children selling newspapers and buns and whatever fruits the wintry landscape could be coaxed to produce. A few men tipped their hats in greeting to Mrs. Flowers; Augusta smiled dimly, not sure whether she had spoken to them once or ten times.

She did not say anything herself, and she didn't expect Joss to do so either. Theirs was a distracted trudge, seemingly locked in silence until the moment they would part at Emily's door. The welcome moment, or the dreaded moment?

Only the question matters, Lord Chatfield would say.

Thus musing, she was surprised when Joss spoke up as they walked. "You said you thought you fit with no one anymore. But there is someone in your life who cares for you just as you are. A true friend."

She stumbled sideways on the pavement, away from

him. Swiftly, he caught her arm and set her aright. "Do not worry; I did not presume to refer to myself. I am speaking of Lady Tallant. She's a true friend to you, and she wants you to be happy. You are not alone."

He was right—yet she felt lonelier than ever with him at her side. A distance drizzled between them, cold as mist falling.

A half step ahead of her, he made the final turn into Queen Square. She looked up at him; his profile was chiseled so sharply that he would have made a beautiful coin. He did not even glance at the manicured garden where they had recently passed a few cheerful minutes.

Feeling out of step, left behind, confused, she hurried after him. The long wool cloak caught around her ankles, flapping sodden and heavy. He seemed so sure-footed as he walked ahead.

At the steps to Emily's house, he bowed a farewell to her. "Be well, Mrs. Flowers."

One of her hands reached from the folds of the cloak and caught his coat sleeve before he could turn. "Why did you kiss me when we were in the mews?"

His smile was harsh and wry. "Because it was unthinkable not to."

"And now?" Breathless, her words were almost a gasp.

His gaze skated away, as though the sight of her pained him. "I am not a fool. It would be unthinkable to kiss you again."

Yes. This was good sense, and so there was nothing to say but: "I see. Thank you for the dinner, and—and for accompanying me home." Releasing his sleeve, she hurried up the steps. She had beat a quick tattoo with the door knocker before she recalled that no one in the house knew she had left.

When the door opened, she slipped inside before the butler could ask any questions. She permitted only one glance behind her before the door closed again.

And this was what she had seen: Joss Everett, his shoulders square and hands folded behind his back, watching her with a face of desolation. He looked like a man hungry for something who had just realized he would never be fed.

Her hands went icy again—which made her realize that, as she walked at his side, they had been warmed.

No, it would be unthinkable to kiss him again. And yet somehow, it was all she could think about.

Fifteen

THIS TROUBLING ISSUE STILL ON HER MIND, AUGUSTA rushed up the stairs to the drawing room. With more force than grace, she flung open the door.

"Emily, Joss Everett said he wants to hold my hand all the time. All the time!"

As soon as she looked about, she realized her mistake: it is a truth universally acknowledged that when one bursts into a room shouting an item of a personal nature, the room will be populated with more people than one expects.

Fortunately, only one person was present beside Emily. Seated side by side on the long velvet settee were the countess and a slightly older woman with scraped-back black hair and apple-round cheeks. Dressed in deep blue serge of a beautiful cut, this unknown person held a stack of pattern books on her lap.

The lamps had been lit against the dim of late afternoon. One sat on a side table, casting its bright circle onto the pages of the topmost book. Emily reached over to turn a page, revealing a drawing of a woman in evening dress. "I like this gown too, Madame. Only perhaps you could make it up with a red gauze rather than a pink."

Then she looked up at Augusta with a most aggravatingly calm smile. "Augusta, may I present Madame Rougier, a delightful designer of gowns? Madame, this is my dear friend Miss—ah, Mrs. Flowers. She is playing a game we enjoy, in which we each state facts that are mildly interesting but also completely obvious. You have stated that Mr. Everett wants to hold your hand all the time. Let me see... Gravity holds people onto the earth. Day is brighter than night. My husband's favorite beverage is chocolate. Do you wish another turn, Mrs. Flowers?"

"You are incorrigible." Augusta's attempted frown flipped into a grin as she and the dressmaker nodded their greetings.

"Another point for you," Emily said. "Well, my wandering, wayward friend, do you care for tea? Madame and I have nearly finished our discussion, and we were about to ring for a tray. Or maybe you would prefer a cold dinner?"

"No need; I already dined."

Emily lifted her brows. Without further comment, she closed the volume and turned to the older woman. "Madame, I find that I have grown ambivalent about the best color for the trim. Let us continue our discussion at another time."

Clearly curious, the dressmaker made a valiant effort to remain. In a low, accented voice, she said, "Your young friend would perhaps like to examine the patterns before I take leave, no? She too is in need of the new gown?"

Augusta looked down at her clothing and realized she was still swaddled in the voluminous cloak. Untying its strings, she dropped it on the hearthrug. The apple-cheeked woman let out a squeak of distress. "No! You must always hang the wool cloak!"

Emily coughed delicately. "Madame, please call again tomorrow and we shall choose all the trim. For the moment, it seems my dear friend is in some sort of distress, so you see that I must aid her. Perhaps you'll take a bit of refreshment in the kitchen before you leave?"

The Frenchwoman looked crestfallen, but she dropped a perfect curtsy. "But of course, my lady. *Comme vous voulez.*"

"A footman will return your pattern books later," Emily said. "Thank you so much for calling on me."

When the door had closed behind the older woman, Augusta and Emily turned to each other. "What was that about?" they both said at once.

Augusta was less polite—or more jittery. She blurted out first, "You're having new gowns made?"

Emily shrugged. "What else is there to do? I must spend my time somehow."

"But your health—"

"One can only drink so much sulfur water. And by 'so much,' I mean 'I never want to do it again.' A bath is pleasant, but it takes only an hour. And most of the callers come for Mrs. Flowers. If she is not at home, they simply trickle away."

In a froth of canary-bright silk, with a gold chain about her neck and rings on her slim fingers, Emily looked the picture of luxury. Yet never had she made Augusta feel vulgar or *less than*. Even now, her mobile mouth was curved in a smile. "This is your doing, dear friend. You inspired me to summon someone to create a new gown for me. You threw my *Lady's Magazine* on the floor, and when I saw it, I thought, *Yes that would do to fill a day or two.* So I sent for the dressmaker everyone wants at the moment. *Madame* is far too busy, yet I kept her here for nearly two hours. Now she shall be even busier, and she shall waste more of my time as she fusses about with interminable fittings and mixes up the orders and runs short of trim with one sleeve left to ornament."

"She will waste your money too."

"Ah, Jemmy told me not to worry about that," Emily said, referring to her good-natured husband. "It's the waste of time that really interests me."

"Having gowns made seems a very…London sort of thing to do," Augusta replied cautiously. This was intended as a coded message: *Are you feeling better? Would you like to go home?*

Emily understood every social code. "If one cannot be in London itself, one must recapture bits of it." *Not yet. But I'm trying to make a good show in the meantime.*

Augusta dropped her into the seat abandoned by Madame Rougier. "How and why must one recapture bits of London?"

"Because days must be filled, though they seem so long. In Bath, at least, I can toss away time arranging a new household. To decide how best to keep the housekeeper from fighting with the cook, and keep the lady's maid from flirting with the footmen. There is no Jemmy to be far too indulgent with the servants or the children or…me."

The countess's eyes were the clear blue green of the ocean; as she blinked, they shone with tears. Yet her voice held steady as she added, "I am grateful that you're here with me. As two guests, really. If I hadn't the entertainment of sorting out Miss Meredith and Mrs. Flowers, I should fall into a decline."

"Thank heavens for my deceitful tendencies, then, for red gauze would never do if you fell into a decline. You should have to have your new gowns tossed out."

She tried to match Emily's light tone, though she understood what her friend did not say and perhaps did not even realize. The countess's distractions, careless though they might seem, ended in helping others. Her blithe cheer made a pleasant household for servants and guests or a pleasant encounter in the Pump Room with their new acquaintances. So easily, she could have tumbled into a deep pit of grief and dwelled on her loss. Instead, she distracted herself through the daylight hours. One never knew when a happy moment would flutter by on vivid wings, hoping to be captured.

The night was more difficult, of course. Augusta knew how endless a night could seem, how a loss could make the world seem dark. But grief paled over time. What was black went gray instead.

And then there were those precious bright moments, so sunlit-sharp that Augusta shied from them even as she craved them. Like a kiss so sweet she could not bear its taste, so hot she felt burned by the thought of it. A dinner invitation, a clasp of hands, a good-bye that had not quite felt like a good-bye.

"I am glad," she said at last to Emily, "that you

summoned a dressmaker. You shall look lovely in her creations."

"Another point for you," Emily said. "Is it my turn to say something obvious, then? What about, 'You have something to tell me'?"

As Augusta laughed, the countess added, "Do you really think you can rampage through my drawing room, shouting about holding hands with an unwed gentleman, and not expect me to be the *least* bit curious?" She shifted a small tasseled cushion and settled against it. "Tell me all about it."

So Augusta did—about her weariness with Mrs. Flowers, and the walk to Joss's house. She did not mention his *dishabille*, though her cheeks went red. Maybe even…warm.

"And then he invited me to dine with him," she added, "and we went to the White Hart. And I gave away my gloves to the barmaid. And he told me that one of his grandparents was Indian." She realized she was blurting and drew in a deep breath. "None of those facts are related. I think. And I *don't* think he wanted to tell me about his grandmother's birth."

"Why ever not?"

"Maybe just because it's something personal." Her brows knit. "I pointed out that the prime minister is part Indian, and then he became huffy and said that the prime minister could wear a dress and bonnet if he wished."

"I will do you both the kindness of assuming you have left out large parts of that conversation," Emily said. "You are quite right about the prime minister's birth. Perhaps your Mr. Everett thinks the same rules do not apply to him as to Lord Liverpool, but I rather think having Indian birth shows that his family is adventurous and well traveled. *And* that they love and marry whomever they wish."

Augusta blinked at Emily. "Maybe. Yes."

"And surely he wouldn't have told you if he didn't want you to know. Which he does, because he said he wanted to hold your hand all the time, or something to that effect," Emily concluded. "Good heavens. While I frittered away the afternoon, you were busy indeed."

They fell silent then, a pondering sort of quiet. Augusta's mind whirled like a spinning wheel, strands of thought knitting frantically together, then twisting into a new form.

He hadn't seemed to want her to know. But was it that fact in particular, or was it a reluctance to tell her anything personal? He didn't reveal much about his cousin Sutcliffe either.

And if he didn't want to tell her anything about himself—why was that? She had meant to listen at dinner, not to talk, yet somehow she had been the one revealing too much again.

She knew quite well that she and Joss didn't belong at the same table. He was the grandson of a baron and baroness; Augusta's grandparents had been grooms and scullery maids before they worked their way into upper service. Her father had worked at the Portsmouth docks as a youth. One day, he had developed a lotion to soothe the chapped, rope-burned hands of sailors. When it caught on at a few pennies a pot, his young wife had convinced him to add floral oils and present it to local apothecaries as a cream for young ladies.

Thus had begun Meredith Beauty more than thirty years ago: a large idea ladled into small jars in a small flat in a large building. Her parents had told her once they could see the dockyard's Victory Gate from their window, flanked by golden spheres. Queen Anne had once passed beneath its lacy iron span. In one direction, it was a gateway to the Channel, in the other, to a different sort of life.

So she had heard. She had never been to Portsmouth. And in the end, her parents had never returned from their final journey there.

Dimly, she noticed Emily drop the cushion tassel she had been twisting. "Now *why* would he permit you to know all about his family background? That, my dear, is an interesting question."

It was a mark of how far into her mind Joss had insinuated himself that when Emily said *my dear,* the words *fake widow* seemed to be missing from the phrase's tail. For a moment, she had to blink her way back from a journey to the coast, from a dinner at the White Hart. "I think," she said slowly, reasoning it out, "he felt he owed me a secret. Since he has been keeping mine."

"That makes *perfect* sense." Emily clapped her hands together. "And that also explains the bit about how he wants to hold your hand until the end of time, or whatever it was you said he said."

"It does?"

In one fluid movement, Emily pulled free the small cushion from behind her back and smacked Augusta with it. "*No.* Of *course* it does not explain that. No, he was either drunk or sincere. How much ale did he have at dinner?"

"Only one tankard." Augusta rubbed at her upper arm. "Ouch, Emily. Have a care with the cushions. And my arm."

Ignoring this admonition, the countess folded herself onto the settee. "Only. One. Tankard." She spoke the words with crisp enjoyment, as though taking bites of a cucumber sandwich. "That is very, very interesting."

"To me, it is—confusing." Augusta wasn't sure that was the right word, but it was as right as any she could think of. "Other than that moment, he seems to want to keep me at a distance." Just as she did to him. "And he does not like Mrs. Flowers."

"The heretic!"

"But I'm not sure I like Mrs. Flowers either."

Emily frowned. "Is this one of those moments where I am meant to disagree and convince you otherwise? Or would you prefer I concentrate on abusing Mr. Everett?"

"No. Neither." She reached for the cushion that had smacked her arm. Silk cloth embroidered with silk thread. Costly. "I think I was rather horrid to him."

She thought so, but she wasn't sure. What would seem horrid to a man who gave no compliments, who had no tolerance for foolishness—unless it came from his employer. And oh, that damnable smile that made her want to kiss him and flee him at once. He was as astringent and bracing as over-brewed tea. "He doesn't know me as well as he thinks he does."

"And whose fault is that?" Sometimes Augusta forgot that Emily was the mother of two young sons. Not so at the moment, when the countess's gimlet stare speared her.

Rubbing at the sleek cushion, Augusta let the silk run soft under her fingertips. Smooth as the old wood of the White Hart's tables. She had stabbed that table; why not leave her mark here too? She found a seam and worked her nails into it until a stitch split.

"It's my fault," she said at last. "But I don't want him to know me. *I* don't know me." *Pop.* Another stitch gave way. "Not since my parents died."

The gimlet stare turned to sympathy. "Ah. So this Mrs. Flowers you are saddled with—she's meant to help you find Augusta again?"

"She was meant to free me from everything dark. But she keeps me from everything real."

"She's like a meringue," Emily decided. "When you, my dear, are like a lovely plum pudding. All colors and sharp flavors, and full of intoxicating spirits."

This dragged a smile to Augusta's face, and Emily added, "I rather think Mr. Everett likes the plum-pudding Augusta, not the meringue woman. Don't you?"

"Your analogy is imperfect, for I am never sweet around him," she admitted. "I feel too…unsettled."

"Bath is a good place to be unsettled. I hope it is a good place to become settled too."

Shadows below Emily's eyes betrayed her fatigue. "You haven't been eating your beef, have you?" Augusta pressed. "You are not yourself yet."

"If I eat any more beef, I shall turn into a cow and trample you," said Emily with some crispness. After a moment, she relented. "I am not myself, no. I feel like only part of myself."

Augusta pressed her friend's fingers. Emily's hand was even colder than hers. Perhaps few outside of

Lady Tallant's family knew what had happened. After the birth of an heir and a spare within a few years of their marriage, she and the earl had not been graced with further offspring. Until a few months ago, when Emily had at last fallen pregnant again.

Friendly with the countess since the previous season, Augusta had begun the habit of calling on her several times each week. Along with tea and biscuits, callers to Tallant House imbibed Emily's friendship, so hearty and pure was it. Joss had been right: in Emily's drawing room, Augusta had felt like herself again for the first time since that week in 1815 when her parents had died and Colin had dropped her like a shameful secret.

One January day, as Emily poured out tea for Augusta, something had gone wrong with the baby.

Augusta had called for the earl, had supported her friend's shoulders and prayed over her rounded belly. A physician had arrived too, but nothing worked. A few dreadful hours later, that was that.

"Looks like you'd have had a girl, my lady," the physician commented. "Nothing to get that upset about. Not with two fine healthy boys in the family."

White-faced under his tan, Lord Tallant marched the man out of the house. Augusta watched as Emily, fragile in a large bed, turned her face away.

A few weeks later, once Emily was strong enough to travel, they left for Bath. And this was why they had arrived together: for both of them, life had changed terribly in one day. There was no need to pretend it was not terrible.

Yet Emily found shining moments—ordering a household, planning a wardrobe. Arranging her friends' romantic lives. She created peace and distraction for herself through control.

Something Augusta's life had lacked for quite some time.

I really must find a lover.

Her plan had nothing to do with sex or love; everything to do with mastery. There was no banishing grief without it, or the shame of being unwanted.

As Joss tugged away her control, with what could she replace it? Their conversation had become intimate, and she could not help but think of their bodies becoming so. Already she had felt his kiss, had seen his cravat undone, had followed the line of his throat down to the dusting of dark hair on his chest. A hint of his masculine strength, unadorned by fashion and frippery.

The idea of an anonymous lover had lost its forbidden charm. No, what she needed was control.

And if she could not control herself around Joss... then maybe she should try to control Joss around herself. It would not be easy, but surely it would not be impossible. Not if he would give her such plain truths on only one tankard of ale.

Not even one, really. She had drunk some of his. She should have drunk far more.

Augusta pressed at her temple, where a tight hairpin had set up a dreadful ache. "Shall I ring for tea, Emily? Or something a bit stronger?"

Ocean-blue eyes met hers, far too knowing. "We could both use something stronger, could we not? Quite a bit stronger."

Sixteen

ONCE HE HAD SEEN AUGUSTA HIDE HERSELF AWAY IN Lady Tallant's house, Joss walked the few steps to Sutcliffe's house. The crowd on the Queen Street pavement unrolled like a dropped bolt of cloth, colorful and sleek as it bounced out of Joss's path. He cut through it, plain and sharp as a pair of scissors.

No one caught his eye. Good.

Joss had never before had the experience of telling a woman he wanted so much from her, only to have his words armor-plated and booted back at him. But he couldn't fault her. They didn't belong at the same dinner table; she was an heiress, and he nothing but a glorified servant.

A footman answered Joss's knock, wig askew and livery streaked with dust. "Mr. Everett!" The footman bowed. "Thank God you're here, sir. He's gone up in the attics, sir, and he won't come down."

Perhaps *glorified servant* had stated his role in too grandiose a form. There was nothing particularly glorified about hunting for Sutcliffe like a child playing Sardines.

Joss summoned the proper expression of indulgent patience. "In the attics, you say. All right. And where is the butler?" It was not typical, even in the bizarre netherworld of Sutcliffe's presence, for a disheveled footman to answer the door in the butler's place.

"Stuck under a wardrobe in the attics, but the other footmen will soon have him free. His lordship had us crawling under ever so much cast-off furniture."

Joss accepted this without further comment. "Has his lordship eaten anything today?"

The footman struggled with his wig, trying to set its crushed mass straight. "I can't say, sir. I know he threw a teapot out into the street, but he didn't mean to. He was trying to toss it up into a chimney pot."

How the devil did he think he was going to do that? would, of course, have been a logical question. *Why?* would be another.

There was no sense in attempting sense, though. "It sounds as though he is in good spirits, then. I hope it did not strike anyone as it fell," was all Joss said.

"No, sir."

"Very good. Have the housekeeper keep an accounting of anything else his lordship damages."

"Yes, sir." The footman bowed. "Thank you, sir."

"Take a few minutes to recover yourself," Joss said. "Then come find me if you need more hands to free the butler. Until then, I shall endeavor to find the baron."

"Thank you, sir." The footman looked almost pathetically grateful. "We shall soon have him free, I think. Thank you. I—I wish you luck with the baron, sir."

As the footman fled, Joss began the long climb up to

the attics. Sutcliffe would probably lose his butler for this. He paid his servants good wages, but there was really no wage good enough to compensate for being wedged beneath a piece of furniture.

"Sutcliffe?" he called as he climbed.

"Everett? In here! Do come see; it is *so* amusing!"

As Joss stood on an upper landing, he tipped his head to locate the source of the voice. It came not from upstairs in the attics, but from below. The second floor. Pounding down the stairs again, he marched through the corridor, flinging open the doors to several bedchambers before he found the correct one.

Pale, rich fabrics and a soft carpet stretched before him. Several candles had been lit, along with a good fire. The baron, resplendent in a coat of—good God, of periwinkle satin and blond lace—had wadded up the room's velvet draperies and crouched in a window seat, peering through a brass spyglass about the length of his arm.

"Everett, look. I can see all the way to the windows across the square. If they would open the drapes, I could see in!"

"You," Joss said calmly, "have caused a great deal of worry. What's all this business about trapping servants in the attics?"

"What?" Sutcliffe lowered the spyglass, blinking dimly at Joss. "Nonsense. I haven't been in the attics for fifteen minutes at least. Why are the servants still up there?"

Joss ignored the question and posed one of his own. "Was there a particular reason you were throwing a teapot? I am merely curious."

The baron brightened, dragging a hand through his fair hair. "As a matter of fact, there was! With a bit of practice, I'm sure I could heave something from an attic window into a chimney pot. Just the sort of unlikely thing I could wager on, you see? I'm sure I could get someone to bet twenty pounds I couldn't do it. No, fifty! Even amid such a bunch of dull sticks as these Bath-ites."

"Bathonians," Joss murmured. "And you would lose the wager, as your thrown items were falling into the street."

"I'll try again later. I ran out of things to throw." Unconcerned, Sutcliffe returned his gaze to the window. "I saw you through my spyglass. You were walking with that woman, Miss Meredith. She was wearing a very ugly cloak, but I recognized her red hair. Bits of it were sticking out from under the hood of her cloak."

"Miss…who?" Joss's heart gave a startled thud. He had been sure Sutcliffe wouldn't recall meeting Augusta, but the baron's hummingbird of a mind sometimes veered aright.

"Oh, wait—you said she got married. No. You said she was a widow. Right?" The baron shook his rumpled head. "She doesn't *look* like a widow."

"What ought a widow to look like?" Joss tiptoed carefully over the words.

"Oh, all swathed in black and crying." He hoisted the spyglass again, leaning so far forward that its lens clicked against the window glass. "She did rather look like she wanted to cry. *Did* she cry?"

She had, just a little, at the White Hart. "No," Joss said in a decisive voice. "You must have been mistaken."

With a sigh of disgust, Sutcliffe set down the spyglass on the window seat. "I can't see *anything* with this. I need a real telescope." He pulled forth his pouch, shaking out the familiar dry blades and popping them into his mouth. As he chewed, inspiration seemed to seize him, for he hopped to his feet and strode across the room. "Everett, help me push this wardrobe to the window so I can climb atop it."

"What will that achieve?"

Sutcliffe gave Joss a pitying look. "Because I will be up *higher*. Now, boost my foot."

"As the wardrobe is not yet by the window, no purpose would be served in your climbing atop it." As Sutcliffe's shiny boots scrabbled for purchase on the side of the tall wooden wardrobe, Joss poked cautiously at the subject of Augusta. "I didn't think you had recognized Mrs. Flowers."

"Yes, I did. I mean, I thought I—*oof*—did." The baron stumbled back, having failed to find a way atop the wardrobe on his own. "She was pretty. I mean, she is pretty. But she was pretty when I first met her. I needed a while to remember where that was. I must have danced with her last season. She dressed like a strumpet."

"I didn't think that sort of thing usually bothered you."

Sutcliffe considered. "You know, it really doesn't. Do you think she'd like a shilling?"

"If by shilling you mean 'twelve pence,' then she probably would. If by shilling you mean 'attention from some nude part of your body,' then no."

Sutcliffe laughed as he returned to the window seat,

plumping onto it. "Damnation, Everett. I wouldn't call that anything less than a guinea."

"I apologize for underestimating you," Joss said drily. "As a matter of fact, though, I am not here to help you spy on the neighbors or discuss your acquaintance with the lady next door."

"There must be a window that looks into their house!" The baron picked up the spyglass with such eagerness that it spun in his fingers.

"There is not. The houses are in a row."

"I could drill a hole through the wall."

"Why do you want to see in the other houses so badly? Are you trying to observe normal human behavior?"

"What? No. Don't be ridiculous." *Toss.* The spyglass traced a neat circle in the air, then was caught again. "I just want to see someone undressing. A woman, I mean."

Joss pressed at his temples, wondering why he had not drunk more ale when he had the chance. "For God's sake, then, summon your wife to Bath."

"Why?"

Joss could not say *So you can pull off her clothes and cease your spying on the neighbors* in reference to a gently bred woman, especially one as put-upon as Lady Sutcliffe. "I thought you might be missing her," he said instead.

The spyglass pointed at Joss. "I need a drink. What do you say?"

"God, yes," Joss said, even though he knew what would arrive on a tray: nothing but a pot of boiling water in which Sutcliffe would steep his *somalata.* "By the bye, the reason I called is to share good news. I met with a man who believes he can locate your blackmailer."

"Oh. Good. Thank you much, Everett. Knew you'd take care of it." He collapsed and reopened the spyglass, lace cuffs bright in the candlelit room, then rang for a servant.

The following minutes proved Joss perfectly correct: Sutcliffe ordered water and a tea service for one. *What do you say* had, as Joss suspected, meant *I require confirmation of my idea* rather than *Please join me in enjoying a beverage.*

As soon as the footman had vanished on this errand, Joss spoke up again. "Is anyone using this bedchamber?"

Sutcliffe frowned. "Of course. I am. It's my spying room."

The so-called "spying room" was larger than Joss's Trim Street lodging. Besides the soft carpet underfoot and the velvet drapes that Sutcliffe had wadded up, there was a large bed with a mahogany frame, the great wardrobe that had proved impossible to climb, and a vanity with a glass. Uncracked, of course. The room smelled slightly musty, as though the linens hadn't been aired for a while, but it certainly did not smell of damp. And it did not appear to leak at the ceiling.

"Your spying room," Joss repeated. "And what of the other bedchambers on this floor?"

"What about them?"

"Are they occupied? Is there a reason I cannot lodge in one of them?"

Sutcliffe stared at him. "Why would you want to do that?"

Teeth gritted, Joss replied, "Because it would

be convenient for us both. Because it would save me money. And damnation, Sutcliffe, because I am your cousin."

"Second cousin, I think. Ah, here's the tray!" Attention entirely diverted by the arrival of the teapot, the baron sat at the vanity and dumped bits of his beloved grass into every dish. Joss took his cousin's place at the window seat. Thus seated, the weight on his mind seemed just as heavy, but at least his feet were no longer tired.

In the past, he would have dropped the question, attributing Sutcliffe's selfishness to the same cause that made it impossible to fault him for long: ruled by whims like a child, he simply didn't *mean* anything by the problems he caused. But if not, that raised a new question. "Do you actually need me in your employment?"

The baron sipped at his favorite beverage, an expression of great relief passing over his thin features. "Of course I do. You answer my letters. Who would answer my letters if you didn't?"

From his seat at the window, Joss turned his head to look through the glass. The view was so different here from his attic window in Trim Street—wide pavement, Bath chairs pulled to and fro, and the neatly ordered garden beyond a still neater wall. "Many men would be capable of such a task. Including you."

Sutcliffe laughed. "Everett, you do enjoy your jokes. Look here, do you want some of my tea?"

Joss recognized this as an expansive offer. "No, though I thank you." He cleared his throat. "To return to the reason for our presence in Bath: are you interested in the cost of finding your blackmailer? I cannot promise that will put a stop to the demands for money, though of course once the person is known, further action can be decided on."

"What do you mean, the cost? You said you would take care of the matter."

Joss turned to look at the baron, who blinked at him with great puzzlement over the rim of his china cup. Joss could blame him no more than he could blame the baron's young son *Toddy*. He simply did not understand consequences.

This was the fault of the whole family. Sutcliffe had been inclined to asthma as a boy, and the health of the precious only son and heir to the Sutcliffe barony had to be safeguarded. Kitty Everett had inherited her Indian mother's fondness for plants and, at the boy's father's request, had prepared a tincture of *somalata* that cured the worst and most frightening of the boy's symptoms.

Sutcliffe had long since outgrown his asthma, but never his fondness for the drug's stimulating effects. Joss had tried in small ways to break his cousin's increasing reliance on it, but Sutcliffe could no more entertain the idea of abandoning this addiction than the others that ruled him.

Thus the fate of poor Jessie the maid. Though Sutcliffe might not mean harm, he caused it all the same.

Respectable employment for a reasonable employer. This was his dream, or so he had told Augusta. She had faulted him for restricting his life to a small circle—but right now, such a wish seemed as distant a prospect as India itself.

Unless he considered taking the position Lord

Chatfield had offered. Would learning secrets to gratify a marquess's whims be better or worse than tidying up Sutcliffe's messes, protecting him from himself?

"You're right," Joss said. "I told you I would take care of the matter of your blackmail, and I will. I'll let you know when there's any further news."

‿◌‿

He soon departed, leaving Sutcliffe in happy abandon with his spyglass and tea service. Knowing that the baron was again spying out the window, Joss tossed it a wave before continuing on his way to Trim Street.

The daylight was all but gone now, and Joss found his way back to his lodging by memory as much as sight. The world was shape and shadow, and he had much to think about as he walked.

For he had grown up not *in* Sutcliffe's shadow, but *as* it. While Joss's mother served as a companion and chaperone to the future baron's six sisters, the future heir was tutored. An indifferent, jittery student, he was steadied by the presence of his younger cousin, who proved a much more eager learner.

The boys became youths became men, and each took the presence of the other—the behavior of the other—for granted. Sutcliffe did what he wished; Joss dealt with the consequences. Yet he had never, it seemed, been regarded as essential. Not if he was of less import than maintaining a bedchamber dedicated entirely to spying.

Even so, Sutcliffe was all the family Joss had. The baron's numerous sisters were indifferent to him, and they all lived far north in Lancashire, where the distaff branches of the family dwelled on parcels of land willed to them through careful settlements.

They were fortunate in that regard. Kitty Sutcliffe Everett had been less so. In a house full of relatives, she and Joss had always been alone, shifted to the outside.

From the outside, one developed a different perspective. One could see a great deal. Perhaps even as much as others could see with a spyglass.

A rueful smile tugged at his lips—and then his lodging house loomed tall before him, lamplight winking like a lodestar from the drawing room window. As he entered, Joss felt in his pocket for coins, wondering if he could order tea. Best not to. He had overspent himself earlier in paying for Augusta's dinner.

He had meant well by the invitation. It had even gone well, for a time. He yearned for her, or for what she meant to him: a woman bright and lovely and able to afford any possibility. There weren't many women such as that.

Well. She certainly knew it. She knew she could do better for herself. And that had been that, hadn't it?

His cold fingers were clumsy with the latch on his chamber door. Stripping off his gloves, he finally coaxed the stubborn thing open—only to find the expected cold, dark room ablaze with lamplight and a generous fire.

Augusta Meredith was sitting on his narrow bed, dressed in pale silk, her hair shining like temptation. "I've ordered a tea tray and biscuits," she said. "But we don't have to eat at all."

Seventeen

IF AUGUSTA COULD HAVE DESIGNED THE EXPRESSION that crossed Joss's face when he caught sight of her, it would have been just this: his eyes widened, his lips curved into a smile. But quickly, he wiped this expression from his face, instead narrowing his eyes. "How did you get in? The door was locked."

"Money." Doubtless he would dislike the answer, but it was the truth. "I gave coins to all the servants. They remembered me as your cousin, and I said it was your birthday and I wanted to surprise you."

"My cousin, you say. And my birthday." He knocked the door shut behind him. "I seem to have come in possession of a great many unexpected items."

"You have not possessed me." She stood, facing him across the small room. "Yet."

"This is most unexpected coming from the woman who wanted only to hold my hand for a single minute, then darted away when I became too honest for her taste. What the devil are you up to, my dear fake widow?"

She deserved every bit of his wariness, yet it still

stung. "I have asked you," she said in a creditably crisp voice, "not to call me that. It is most insulting to be called fake all the time."

"There's more to the phrase than that." Joss stepped toward her once, then again, until they stood almost body to body.

Her eyes were at the level of his jaw: that clean, hard line he had shaved this afternoon, now just beginning to show a shadow of stubble. She wanted to touch it, to lean her head against his chest and catch his sandalwood scent, to let the beat of his heart carry her away. "I'm not a widow. So is it the 'my' part or the 'dear' part in which I am meant to believe?"

"I could never call you mine. You just informed me of that fact."

"Dear?" This was nothing but a whisper as she swayed closer.

"Damnation," he muttered. "I can't—no, Augusta." He stepped backward so quickly he stumbled a bit, then crossed to examine the fire. "Quite a generous allowance of coal. Did you pay Mrs. Jeffries for an extra bucket, or shall I have to hock something to cover the debt after you leave?"

"I paid for it. And the tea tray. I thought"—she took a deep breath—"we would want the room warm when we removed our clothing. If you must know."

He went still, hands gripping the rough board mantelpiece. "That does seem the sort of thing I ought to know." Without looking at her, he strode to the desk, poured out a cup of tea, and gulped it with a wince.

"I—"

Clack. His teacup hit the tray with ringing force.

"What is going on, Augusta? Why are you tormenting me? You reject my politeness and seek to upend my honor, then you offer the ultimate intimacy as though it means nothing."

She sat again on the bed. "We have a different idea of what constitutes the ultimate intimacy." This seemed an inadequate reply, but what else could she say? *I know I am tormenting you. I am tormenting myself too.* She was not feeling very wise right now, but she had wisdom enough to keep that particular thought to herself.

"Do we?" He began to fiddle with the items on the tea tray, his voice low and carefully steady. "Perhaps we do. To me, it can indeed involve undressing, just as you suggested. Or it can be experienced with the removal of no clothing at all. The *ultimate intimacy* happens when two people want nothing more than to be together, and when being together is a pleasure in itself. When the joining of bodies is more than a lust slaked; it's heart to heart and mind to mind."

As he spoke, he created a spell. Its ingredients were his low voice, the warm scent of coal, the slope of the ceiling like a secret cave over their heads, the rich sleekness of the old coverlet beneath her fingers. They were alone, they were together, and his voice was twining through her frozen depths, cracking shards of ice free. They were so sharp, like tiny knives.

She closed her eyes and pushed the feeling aside. Let him wake her body; let her mind sleep.

"We don't have a different idea of the ultimate intimacy, after all," Augusta said. "But that's not what I'm offering you."

The china cup on which his fingers rested rattled in its saucer. His fingers were trembling, then—and Augusta knew what it meant when one's face was stern but one's fingers trembled. He was hurt. She had hurt him.

Her heart thumped a protest. "I can't offer it to anyone," she rushed to explain. "I'm not capable of it. But I want to…" What would the right phrase be? It could not be *make love* without love. *Rut* and *swive* sounded so vulgar.

"You want to…" He prompted, lifting his hand from the treacherous china cup. "Ah, you are blushing. Permit me to guess what you want, then. You want to revenge yourself on your wretched former lover through me, even though he will never know or care. You want to be wanted yet not do any wanting in return. You want all the power, all the advantage. And then you want to be able to back away, done with me, and say that you've had enough."

"All correct," she said. "Except for one thing. I want you very much indeed."

She did; she *knew* she did. That was why she had traipsed through the streets of Bath and strewn coin on every floor of this lodging house. She had wanted to make him hers; she had not expected him to mind.

But he did, and that hurt too. Many things hurt now that the ice had begun to crack.

Could this truly be the same day she had fled Emily's house in a borrowed cloak? She had run to Joss, then from Joss, then been brought back by Joss. She could not get away from this man, no matter how much she wanted to.

Obviously she did not want to.

Silently, he had crossed the room. Now he sat next to her on the small bed, ropes creaking as he settled. "Good lord," he said quietly. "What *did* he do to you, this man from your past?"

The mattress sank beneath his weight, tipping Augusta closer to the wall of his chest. "Too much," she said. "Or not enough. The end result was the same. But there's no room for someone else right now. Not here."

Joss's mouth made a grim line. "I certainly don't want to be joined by another man, either in flesh or spirit. But can you forget him while you are with me?"

With no one but you. "That is the reason I'm here." Her voice sounded hoarse, choked. Her breasts were heavy; her sex clenched. Her heart was a frantic flutter. Why had she thought she could control Joss? She couldn't even control herself.

With a gentle forefinger, he turned Augusta's chin toward him. Eyes as dark as smoky quartz searched her, looking so deeply into her she felt as though he had seen the thoughts she did not speak. Closer, he bent, and when his lips parted, she closed her eyes. *Yes.* Now it would begin. He would kiss her again, and she would kiss him back, and somehow she would be knit back together.

But no lips touched hers, and her puzzled eyes opened. Instead, fingertips danced over her temple. "This hairpin must come loose." With one little yank, he had it free, then pressed the curved pin into her palm.

At once, a band of tension she had not known she

carried began to relax. She searched his face, dark and clever and impatient and wry. His eyes were kind. Too kind. Even pitying, maybe.

He had not told her yes. But he had not told her no, either.

She heaved a deep breath. "Will you take out some more pins?"

"Certainly." Joss tugged more hairpins free, slipping his fingers through her locks, pins pinging onto the floor like tiny hailstones.

"It's such a trial to be female," she said. "When I was preparing to debut in society, my mother often said, 'You have to suffer to be beautiful.' And I told her, 'It's not worth it!' But of course it was, for a while."

Ping. Another hairpin dropped to the wooden floor, a delicate sound. A shiver raced through Augusta's chest, her belly. She was not prepared for the eroticism of such a tiny noise: an unmistakable sound of undressing.

The last time she had undressed for a man, she had thought herself in love and beloved. She had been so innocent. The contrast was painful, yet she would not go back. Now that she had drunk of honesty, bracing and brave, she wanted nothing else.

So she must be honest too. "I shall tell you what happened," she said behind the red fall of her hair. "The man—he was a master forger, feigning love so well I never suspected I was being deceived. I helped, too. I wanted to be loved, and so I was ready to believe."

And she was the one to spin the spell now, as she told Joss the truth. The meetings in secret that seemed so romantic. The kisses and promises he extracted, the physical passion that began to enslave her. She agreed to marry him, but the trip to Gretna Green was put off for one reason, then another.

She was ensnared; she could think of nothing but him. She would go along with his every suggestion, falling deeply without knowing it.

"It was my fault," she said. "My foolishness to believe him. I cannot trust myself to know what's right."

"And you do not believe anything anyone says unless it is horrid." Joss sighed. "You never made it to Gretna Green, I assume. Unless you had him killed, and truly are a widow?"

The idea brought a smile to her face, swift and wolfish. "Would that I had finished him off, though it wouldn't be worth the chance of being executed. No, we never eloped. And I never…ah, fell with child. In both instances I now consider myself fortunate."

She shook back her hair so she could look Joss in the face. So far the pain of honesty had been like pinpricks, swift and sharp. Now she lanced herself. "When my parents died and my fortune fell under the control of trustees, he abandoned his suit." Her heart gave its usual squeeze, hard and hollow. "He had, apparently, been courting someone else all along. Someone better."

The stark, bare details were enough to sketch the picture for Joss. In her mind, though, the memory spread like watercolor bleeding over paper. The news of her parents' accident arriving at the London house, instead of her parents themselves. Their clothes still in the wardrobes, their shoes and boots cleaned and lined up, waiting for them to step back in. This was the worst part: the reminders of how swiftly they had vanished.

She had just returned from Colin's lodging when the messenger arrived from Portsmouth with the tale. Her parents had arranged a quick sail for pleasure; city-bound folk, they could not resist the chance to ruffle the open water they missed so much. But a sudden squall, or maybe no more than the wake of a larger boat, tipped their vessel.

City-bound folk, dressed in costly, heavy layers. They could not swim to safety.

As she listened to the message that upended her world, her skin was still pink and sensitive from Colin's stubble. He had scratched at her as he uncovered, kissed, licked every inch of her body, but it was not for this reason she felt unbearably raw. The marks had still not entirely healed when a servant mentioned a few days later that "nice Mr. Hawford" was now betrothed to a sugar heiress.

It was embarrassing. It was shameful. That was the moment she realized she had thrown her heart after someone who did not want it. She had lost everyone she loved at once, and she felt she had lost herself.

Desperate, she had tried to bring herself back by coloring in the lines more brightly: clothes, gaiety, flirtation. But society had faded away until she was alone, her flash and dazzle only making the darkness about her more unrelenting.

Taking a deep breath, she explained to Joss, "No one thought to keep his betrothal from me because no one knew he was courting me. Which means, I suppose, that it was never courtship at all. I think he was pursuing both of us, and whoever was the easiest to topple would become his wife. Or maybe I was *too* easy to topple."

Joss looked as he always had: wry and wistful and wicked all at once. "Are you sure you do not wish him killed?" He reached behind Augusta's head, sliding his fingers through her hair. *Ping.* Another hairpin fell to the floor.

"I wish him gone," she said. "That's what I wish. But I was the one who vanished."

Somehow, she thought he would know what she meant: he, who spent his life at the whim of a relation who scarcely acknowledged him. It was easy to vanish—far easier than one might expect.

"I understand," Joss said. "But you are here now, entirely present. And you are worthy. Just as you are."

❧

This woman would be the death of him.

If Joss had one guiding principle in his life, it would be: *don't use women for your own selfish pleasure.* Men who did not agree ended by ruining lives. Joss's mother's. Jessie the maid's. Augusta was, as she had said, lucky to have escaped with no wounds to her body. Even so, her mind and heart and reputation had all suffered.

And tonight, she placed them all in his hands. She meant to use him—but did that not also mean she trusted him to make things right for her? He had no idea what to do with such trust.

So he plucked more hairpins free and flicked them to the floor, trying to ignore the delicate floral scent of each tumbling lock. Running his fingers through her dark-red strands merely to check for further pins. Certainly *not* noticing their sleek texture, or the way the long strands fell like gossamer once he released them.

He tried. He tried to close his ears to the deep breaths Augusta took, the faint "Oh" of pleasure when he removed a particularly tight pin. Though it was difficult indeed to let that last one pass. The little catch of her voice vibrated through him, plucking at his resolve. To unbind a woman's hair—to be allowed to run his fingers through it—*God*. His few partners of the past had never permitted him such intimacy, nor had he wished it.

Now not only his thoughts were disobedient, his body was too. Heated and eager, an erection threatened to scatter all thought and replace it with need.

He curled his toes within his boots, pressing them into the hard sole. Discomfort. That was what he needed. Discomfort and calm and gritted teeth and *for God's sake why must her hair smell so good*? It was like the scent of the country in spring, bottled fresh and sweet.

Inhaling deeply of the scent, he cloaked the breath as a sigh. "That's all the pins, I think."

"What do we do now?" She turned to face him. Her eyes were the color of luxury: a fine French brandy, a gemlike cabochon of amber. Sandalwood oil.

"You're the one with the grand plan," he said roughly. "You decide."

"I trust you," she said.

And that was that: resolve vanished. Or maybe it only transformed, turning from something leaden and determined into the sweet clarity of hope.

She trusted him. Did she realize how she had rocked him with three small words? Did she realize what a difference that made? Her reason for sneaking into his room was dark and sad—but she trusted him, and trust was light and precious.

And she *wanted* him. And by God, did he want her. He'd been fighting against it since her first *you would do.* Now that he knew her impossibly bright, willful, generous mind, *you would do* sounded like a benediction.

"I will do anything you want," Joss said. "Anything at all."

Augusta beamed at him—then hesitated, half turned toward him on the bed. "I should have prepared beyond this point. I don't know what to do."

"Might I make a suggestion?" Somehow he managed to sound light, but he could not remember ever asking a weightier question.

"Yes. All right." She smiled. "You may suggest it, and I will tell you what I think."

"Naturally. So you can be mistress of this encounter."

"Naturally." Her smile tilted sideways, a wistful little curl of lips.

"Well." He cleared his throat. "Having kissed before, there seems no reason not to do it again. That particular barrier has already fallen."

"Very true," she said. "All right. Let's kiss, then."

From an arm's length apart, they stared at one another, each waiting for the other to make the first move. At once, they broke into nervous laughter. "This is about as erotic as adding up expenses in a ledger," Joss finally said. "Perhaps we ought not to discuss each step in such detail."

Augusta twisted her long, coppery hair into a rope and slung it over her shoulder. "No, let's not discuss it." Reaching for his shoulders, she pressed back, back, until Joss had to sink to one elbow or lose his balance. "I think I do have an idea, after all. Will you close your eyes?"

He raised one eyebrow, which he knew she hated—or maybe she loved it, because she gave him a wicked laugh as her fingertips grazed his face. Low and secretive, a throb of joy, and he shut his eyes as bid, ready to learn what she had in mind.

Loosened strands of hair danced over his features, light as spiderwebs, tickling his skin. She was…good Lord, she was crawling atop his lap. His hips shifted, and she let out another of those magical, intoxicating moans just as when he had pulled free her hairpins and run his fingers through her uncoiling hair.

Which was another idea, wasn't it? Eyes still closed, he let her press him flat to the fortunate surface of the bed. His fingers whisked down, finding the curve of her breast, then reluctantly moving left until they located her long rope of hair. Up, up, he followed it until he cradled her cheek in his hands. Then with deliberate force, he skated his nails into her scalp, working free the tension, rubbing the sensitive nerves. Pulling her face closer to his.

"Oh," she moaned again, and within two seconds—maybe less—Joss had yanked her flat atop him, full breasts crushed to his chest. The silk of her gown was as smooth as a coin, her warm breath at his throat like the memory of summer.

It was so easy now, so natural, to find her lips with

his; to press them, tease them, torment them as she so beautifully tormented him. He sipped at her, full and sweet, his hands fisting in the skirts that tangled over her legs. She moaned her pleasure again, or maybe he did too, as mouths fit together and hands slid and traced the planes of bodies through far too many clothes. He lifted his head, catching her mouth more deeply, nipping her lips and grinding his hips upward into hers. There was no way he would ever be done kissing her, this flower-scented goddess…

Until she put his hand on her breast. "You can look," she panted, "at my dockyard. If you want to."

His eyes snapped open.

Augusta filled his sight, all firelight-gold skin and brandy-gold eyes and bronze-gold hair. So much gold he had to shut his eyes again, a quick squeeze. When he opened them, she had shifted. No longer a gilded goddess, she was a beautiful woman with parted lips and a questioning expression on her face.

"You have forever improved that word, as far as I am concerned," he said. "Never again shall I be able to visit the coast or the ports of the Thames without being overcome by a fit of fleshly lust."

"Oh?" She pressed a kiss to his throat, shifting the line of his cravat to dart the tip of a hot tongue over the sensitive skin. "Is that how you are feeling now? Overcome by a fit of fleshly lust?"

"Not quite," he said. "Not quite overcome. I know perfectly well what I am doing and saying and thinking. To you. With you. About you. "

"Oh," she said again. "Do demonstrate, if you please."

Eighteen

Do demonstrate, if you please.

It was an order, yet a sort of abandonment—and the combination gave Augusta a sense of power of a sort she had never known.

Until Joss laughed at her. Of course he did. She didn't even need to see his face to know the curve of his lips, the leaping line of his dark brow. "What shall I demonstrate? The speed with which I can divest you of your bodice?"

"That would be acceptable," she murmured, head still pillowed on his shoulder, against his throat. She would never be done breathing in the scent of him, so unique yet so familiar.

"Acceptable, you say. That is hardly a hearty endorsement. I shall have to think of something better."

"Demonstrate…" She trailed off, thoughts floating in a scatter like dandelion seed. "Demonstrate what it would take to overcome you."

Lifting her head, she looked down at him. Rolled herself, rubbed herself, over the long hard planes of his form. His eyes were dark and deep as the night sky, and she imagined them full of stars. "Not much," he said. "Not much at all."

Over her back, his hands roved, finding the small buttons of her silk gown. The buttons trailed to the gown's waist, a row of pearls, and as his fingers slipped smoothly over the precious orbs, she wondered whether she had thrown money away on useless things.

But as Emily had said, it was time she truly wanted to vanquish, thought she wanted to break, a memory she wished to reduce to a glassy shell that she could stomp on, victorious.

And under Joss's fingers, time seemed at last to vanish. Not she but he was the victor as the silk parted and his strong hands skated over her stays, her shift. Or maybe they both won, as his fathomless eyes closed and as hers flew open wide, startled by the unaccustomed pleasure of another person's hands grasping her with tenderness. As Joss pushed her up, tugged her bodice down, eddies of air cooled her pleasantly. In this room, she had at last thawed in the heat of her desire and of Joss's body so close to hers.

In another minute, he had coaxed loose the laces of her stays, pushing the mass of linen and boning away. Her shift soon followed. Then she sat bared to the waist, a voluminous mass of crushed cloth about her. Shivering with anticipation, she hitched one knee onto the narrow bed.

And all he did was look, and look, and look. As though she were a feast he was not permitted to eat— at least, not quite yet. Her nipples hardened; her sex pulsed, wet.

"You look edible," he said at last. "Delectable."

"Like a peach?" A silly thing to say. But she was nervous, deliciously so. And being nervous—uncertain yet not afraid—was a sort of fizzing excitement in itself.

He grinned, sweet and sincere. "Far more luxurious and luscious than any foodstuff imaginable."

"I *did* wear a peach-colored gown." She watched, eager, as one of his hands extended toward her. "So you would want to nibble me up."

"Or lick you?" Lightly, one fingertip brushed her nipple. The touch was shocking in its pleasure, so careful, so quickly over. And then he bent his head, cradling one breast in his palm as he took the other nipple between his lips. Nipping, tasting, with gentle abrasion of teeth over sensitive skin.

"Yes," she murmured. "Or lick me. Whatever you choose—*oh*. Please choose that again."

"Why do you always smell so good?" he murmured.

"I use"—she caught her breath as he did something particularly ingenious with his lips—"Meredith Beauty's finest cold-process soap, made with oil of honeysuckle. It is expensive and impractical, but then, I can be."

"Can be what?" He looked up at her with mischievous eyes. When he pinched lightly at one of her nipples, she sagged back against the wall.

"I have no idea," she said. "Were we talking about something?"

"Nothing of consequence. Now, do let me touch you some more." He returned his full attention to her breasts.

Sensation jolted through her like lightning, shocks

of pleasure almost startling in their intensity. The persistent chill she carried about with her was gone; he turned her liquid with his strong hands, his hot mouth. His tongue touched the valley between her breasts. Without thought, she pressed herself more firmly into his hands, his mouth, wanting him to claim her further.

His hands slid down, fisting in the yards of costly fabric, tossing them back. Peach silk slapped Augusta in the face, making her laugh. She escaped the luxurious barrier by sinking to her elbows atop the scrapped-together coverlet, the mattress firm but yielding beneath her.

As Joss fought his way through the fabric, he began to smile. "My dear fake widow, you are not wearing drawers."

"I usually do not."

His smile widened. "Augusta, you will slay me."

Her name on his lips was another shot of pleasure, far more intimate than any falsehood or nickname. "That was never my intention. But if you die of pleasure, that is not such a bad end."

He stroked the outside of her thighs, hands sliding hard over the sensitive skin. Her knees parted as though unlocked. He had always held the key to her undoing, had he not? Or was this her remaking instead?

Beneath the crumpled silk and linen of her clothing, he held her hips. "I want to taste you." With the firelight a halo behind him, his dark eyes burning hers, he looked like a beautiful fallen angel.

"Let the record show that you proposed this. I but agree, though quite gladly."

"Ever the shrewd woman of business." Then the laughter fell away, leaving him serious. "I will give you the pleasure you seek, also quite gladly. And then we shall see if you still want anything of me."

"Of course I—"

"Don't answer yet. Not even if you're sure it's true. You won't know until you've taken your satisfaction. So just—wait. And see."

Unblinking, he looked at her without touching—curse the man. "All right," she said. "We shall see." She would have said anything to claim him.

Sinking back onto the mattress, she let her legs fall open wide. Let him do what he would; she had given him permission. Whatever he took or gave was on her terms.

He didn't touch her right away, and she lifted her head to peek at him. "I am ready."

"You might think so." His voice held amusement. "But I shall make sure of it."

The faint shush of cloth against cloth sounded, then he laid fabric over her eyes. Running a hand over it, she felt creases and starch and smelled that smoky-sweet sandalwood. "Your cravat?"

"It will be yours for a little while. Hold tight to it, now."

How odd. He *wanted* her eyes covered, as though surprising her was important.

She liked that, liked that he wanted to surprise her, and that he had undressed a bit too. Easily, she recalled the sight of him with his shirt gapping open to reveal collarbone and a hint of dark hair on his chest. "I want to see you." She lifted a hand to peel back the cravat.

He caught her about the wrist. "I'm glad to have divined something you want. Maybe later you shall have your way. Right now, take your pleasure from me."

Strong hands slid downward, tracing her form, then trailed to her inner thighs. So long untouched, she shivered when he only trailed his finger lightly over her skin. When he reached her private curls, her toes clenched. When a fingertip parted her, pressing within, she moaned.

Oh, the seduction of control; it made her slick and hot and needy. Who was in control, though? He was hers; she used him for pleasure—and yet she was the one naked and splayed. She strained for his touch, hearing him laugh low as she pressed blindly against the cloth over her eyes. Tension coiled spring-tight within her as he played over her folds, sank a finger within her, withdrew it and pierced her with two. She could not open her legs wide enough, she could not take him deep enough. She wanted him all, unbearably, desperately—

And then he pulled back. "Do you remember what I said I wanted to do?"

She groaned. "No. I shall murder you if you stop."

"Oh, I have no plan to stop." The mattress shifted, the ropes beneath it creaking as he changed position. "I'm going to taste you now."

And then his mouth was on her. The sensation was so intense she did not recognize it as pleasure at first. Shocked, she shook and twisted away. When he laid one hand over her belly, she trembled, then settled under its warmth.

And he undid her. With fingers he parted her, with

tongue and lips he stroked her. Each tiny movement on her sensitive flesh sent a wash of pleasure through her. Tightly, his fingers filled her and coaxed her; wickedly, his hot mouth pulled at her. It seemed there was no place he did not see and touch and kiss, and this claiming was startling, too, in its pleasure.

So tight, he wound her; so far, he drew her along; so high, he tossed her. She could not bear his touch another instant; she could not stand for it ever to end. And then one final, marvelous movement with his tongue and fingers sent her cresting in harsh waves, flying into a great endless freedom.

When she fell, gasping and damp with perspiration, he was there to catch her. "You are a marvel." He pressed a kiss to her thigh.

The intimacy made her shiver; she pulled him up, closer, for an embrace.

He wound himself behind her on the bed. Strong arms enfolded her, pulling her against his chest. She could feel his heart beating quickly, as though he had shared the ecstatic flight with her. But he had not: a hard ridge pressed against her back, the insistence of desire unfulfilled.

Who had used whom? And what ought they to think of each other now? She was his in a way she had never meant to be, and she had mastered him not at all.

Though he still held her within his arms, his breath coming shallow and ragged. Maybe he did not wish her to go.

Maybe. The word woke desperate thought and terrifying uncertainty. And she kept falling and falling, so fast she had to close her eyes against the dizziness of it. The peach silk that had seemed so luxurious was too hot and too clammy, and she felt foolish in her nakedness.

Best to make him naked too. She turned in his arms, face to face on the narrow bed. If she pulled the cloth from her eyes, it would be impossible not to kiss him, impossible not to search for his heart in his gaze. And what if it was not there?

She held the cravat tightly over her face, breathing in his scent. They had made the room smell of desire, musky and intimate, and her own heart seemed to stutter its wish to stay. This slope-ceilinged room made an unlikely cocoon, but she could not remember ever wanting to remain in a place more.

She must keep him here. "I like your kind of demonstration," she murmured. "Now let us demonstrate together." Her hand sneaked to the fall of his breeches, which strained against his obvious arousal.

He snapped back, and she heard him shift away from her on the bed. "Not that." Hazily, Augusta dropped the cloth from her eyes and raised her head. Joss crouched at the end of the bed, a man of knots: neck corded, jaw tight, fists clenched. "No, Augusta. I can't stand up to that sort of demonstration."

"You needn't stand. You could just lie down." Her wet skin felt clammy, missing the heat of his frame behind hers. When she sat upright and leaned toward him, he clambered off the end of the bed.

"I really cannot, Augusta. I can't—do that particular thing with you."

He shook himself like an animal shuddering off

water, top to toe. His shirt gapped at the neck, and she saw a hint of olive skin, the valley of his collarbone. He wouldn't let her touch him? She had never wanted anything more.

"Please." She didn't know what she was asking for, hands outstretched. Anything. Her hands on him, his on her. His body within hers, the deepest claiming for them both.

He turned to the desk, picked up the brown glass vial and held it to the firelight. "You did ask me to demonstrate what I wanted of you, did you not? I believe I have done so. My desire for you has never been in question." Setting the vial down again, he folded his arms tightly across his chest. "The better I know you, the more I want you, until I think I will expire from longing."

"You can have me," she said unsteadily. "I want you to have me. Please." Did she sound as though she was begging? She almost felt she could weep.

"Not lust, Augusta. I'm talking about *longing*. You are bright and cunning and beautiful and brave. I want your body, but I want the rest of you too."

"What do you mean?" Her lips felt numb.

"We're together on the outside, you and I. You know me, and I know you, better than anyone else." His hands fell, then moved in helpless circles. "I want…I want to scheme with you and laugh with you. I want to be the man you wake up next to every morning. I want to buy you a plain dinner and watch you give away gloves. I want to unpin your hair and stroke my fingers through it."

She became aware of her unbound hair spilling over

her shoulders and breasts. An odd tickling sensation. When she shook its length back, an expression near pain crossed his features.

"You want a great deal," she said faintly.

"I do. And I have already been given more than I have any right to. But have you ever known a man who was satisfied with what he had a right to?"

"I—" She shook her head, fumbling for words. What did he want? What did it all mean? And what did *she* want? She had intended to flick away the scab of her old wound, but that was a dreadful and wholly inadequate description for what had just passed between them.

At her fumbling silence, Joss smiled, dark and humorless. Then he turned to the fire, crouching to study its blaze. It didn't need tending, but likely he wanted something to do with his hands.

The moment wound tight, as though somehow she had wound up atop the cliff again, but it was crumbling. There would be no flight this time—only a fall or a retreat. His cravat was a crushed rope in her hands; still more tightly, she twisted it.

"Lord Chatfield," Joss spoke up suddenly, "is of the opinion that the question matters more than the answer. But I believe in some cases the answer is of great importance indeed."

He stood, then turned to face her. "Do you love me?"

❧

For a moment, as Joss stood mostly clothed, painfully aroused, and ridiculously vulnerable, he thought she wasn't going to answer him.

Then she drew up her knees, making herself a tight

ball of crushed silk and flowing hair, and asked, "Do you love me?"

Maybe Chatfield had been right. The question told him all he needed to know: that her answer was not *yes*. "God help me," he said, "I think I do."

The admission was both more and less than he had expected. It slipped from his lips easily, but the silence that succeeded was leaden. He had never loved before, never trusted a woman with so much of himself. It seemed it was too much for her.

And though this realization slashed and burned within him, he would not betray her trust. He would hope only that she might one day bestow it.

He pulled forth the chair from his desk and sank into it. If he sat with her on the bed again, he would never be able to restrain himself from pulling back that curtain of hair to see her beautiful skin, lightly freckled at the shoulders. He could never resist touching her, and if she reached for him once more, begged him to make love to her—

Well. That was just the problem. If she didn't love him, it would not be making love.

"What do we do now?" Her eyes were wide and puzzled.

"What I *want* to do is not in question." He shifted his weight; his erection made his breeches uncomfortable. "What you want to do, I've no idea. And what *we* shall do? I don't know about that either."

When her hands lifted, her breasts raised and bobbed enticingly. She twisted her hair again into a fat rope, exposing her peachy nipples to his view. "Can I not persuade you?"

"I'm sure you could. It takes every bit of my control not to remove your gown entirely and feast upon you again and thrust into you until we both scream with pleasure."

A choked sound issued from her throat, and she dropped her rope of hair. "Why will you not, then? What's wrong?"

He shut his eyes and tried to remember every reason he could not. There were so many; a lifetime. "If you really want a reason—if this isn't just petulance—then it's because of my birth."

In a few quick sentences, Joss sketched out the family history: his arrival so shortly after the hurried marriage of Kitty Sutcliffe to the charming wastrel Jack Everett, who had soon left his wife and son to pleasure-seek himself to death in France. "And so I believe that women should not be dallied with," he finished. His past lovers, graceless and brief, had dallied with him. The encounters had slaked lust but left him feeling low.

"Not even if I want it?"

"Not even then." He sighed. "If anything should happen—if there should be a scandal or a child—you would suffer far more than I. You would bear the loss of reputation or the burden of an unwanted child. I will not risk tying you down in that way. I won't have you forced into a choice you don't want."

For if she suffered, he now knew, he would too. He would feel it as his own. And it was suffering enough to know that she did not love him back.

"But it's my choice to make," she insisted.

"Not only yours," he said. "It's mine too."

And that would be the end of it, he knew. He had pressed his love upon her, and she had pulled away. She wanted a quick tumble; he wanted a lifetime.

Augusta Meredith could buy the world, and the possibilities radiating from her made him forget the shape of his own life. What should a man such as he wish for? His dreams were small out of necessity. When he over-reached, he was sure to get pounded down.

"Come, let us do up your dress," he said. "I should see you home now."

Her only reply was silence; he could not tell whether it was wistful or angry or disappointed or... God only knew. Unresisting, she tolerated his hands at her waist, her chest, as he tugged her rumpled clothing into place. The hairpins were quite another matter. He picked up the scattered pins from the floor, but he had no notion how to fasten them into her hair again. In the end, he found a clean handkerchief and wrapped them up for her, setting the bundle in her lap.

"That's everything," he said.

"Yes," she said faintly.

And then the door slammed open. "Everett! I remembered how to find your lodging all by myself!"

Only one person could be so proud of such an inanity. "Sutcliffe." Joss turned to greet his cousin.

The baron—now dressed in a coat of red-and-white pinstripes, like a candy stick—clapped Joss on the shoulder. "I got another of those blackmail letters, and I spied on the person who delivered it. And now I know where they're coming from!"

Just as abruptly as he had entered, he abandoned this topic to peer past Joss. "Your landlady said your cousin was here, but I knew it wasn't me, because I wasn't here yet. So I thought one of my sisters must be here instead. I wasn't expecting to see you, Miss Meredith. Wait, that's not right. What's your name?"

"She likes to be called Mrs. Flowers." Joss had tried to block Sutcliffe's sight of the woman sitting on his bed, but it was no use.

"Is she an Indian cousin of yours?"

"I am no relation." Augusta spoke up in a colorless voice.

Sutcliffe grinned. "You were fornicating! I say, were you finished? I brought my spyglass, but I never thought to turn it to your window."

"We were quite finished," Joss said firmly.

"Are you sure? I could give you a shilling." The baron winked.

"There is no price," Joss said, "that you could set on this encounter. Please go, Sutcliffe. I shall meet you at your house directly."

Still craning his neck, the baron hesitated. Augusta said, "Do *you* want a shilling?" When he laughed, she rummaged for her reticule and tossed him a coin.

This did the trick: Sutcliffe bowed, then turned to depart. "I'll see you back at Queen Square!" Then he thundered down the stairs, whistling.

Joss strode to the door and banged it shut, then leaned against it. "I'm sorry. I forgot to lock the door. I must have been…distracted. When I saw you waiting within." Sentences stumbled slowly; his head thudded with fatigue and thwarted desire and the heaviness of an unwanted heart.

"There's no point in shutting it now, if I ought to leave."

"Stay if you like. As long as you like. I will let a servant know you'll require a Bath chair later, if you wish some time to compose yourself. I must go, though. If Sutcliffe has truly identified his blackmailer…"

There would be no more reason for Joss to stay in Bath.

Augusta spoke up in that same colorless voice. "You leave me very easily."

This hurt, like a punch thrown after the fight was supposed to be over. "For what reason ought I to stay? He has a purpose for me right now, which you have made quite clear you do not. At least nothing with which I can assist you."

"I'm not sorry for what I want of you."

"And I'm not sorry for what I've done or what I haven't done. I can manage a bit of sorrow about the aftermath, though." He needed to get away from her, now. Had she brought a cloak? Yes, there it was, tossed over his trunk. Impatience and anger welled up within him—she had everything, yet she wanted *more*—and he grabbed up the cloak and flung it in her direction. "I know you've never wanted anything from me but to own me. Other men, you might buy, but the cost of my pride is too high. Instead, I decided to give myself to you, and I was the one who paid."

She stood, shrugging on her cloak and shoving the handkerchief full of hairpins into a pocket. The hood covered her tumbled hair; no one would know what had passed between them. "I could say the same to you," she said. "But you would not take what I wished you to. Do you not think of what that costs me?"

That was too much; he laughed bitterly. "You're an heiress. You can afford it, can't you?"

For a long moment, she stared at him with those amber eyes. And then, without another word, she gathered the cloak about her and turned toward the door.

As she passed by the desk, the heavy fabric of her cloak brushed his glass vial of sandalwood oil. It teetered and rolled, then fell to the floor and shattered.

Nineteen

As he strode through the twilit streets of Bath, Joss's arousal was replaced by a deep gray feeling. If he had to put a word to it, it would be disappointment, maybe. Disappointment in Augusta for trusting him, but not enough. Disappointment in himself for hoping for a beginning, when what passed had instead felt like the end. He offered his heart, but because she could not decide its value, she had no use for it.

There was no time to lick his wounds and pity himself, though. He had work to do.

Once admitted to the baron's Queen Square house, Joss refused to meet with Sutcliffe in the spying room.

"I shall see him in the drawing room," Joss told the flabbergasted butler. "That is, after all, where barons customarily entertain callers. *Not* in a random bed-chamber that serves as host to nothing but a spyglass."

When he established himself in the flower-papered drawing room, he requested a pot of tea, a plate of biscuits, and a tray of sandwiches from a servant. Why not a bit of gluttony? He was already full of lust, pride, wrath, and envy. Greed too, if one counted his wish for Augusta Meredith, heart and hand, mind and body.

Sloth was the only deadly sin of which he was not guilty today. At least that.

As an afterthought, he ordered a pot of hot water for the baron.

When Sutcliffe entered the lamplit drawing room, petulant about having to abandon his post at the spying room's window, Joss stood. "The hour is too dark for spying, Sutcliffe, and I am in a dreadful mood. But as it's not your fault that everything is horrible right now, I ask you calmly: what have you learned today about your blackmailer?"

"Oh, ho. I have a secret from you!"

"If you do, it is much more difficult for me to help you. And I did promise to help you."

"I don't need your help anymore. I figured everything out all by myself, using my spyglass." The tea tray arrived just then, and a confused expression crossed the baron's thin face. "What's this, then? I didn't order all this food. Take it away, servant."

"Wait. Please." Joss caught the eye of the footman balancing the tray above a tea table. "I ordered this, and you may leave it. Thank you."

As the liveried young man bowed out, Joss added, "There's hot water for you, Sutcliffe. I know how you do enjoy a steaming cup of grass clippings."

"By Jove, yes." He drew out his ever-present pouch and shook forth the dry blades.

Once this oft-repeated process was complete, Joss prodded. "And the blackmail letter?"

Sutcliffe sipped at his teacup. "With my spyglass, I

saw a young woman deliver it. She was dressed like a maid. Since she was pretty, I ran down the stairs and gave her a shilling."

"Of course you did."

"Then she went into the house next door. She didn't see me because I had closed the door and run back up to my spying room. I'm very fast on my feet."

"Of course you are."

"So," the baron concluded, "the blackmailer must be Lady Tallant. Or one of her servants. It might even be that redheaded woman you were fornicating with."

"I was *talking*. I was *not*," Joss ground out, "fornicating."

Well. Maybe he had been. Did it still count as fornicating if his mind was clouded by love, marriage, forever? Or if he had slaked his own passion not a bit?

"What were you talking about, then?" Sutcliffe asked.

"Nothing of significance." True enough for the purposes of an answer. Joss's feelings for Augusta were not significant to her, and certainly her feelings for him were nothing of the sort.

Moving toward the fireplace, he stretched out his hands and let the warmth lick his fingertips. An eggshell-thin porcelain vase atop the mantel held a few hothouse blooms in shades of orange and red. Their scent struck him as heavy and oversweet; Joss turned his face away.

A spark popped from the too-high fire. Joss stepped from its embrace toward the settee of which Sutcliffe had once complained because its velvet upholstery dared show a bit of wear. Its frame was built of satin-wood, decorated with acanthus carvings and gilt.

For all that costliness, it really wasn't comfortable

to sit on. Or maybe his discomfort seeped out from within. "Nothing makes sense, Sutcliffe."

"I agree," said his cousin. *Second* cousin. "What reason would Lady Tallant have to blackmail anyone? She has pots of money."

Joss shook himself back to the subject at hand. "Are you absolutely certain of the house the woman entered?"

"I can see everything with my spyglass."

"That doesn't answer my question."

Sutcliffe blinked, then set down his cup on the tea tray. "You are a dreadful grump, Everett."

"Habitually? Or only at the moment?"

Sutcliffe gave the question careful thought. "Habitually. But extra much at the moment."

Joss had to smile at this. "Yes, I'd have to agree with you. Show me the letter the maid delivered, won't you?"

The baron tossed over a wadded paper which he had, apparently, stuffed into his coat pocket next to his precious pouch of herbs. As he'd indicated, it bore no marks of having been handled by the post. The hand-delivered note was gummed shut with a wafer; when unfolded, the text was simple.

> On the last day of March, your lady learns all. You should hope, reckless fool, that she is more forgiving than I.

"No demand for money," Joss mused. "Very odd."

"It's good news, though, isn't it? If there's no more trouble over money, we can leave Bath at once."

Joss refolded the paper, then rose to hand it back

to the baron. "You are free to leave anytime. But if a maid from Lady Tallant's household is depositing threatening notes at your doorstep, then I ought to speak with those servants."

"Or the redheaded woman."

"She likes to be called Mrs. Flowers," Joss said. "But as a matter of fact, I know the lady's writing, and this is not it."

So easily, his thoughts flew back to Augusta. Had she made her way to Queen Square yet, or did she remain in Trim Street? He had left her behind in his lodging, a jewel amid dross. And he had fled her to sit on velvet in Queen Square, only a spyglass's span from where she belonged.

For the time being, they had switched worlds, though they would switch back soon enough. But he was not dross among jewels, and it was time to make that clear. Starting with Sutcliffe.

First he poured himself a cup of tea, adding lump after lump of sugar. Then he piled up a plate of food. And then he spoke. "At the end of the month, Sutcliffe, I will leave your service."

The sentence was as easy to speak as had been his words of unwanted love to Augusta. This time, he didn't need to wait on an answer. It was not a question.

Sutcliffe stared at Joss for a long moment, then he laughed. "And here I thought you were in a gruff mood! Everett, you are a funny man."

"Thank you. If you would like to hire a successor at once, I will do my best to train him in your"— *eccentricities, whims, addictions*—"preferences before I leave your service."

The baron laughed again before gulping the rest of his beverage. Joss took a sip of fragrant tea. He grimaced—he had added too much sugar, an unaccustomed luxury. But who could pass by a chance for unaccustomed luxury? Drinking it down, he then turned his attention to his plate of food.

Sutcliffe followed his every gesture with wary blue eyes. "You're serious?"

"Quite serious." Joss bit into a sandwich, savoring the fine-textured bread, the salty meat. Why had he never ordered his own tea tray before? The baron did not mind. He did not protest beyond his initial confusion. Why had Joss resigned himself to being starved in any way?

He had been party to his own servitude. He had let himself be pushed to the side, not pushing back.

He set the sandwich down, appetite gone.

Sutcliffe's usual armory of fidgets stilled, his shoulders slackened. He looked like a marionette whose strings had been dropped. "Everett, how *could* you?"

The same question Augusta had once asked Joss when they were skating perilously through a conversation about lovers. His answer now was not much different. "There's no longer any hope of meaning." He smiled. "I don't leave you with ill will, cousin. But I don't think we can do each other any good anymore."

As Sutcliffe poured out another cup of hot water, his hand shook, rattling porcelain against porcelain. "You called me cousin. Why now?"

"It's what you are to me. It's what I am to you." Joss set down his plate, leaning forward. "I should have called you cousin much more. I should have destroyed the *somalata* when you were a youth, as soon as your asthma no longer troubled you. I should have—well, I should have done many things differently. As should you have. But I suppose we formed each other over the years."

The baron looked bewildered. "But…what will I do?"

What will I do, Sutcliffe wondered. *Not what will you do*. Well. One could not expect a perennial dependent to grow selfless all of a sudden.

"You'll be a baron. And I hope you'll go home to your baroness and treat her kindly. She's a good wife to you."

Sutcliffe looked much struck. "She is, isn't she? Do you think—"

A knock at the door interrupted this sentence. It preceded the entry of the butler, who bore a note on a silver salver. "A message for Mr. Everett."

"Thank you." Joss took the note, insides dancing a cotillion. Augusta had written, she said yes, he would meet her tonight…

No, she had not written: the angular script across the note was unfamiliar. His insides dropped into sedation again, though his fingers tingled from the aftermath of the sudden dance as he cracked the seal.

> To Mr. Everett, who is at this moment in company with Lord Sutcliffe—
>
> In accordance with your request that I investigate the matter of Lord Sutcliffe's difficulty, I have made certain inquiries. As a result, I have summoned Lady Sutcliffe to Bath. She will arrive at the Pump Room by private carriage tomorrow morning. The matter

*of Lord Sutcliffe's difficulty will, I am confident, be
sorted out at that time.*

   *It is possible that the baroness will wish to
remain in Bath following her journey; it is also
possible that she will not.*

   *At your convenience, we shall meet to discuss
the matter of how you shall pay for the service I
have provided.*

>   *Yours,*
>   *Chatfield*

"Chatfield," Joss murmured. "Good Lord, he
works quickly. And he really does know everything."

Such wonders could be achieved with determination and deep pockets. Working as an information
hunter for Lord Chatfield would bring variety to one's
life, to say the least.

"Let me see." With a whoop, Sutcliffe snapped up
the note.

"If Chatfield knows I am here," Joss mused, "then
he might also know about your most recent blackmail
letter, or—hmm. No, it's too much to hope he has
news of it."

"Why would he not? The maid brought the letter
before you arrived. So if he knows you arrived, then
he knows about the maid, which means he probably
knows about the letter."

Joss's brows knit. "That…actually makes sense."

"Do you know where he lodged? Do you think
he's watching the house right now? Perhaps we should
wave out the window."

"No." Joss caught Sutcliffe's wrist before the baron could parade before the lamplit window in his candy-striped coat.

Sutcliffe sank to the settee at Joss's side, the note dangling limply from his fingers. "I wonder whether Lord Chatfield has a proper telescope."

"I wonder what you think of your wife's arrival."

"What about my wife?"

"She will arrive in Bath tomorrow. And one way or another, Sutcliffe, the truth will come out."

"Why?"

"Because somehow her arrival is tied to the blackmail. And you are quite sure someone next door is connected with it." Joss shook his head. *The first letter had been posted in London.* Impossible. "It must be one of the household servants. The blackmailer's penmanship is rather rough, isn't it? That might fit. Did any of them come from Lady Tallant's London household, or were they all hired in Bath along with the house?"

"How the devil should I know? I've no head for anything but magic tricks and pretty ankles."

This was so suddenly honest that the two men blinked at each other, equally surprised.

"Yes, well." Joss cleared his throat. "Lord Chatfield, who has a nasty habit of being correct about things, seems to think Lady Sutcliffe's arrival will unravel this whole mess." He drew in a deep breath. "You'll have to tell your wife about Jessie. The *maid* who will bear *your child* in about two more months," he added sharply, seeing his cousin's expression turn bewildered.

"But Lady Sutcliffe will get angry with me and cut off my funds."

"And so the means justify the end," Joss murmured. When Sutcliffe looked yet more puzzled, he added, "She *should* get angry. And so should Jessie. You treated both women terribly; you betrayed their trust."

So much, so many women. Was Jessie the first servant to carry a baby by Sutcliffe? Whether he promised her love or forced her—whether it began with a great lie or a great wrong—it ended in her suffering.

Joss's mother had died of measles when he was just a boy. Would she have died so young and lonely if Jack Everett had never got her with child? What if she had been able to marry someone wealthy and kind instead, someone who would cosset her and adore her?

And would Augusta have trusted Joss more, or sooner—or maybe even loved him—if she had never been scarred by the betrayal of someone to whom she'd given her heart?

There was no way to know; no way to change the past. And as Augusta had once pointed out, the past made them all. If Jack Everett hadn't been a seductive scoundrel, Joss would not exist. All things being equal, he would rather exist than not.

And if Augusta's past lover had coaxed her to Gretna, Joss would have met her only as a married woman, if at all. He must be selfishly glad that the path of her travels had crossed his.

But it now diverged, as it must inevitably when two people lived such differently winding lives.

As Joss stared at the leaping fire, the world seemed gray again.

"This note, Joss." Sutcliffe waved the paper before his eyes. "To what is Chatfield referring? What payment?"

With an effort, Joss focused his eyes and mind back on the present. "Don't trouble yourself about that," he said. "I told you I would take care of the matter, and I will."

He stood, then held out a hand to help Sutcliffe to his feet. "Do call back the butler, won't you? You must order a bedchamber prepared for your lady."

"Yes, you're right. But not the spying room."

"No," Joss agreed. "The spying room would never do."

Twenty

THE NEXT MORNING'S PROMENADE AROUND THE PUMP Room felt to Augusta like putting on a glove: a bit restrictive, but so familiar one hardly noticed the resulting loss of sensation. The immense room's corniced tray ceiling stretched high overhead; the Corinthian half columns marched down the wall, keeping watch over the health seekers who eddied around the urn-shaped fountain that gave the room its name.

As she threaded through the crowded room at Emily's side, the room dulled her with its sameness. Always the hushed voices, the bubble and flow of greetings, the sulfurous scent of the mineral waters.

Unfortunately, she was insufficiently dulled. Just as gloves did not always keep hands from being nipped by chill, so the cocoon of the Pump Room could not keep Augusta from piercing herself on the shock of last night's passion, of Joss's confession of love. She was rather glad Lord Sutcliffe had interrupted her and Joss, saving them from causing one another further pain. She should have known—had always known—that Joss would demand more of her than she was able to give.

She resented him for mentioning love—yet she admired him for being unsatisfied with less. Joss was honest, always, about what he wanted. And there was no denying that he wanted her. *Longed* for her, he had said.

"I need to sit down," she said weakly.

At her side, Emily walked with sure steps, having recently abandoned the wheeled chair as "far too much fuss." Without a word, the countess grabbed Augusta's arm and marched her to the far end of the long room, in which chairs and benches were scattered under the watchful gaze of statues in wall alcoves.

Emily deposited Augusta in a chair, then plumped down next to her. "Finally, a moment to speak. I feared we weren't going to talk at all about what happened yesterday. I've nearly chewed off all my fingernails."

"You have not. And I didn't say I wanted to talk." Augusta pressed at her temple. "I said I needed to sit down."

Emily signaled for a servant, then turned to Augusta. "So you say. But I am sure if I ever came home alone in a Bath chair after dark, with my hair all tumbled down my back and a suspicious scrape on my cheeks as from stubble, I would tell you all about it."

"Because you would have met with your husband? My, what a scandal that would be." Augusta trailed a hand down the side of her face. "Are my cheeks truly scraped?"

Emily ignored this, shooting a dazzling smile at the liveried servant who drew up to her side. "My friend is not feeling well. Would you be so kind as to bring her some of the marvelous medicinal mineral water? Let us say…a pint. No, a quart."

This was most unkind, as the water was ordinarily drunk out of small glasses.

"I was not aware that you hated me," Augusta muttered as the servant went off on his errand.

"Hate you?" Emily was all innocence. "By no means, dear friend. Your uncharacteristic behavior last night, and your silence about it this morning, prove to me that you are ill. I simply want to help."

"I am *not* going to drink the water."

"We'll see." As the servant returned from the pump with a silver tray full of glasses, Emily handed him a coin from her reticule and accepted the burden in exchange. "Thank you. This will have her feeling better in a trice."

"*Honestly*, Emily. I am not going to drink it."

She expected Emily to press the matter, but the countess looked down at the tray full of glasses as though puzzled. In her simple day dress of yellow muslin, sprinkled with flowers and banded at the sleeves and waist with velvet, she looked much younger than her thirty years, but her eyes were old. "No," she said. "There's no purpose to it, is there? It doesn't help."

Emily's voice was so quiet and suddenly bleak that Augusta reached out for a glass. "Maybe not, but it won't hurt. I will drink it if you want me to. Well— not all of it, but some."

The countess gave her an odd little smile. "No need. It was nothing but a petty revenge on you for keeping secrets from me. But you've a right to your secrets."

"I've a right to my secrets? Have I heard you correctly?"

"You have. What you did not hear me say was, 'I don't wish to hear all about it.' Because, my dear, I do." Emily hefted the tray of mineral water glasses and laid it on the floor before her chair. "I could use the distraction. And *you* could stand to be less distracted."

"What do you mean?"

Emily narrowed her eyes at Augusta. "I mean— you're running away from everything. You ran away with me to Bath, and you ran away from your own name. You keep seeking out Mr. Everett, but then you run away from him too. It's terribly unfair."

"Unfair, you say." Augusta narrowed her eyes right back. "It's unfair that I—what? That I told a lie that doesn't affect you at all?"

"To what do you refer?" Emily's voice took on a crisp edge. "To whatever nonsense with which you fobbed off Mr. Everett last night, or to the fact that you are using my name as protection for your false identity?"

Darting her gaze around—good, it did not appear anyone was close enough to listen—Augusta fumbled for a reply. "The...the second thing you said."

This brusque Emily was a formidable creature. Gone was the softness of uncertainty, the shadow of fatigue. Her chin held high, she looked down her nose at Augusta. "You think that doesn't affect me, merely because I permitted your falsehood to stand? I allowed your lie for your own inscrutable reasons, but you trade on my reputation every day. All of Bath knows that Lady Tallant has given house room to Mrs.

Flowers. And when Mrs. Flowers comes home all of a tumble, Lady Tallant damned well has the right to know what is going on."

"You want to know?" Augusta could lift her chin too, all the higher to avoid the crawling feeling that Emily was quite correct. "Fine. He told me he loved me and he did…things."

Emily's imperious posture loosened a bit. "Nice things?"

"Very nice things."

The tautness in the countess's posture melted away. "Good. And what did you tell him in return?"

"Ah—nothing."

"What did you do, then? Nice things?"

"Well…no." Augusta pressed at her temple again. How lovely it would be if she was alone with Joss again, and he was pulling the tight pins from her hair. This time, she would be ready for him; she would…

What? What would she do differently?

"I did not do anything to him." She squeezed her eyes closed for a moment. "But I think I hurt him very much. And I—I don't know how else to be."

Emily patted Augusta's arm. "I know. You have forgotten. And that's why I allowed you to pose as Mrs. Flowers. But you are still you, Augusta, and thank heaven for that. You must find yourself again."

In a fidget, Augusta stretched out her legs and bumped the tray of glasses on the floor. A clatter recalled her, and she collected her posture into a neat bundle: ankles crossed, hands folded in her lap. A perfect lady from the outside, just as her mother had always wanted her to appear.

And just like that, a damp blanket of gloom descended. "Most of the people who loved Augusta are dead. Or they never existed at all. Why shouldn't I be Mrs. Flowers for good?"

Emily arched a brow. "Who would you like to be?"

Six words. Six syllables. Such a small sentence to hold such a large thought. And Augusta had no answer; she could only stare.

"I beg your pardon." A masculine voice, low and beautifully familiar, broke into her surprise. "Lady Tallant. Mrs. Flowers."

"Joss." The name escaped Augusta like a sigh.

"Mr. Everett." Emily covered the lapse in formality with a perfectly polite smile, a hand outstretched to shake.

And all Augusta could think was: *Joss. Thank God you are here. Joss.* He stood before them with hands folded behind his back. In his plain black coat and waistcoat, his gray pantaloons and worn boots, he looked as elegant as a prince.

Who would you like to be? Had Joss ever doubted the answer to this question? No, he had told her his dreams with utter certainty. He knew the direction of the path he wanted to take, now and next and onward.

"Joss," she said again in a voice that sounded cracked and hoarse. "How are you?"

He ignored this lukewarm greeting. "I shall be leaving Bath in the next few days, and I wished to give you something before I departed." From behind his back, he brought forth a few folded papers. "These might be of use to Meredith Beauty."

Augusta held out her hand, mystified. The papers

were covered with Joss's elegant writing: notes on plant extracts and fragrances. She flipped a page, skimming a description of *shikakai*, which appeared to be a powdered plant compound used for cleansing the hair. "What is all of this?"

"My transcription of my grandmother's notes." His hands tapped the line of his thigh, belying the smooth calm of his voice. "My Indian grandmother. She was fascinated by plants, and she recorded many of her observations. Some are in a Hindustani script I cannot read, but some were written in English. These—I—if you think you can use them, you ought to take them."

She did not realize until he folded his hand over hers that she had extended the papers back to him in confusion. "Whether you trick Meredith Beauty's trustees into thinking these are their notions," he said, "or whether you beat them over the head with your brilliance, just take these notes. If you think you can use them."

"You are repeating yourself, Mr. Everett," Emily observed.

The paper crackled, dry as a husk between Augusta's fingertips. Her throat worked, blocked by a lump. "Why?" The word was nothing more than a whisper.

"Because you have your parents' curiosity. Because they wanted the best for you, but most of all, wanted you to be happy." His smile was unfamiliar. Tight. "Maybe if you make things that help women become aware of their own loveliness, you'll become happy. Or maybe you won't, but you could still make the company good. It is yours, after all."

Like a soldier, he snapped upright before bowing

over Emily's hand. "Lady Tallant. Always a pleasure to speak with you."

"But I hardly said anything," Emily protested. "Here, I could leave you two to your conversation. Let me leave. I could—ah, promenade toward the fountain."

"Do not distress yourself. I came only to give Mrs. Flowers those papers. I must go now; Lady Sutcliffe will be arriving at the Pump Room at any moment. I am to help her become situated, then I shall prepare to leave Lord Sutcliffe's employment."

"A great misfortune for him," Emily said politely. "He will miss you, I am sure."

Leaving. "I—did not know," fumbled Augusta.

But she should have known. He had left last night; he would leave again. No one stayed in Bath.

She had not thought of how this moment would feel, though. She had never expected to run out of chances, to have a conversation be their last.

Then he looked at Augusta, deep and full in the eyes. "I understand why you could not say yes. And it is for the best."

He understood? How could he when she herself did not? Joss had shaken up her world, making its chilly sameness ebb. "No," she said. "No."

It was not for the best, but what was? Not Joss, turning on his heel after a perfunctory bow. "What will you do?" The words burst from her lips like a sparking fire.

He paused. "Lord Chatfield has offered me employment."

And then he was gone, a blade cutting through the crowd. He seemed to have sliced Augusta as he left.

Though he had done so with kindness, this handful of papers was no substitute for…for something she had told him she did not want.

Before she could ponder that deeply, a mellifluous male voice rang forth. "Dear ladies!" Leaning on his cane, Lord Chatfield hove into view, stocky yet impeccable in deep blue and a gilt herringbone waistcoat. With a groan, he settled himself heavily into the seat on Emily's other side. His wooden leg, Augusta knew, often pained the knee to which it was strapped.

"Good morning, my lord," she said. "Would you care to take the waters?" She gave the rejected tray full of glasses a nudge with her slippered foot.

"Not at all. I am here for the entertainment."

Emily looked bemused. "What entertainment is that? Is a concert to take place?"

The marquess's full face broke into a grin. "It might be a concert of a sort, if one counts wailing and gnashing of teeth. The Right Honorable Lady Sutcliffe is to meet her husband for the first time in several weeks, and I believe we have excellent seats to the show."

"A show?" Augusta was still following Joss with her thoughts; she could not trace the marquess's meaning.

"They both possess a secret from the other." Atop his cane was a sphere of amber; he clutched this, rotating it within his grip. "When they meet, they shall learn this. I expect something rather like the reaction of sodium and water."

Emily looked blank. "Which is?"

"A conflagration." Chatfield lingered over the word, savoring it.

"Dear me." The countess lifted her brows. "How

fortunate that we are near a door if we must escape the flames in a hurry."

"There will be no need to escape," he replied. "The fire will burn out quickly. But will it be the destructive or cleansing sort? That, I admit, is what I am curious to learn."

As he scanned the crowd, his avid expression reminded Augusta of nothing so much as a parent looking for a child of whom he was proud. His carefully hoarded knowledge was all the family he had, and he took undeniable pleasure in seeing his information translated into results.

There was something unfeeling, though, about Chatfield's clockwork determination to see a scheme to fruition. What if Lady Sutcliffe should not wish to be observed as she met her husband? Any public outburst would end in someone's humiliation.

But Joss would be at the baroness's side, Augusta recalled; though he planned to leave Sutcliffe's service, he would not shirk his duty to his employer. His family. "You have my congratulations," she said to the marquess. "We have just spoken with Mr. Everett and have learned that he will soon take up employment with you."

Chatfield leaned forward to meet her eye around Emily's form. "Have you indeed learned that? How interesting."

"In what way?" Emily leaned forward too, not wanting to be overlooked.

"I offered him a position. He turned it down."

Emily shot a quick sidelong glance at Augusta. "Ah, indeed? We must have misunderstood."

Had they? What had Joss said to them? *Lord Chatfield has offered me employment.* He had not said he accepted it, though. Oh, the canny man.

It seemed Joss was done with her; he had unburdened himself last night and did not wish to pick up the weight of her company again. Better that she had not said yes, better that she knew nothing of where he went next.

So he said. But she disagreed.

She turned her head, looking down the row of chairs at Emily's serene elegance, at Chatfield's bated eagerness. They represented England's elite; they were wealthy and influential. Yet even so, they had suffered. A scion of the nobility could lose a leg; a countess could lose a child.

An heiress could lose her parents, then a false suitor too.

No one had a perfect life. Everyone lied sometimes, even if only when they said *I'm quite well, thank you.* Augusta had been selfish, so selfish, to act as though her pain was worse. As though she had no hope of recovery. To convince herself that, because she had not been loved once, she could not be loved, and so words of love ought never to be trusted again.

You are worthy, Joss had told her. *Just as you are.*

And this was the other direction in which life could slope. A man could be knit together in trickery and scandal, yet become steadfast and honorable.

And wickedly, beautifully honest.

"You asked," she murmured to Emily through a tight closed throat, "who I want to be. I know who I do *not* want to be. I do not want to be afraid anymore."

She hated being afraid. Of pursuing not out of want, but out of the fear of what chased her. Seeking a lover to evict Colin Hawford. But that would never happen unless she let someone into her heart more deeply than Colin had ever delved. Deeply enough to touch the bedrock of love on which she'd built her life: her family, lost but always remembered.

"Not wanting to be afraid is a good start," Emily replied, equally low. "Being Augusta, whether afraid or not, would be an excellent next step."

As though the entire Pump Room had overheard Emily's advice, a piping voice rang out. "Lady Tallant—what a pleasure. Ah, and Augusta Meredith. I thought I recognized you!"

Toward the chairs walked Little Bo Peep: a golden-curled, doll-like woman garbed in icy, elaborate pastel silks.

This was not, of course, a figure from a nursery rhyme. It was Lady Sutcliffe, a very real figure who had, apparently, a better recall for names than her husband. "My lady," Augusta said weakly. "I am now known as—"

"As the greatest tease in London?" The baroness trilled, a brittle smile on her lips. "Ah, my dear girl, not so anymore. For you see, Lord Sutcliffe has surpassed you. He has been to Town and teased all his creditors by appearing in new waistcoats."

Lord Chatfield murmured, "Conflagration."

Never before had Augusta heard the phrase "my dear" uttered by someone who seemed to mean it less. Despite the beauty of her clothing and her elaborate butter-gold coiffure, her features wore a pinched, hunted look. The laugh that issued from her lips was like dropped glass, shattering and sharp.

As though they were spectators before a stage, new players joined the scene. Joss reappeared, dragging Lord Sutcliffe by an elbow. "But I forgot my spyglass!" bleated the baron. "I can't be without it." His eyes went wide. "My pouch! Where's my pouch?" He slapped at his violet brocade coat. An expression of relief crossed his face as he apparently found what he sought.

"My lord." Lady Sutcliffe gave her husband the tiniest of curtsies.

"Lady Sutcliffe?" Sutcliffe stared at her until Joss nudged him. "Oh. Ah—greetings to you, my darling wife. I say, can a man get a pot of ordinary hot water in this room, or do they have only that terrible stuff that smells of dirty feet?"

The baroness's small frame went so stiff that it practically vibrated with tension. "Is this all I am to expect by way of greeting? You summoned me to Bath. I thought you must have something of import to communicate."

"What?" Sutcliffe blinked.

She stamped her foot. "Sutcliffe, *do* pay attention."

"What?" he said again, then seemed to notice his surroundings. "Yes, quite right—something of import. Look, Everett, there's that widow I saw you with last night!"

The surrounding people seemed not to know whether to gasp or not. Augusta tried to smile, but a sick, slapped feeling raced over her skin. At her side, Emily went carefully still.

Joss leaned toward Sutcliffe and whispered

something in his ear. "No." The baron shook his head. "I'm not mistaken. Look, she's right there. Don't you recognize her? The redhead. Miss Meredith. Oh, no, I forgot—she's not called that anymore."

Lady Sutcliffe tilted her head. "Yes, she is. What sort of rot are you talking, Sutcliffe? She was in the gossip columns in London not a month ago for being a madcap flirt."

It was as though everyone in Bath who had met Mrs. Flowers overheard this exchange, their heads turning like chickens sighting a farmer bringing corn. Suddenly everyone in the Pump Room was drifting in the direction of the Sutcliffes, of the three figures in chairs before them.

And then the clamor started.

Emily said something polite and soothing, Joss tried again to silence the baron, and Lady Sutcliffe insisted more loudly that she knew of what she was talking and that her husband had got things wrong again. "I'm not talking rot!" Sutcliffe shouted, and then he called for his spyglass—what spyglass?—and over all, the master of ceremonies could be heard to call, "What's all this, then?" A servant hawked mineral waters, a crush of people pressed closer, and the words *flirt—widow—lied—true?—impossible* mixed into a cacophony, layer upon layer of sound beating at Augusta's ears until she felt she must crumple.

Everyone lied sometimes. But not everyone lied as much as Augusta had, and now she was found out. She had just said she didn't want to be afraid anymore—but wanting wasn't the same as having, and the weight of crashing public opinion pressed the breath from her lungs.

"I must go," she said to Emily. "I think I am ill."

Coward. Yes, she was. But so many eyes blinked, so many people knew her for a fraud, a nothing, a fake. And in the midst of them all was Joss, watching her come undone.

It was for the best they had nothing more to do with one another. He had said so.

She staggered to her feet, the curious crowd pressing back, all a-whisper as though she were some spectacle in a carnival. "I must go," she said again.

As she took a step, her foot hit the tray of mineral water glasses, sending them crashing and spilling. She slid in the puddle, then stumbled over her long skirts and lost her balance. If she hadn't been clutching the papers from Joss so tightly, she might have arrested her fall before she struck her head on the floor and all went dark.

Twenty-one

AUGUSTA BLINKED INTO HAZY DARKNESS BROKEN BY blobs of light. When she squinted, the lights resolved themselves into the flames of a fire and a lamp. Glancing around the room, she recognized the dark trellised wallpaper as belonging to her Queen Square bedchamber.

She lay in the bed with the coverlet pulled up to her chin; she was perspiring; her head ached. Trailing light fingers over the painful spot, she located a knot on her forehead that felt as large as a duck egg.

"What in God's name happened to me?" she murmured, tossing back the covers.

"You slipped on spilled mineral water."

Augusta started at the sound of Emily's voice. She sat up and saw the countess reclining on the bedchamber's short settee near the fireplace, a book in her hands.

"What time is it?"

"Five o'clock in the morning on the fifth day of April. You've been unconscious for weeks."

"Impossible." Augusta glared at Emily. "Ouch. Glaring at you pulls at my bruise."

Emily laughed, then shut her book. "All right, only teasing. Your fall looked rather horrible, but you weren't unconscious long. It's just after noon."

Augusta thought back. "The Sutcliffes were shouting. No—everyone was shouting." *Flirt—widow—liar.* "All of Bath was shouting."

"Close to it," Emily said blandly. "Here, have some water." The countess poured out a glassful from a pitcher, then tugged back the drapes to let daylight into the chamber. "I have never been convinced of the health benefits of Bath's mineral waters, and today they nearly broke open your head. The positive side is that now you are an invalid and you may be as demanding as you like."

"Oh? Are you going to cater to my every whim?" Sips of water—*not* mineral water—were pleasant on her parched throat before she set the glass aside again.

"Perhaps not I. But I'm sure I can find someone who will." Emily sat on the bed. "I could hardly tug the papers from your hand even after you hit your head."

"Where are they now?"

"I tucked them in my book." Emily waved a hand in the direction of the settee. "Were they worth breaking your head over?"

"As they effected my removal from a shouting mob, I should say so. How did I get back here?"

"With the combined efforts of Mr. Everett, a few footmen, and a Bath chair. Lord and Lady Sutcliffe were beginning to brew a grand row, though they managed to bottle it and follow our progress to Queen Square." Rising, Emily retrieved the volume from the settee, then returned to press it into Augusta's hands.

"Mr. Everett has rejoined them, and I cannot imagine how he intends to make peace between them. But that will not be his concern for much longer."

"No, I suppose it won't." Augusta traced the tooling on the small book's binding. "You were attempting to read William Blake again?"

"Attempting it, yes. I was able to read all of 'Infant Joy' today without even throwing the book into the fire."

"'What shall I call thee?'" Augusta said. "'Sweet joy befall thee.'" The poem that had sent Emily into tears not so long ago. The evening of the assembly, when Augusta had encountered Joss Everett and he had peeled away the first of her secrets.

It seemed ages ago.

"'What shall I call thee' reminds me of something I meant to tell you." Emily sank onto the edge of the bed again. "Augusta, I admit that I was angry with you earlier. Not because you expected me to let you pose as Mrs. Flowers—though you *are* fortunate that I'm up for such a lark."

"A lark that is certainly done with now," Augusta said drily. "It is for the best, though I expect the aftermath will be dreadful for a while. I thank you for giving me room to recover my wits, and I only hope the scandal does not affect you much. But what angered you, Emily?"

Emily looked at the cover of the small book in Augusta's hands. "Because you persist in thinking of yourself as weak and wounded, and you have thrown away much good as a result. You've had much to grieve, there is no question. Were you a man, you might have coped by destroying your health and fortune with drink and gambling and whores. All things considered, dear Augusta, I think you must give yourself credit for being quite strong. Quite strong indeed."

This was so unexpected, so unlikely, that Augusta had to laugh.

"Ah, you are trying to ignore what I'm saying. But I'm serious. You must choose for yourself in the present, not to chase away the past. Because making decisions to chase away the past..."

"It stays," Augusta sighed. "It stays and stays, every time I try again to forget it."

"That is why I read 'Infant Joy' again," Emily agreed. "Only think of this: you have a chance at love, Augusta, yet you keep yourself hidden away from it."

"And you," Augusta could not help but reply. "What of you?"

"*Touché, ma chère.* You are quite right; I have been hiding too. But I wrote to Lord Tallant this morning, asking him and our sons to join me in Bath for a few days. And then, I think, we will all return to London together."

"You are ready for that?"

"Yes, I believe so. I'm not done grieving. But I'm done grieving alone."

Emily was good, so good, at capturing shining moments.

Oh, this was not such a moment, not with Augusta's head aching, a scandal prowling the streets of Bath, and a poem that would forever remind Emily of the daughter she had lost. Yet as the women sat together, quiet and still, Augusta thought there was something solid in the moment. It was, as she'd said of the White Hart, *true*.

She was ready for truth.

Emily patted Augusta's arm, then stood. "And now, the former Mrs. Flowers, I shall leave you and your precious papers. Do you think you could see another caller in a little while? Say, a handsome bachelor caller?"

Augusta dropped the book.

"Very good. I'll have him summoned." Emily smiled, then left Augusta alone.

The folded papers had slid from the book when she dropped it, falling in a sheaf to the coverlet. Joss's handwriting, careful and elegant. He had left her with this, intending it to be a final gift, a good-bye.

But the closely written pages gave her an idea instead. And when he called later, she would have much to tell him.

❦

"Into the drawing room," Joss said when he and the baron and baroness entered Sutcliffe's rented house. "Both of you. Upstairs. No, Sutcliffe, you will not need your spyglass."

The past two hours had contained a series of unrealities. Giving papers to Augusta—papers written from his family and his heart—as he intended never to see her again. Watching Lady Sutcliffe's foray into the Pump Room in full battle regalia of watered silk. The public fight that threatened to spill forth when she saw her husband—and the secrets that had been spilled instead.

When Augusta slid and fell—*God,* watching her slam to the floor had made his heart hurt—Joss had helped Lady Tallant see to her safety and transport back to Queen Square. And then he marched the Sutcliffes from the gawking crowd in the Pump Room.

As he had passed by the seated Lord Chatfield, the marquess caught his arm. "Conflagration" was what it sounded like the man said; Joss shook his head in confusion. More loudly, the marquess said, "Once you've seen to the present needs, let me know how you shall pay me. My offer of employment stands."

Joss hardly knew what he had said by way of reply, so desperate was he to follow the Bath chair that carried away Augusta's still figure.

He was certain, though: he could not carry out this sort of work for the marquess. He could not bear to earn his bread by searching for clues to people's undoing. Watching the undoing of one family—this family—was too much already.

Once Lord and Lady Sutcliffe had drifted into the drawing room, tension vibrating as though a spring ran between them, Joss arranged each spouse in a slipper chair before the drawing-room fireplace. Then he faced them both, and, drawing a deep breath, prepared for painful truths. "Lady Sutcliffe, your husband has been receiving blackmail letters. You have been sending them, have you not?"

The diminutive baroness sat up straight, her feet hardly brushing the floor. "Yes. I have."

Sutcliffe sprang to his feet. "Impossible! A maid delivered one only yesterday, and she was much too tall to be you. I know, because I gave her a shilling."

Given the time, place, and subject of the conversation, this was not a wise confession. The baroness's pale skin went the color of chalk. "Shillings for maids," she spat. "How generous, especially considering all your money is really mine. But it doesn't stop with coins, does it? No, then you begin your magic tricks. Flirtations. Seduction. Or was it rape?"

Gingerly, Sutcliffe perched again at the edge of his chair. "I've never forced a woman."

"It should never even come *close* to that." Red blotches appeared on the baroness's face and neck, but her voice remained under careful control. "You cannot imagine the humiliation of knowing that you stray. Knowing that you would rather gamble and shop than spend time with your children or your tenants. Yet as humiliated as I am—as *angry* as I am—I am not the one most wronged."

Joss was beginning to feel superfluous, until Lady Sutcliffe turned to him. "How did you know it was me?"

A ghost of a smile touched his lips. "I gave the maid a shilling."

The baroness made a disgusted sound. "I did not think she would be so easily bought."

"She was not. Lord Chatfield had also paid her for her secrets, as it turns out, and a great deal. Information is worth far more to him than mere coin." Following his departure from Sutcliffe's house the night before, Joss had knocked at the kitchen entrance of the house next door. After a short survey of the servants, he had picked out the maid who had drawn his cousin's notice. And the story flowed out from there: Lady Sutcliffe had hired a maid in Emily's service to post a few letters. Once her messages were delivered to the maid, Jill, they were recopied in Jill's hand—unfamiliar to the baron—then sent on to Lord Sutcliffe. Thus came the letters from London, then posted from Bath, then carried by hand.

"It was a clever plan," Joss added. "But—why?"

Lady Sutcliffe set her jaw. "Because I have nothing that he cares for but money, and so the threat of impoverishment is the only hold I have over his behavior. I thought to shock him into respectability, but instead, he has dragged you down with him."

Joss bristled. "Any action I took in the service of Lord Sutcliffe was intended—"

He cut himself off before adding *for the ultimate good of your family*. Because it wasn't true, was it? He had meant well; he had urged Sutcliffe to confess, to mend his ways. But when had Sutcliffe ever done something just because someone told him he ought? Joss should have known that, but it was easier to make a small effort, to keep his head down and plow forward.

He ought to have done what he knew was right, even though it was not easy.

"I'm so sorry, my lady," he said to the baroness. "You are right. You deserved to know the truth. I ought to have told you."

Her small frame sagged against the back of the chair. "My children shall have a half sibling that they can never know."

Awkwardly, hesitantly, Sutcliffe reached out a hand and patted that of his wife. "Now, Celia, it's not as bad as all that. We could take the children to visit Jenny and the baby—"

"Jessie," said Joss and Lady Sutcliffe at once.

"And no, Sutcliffe, we could not," she added. "It would be cruel for you to force me to face the physical evidence of your adultery. At least, Mr. Everett, you were not so far gone in sense as to neglect to make provision for the poor woman."

"I believe she shall be well," Joss said. "She will receive an annuity for life."

"To be paid from my fortune," sighed the baroness. "All of our money was my money. And so I pay for your wrongdoing again, Sutcliffe. When will it end?"

Joss sidled toward the door. "Let me ring for some tea."

"Hot water for me," piped up the baron.

His wife made another disgusted sound.

Joss rang for a servant and ordered the tea tray, *not* a pot of hot water. Then he turned back to the baroness. "When you return to Sutcliffe Hall," Joss said to her, "I suggest you have the contents of the conservatory destroyed."

She tilted her china-doll head. "Are you certain? That is all you have left of your grandmother and mother."

Joss stared. She had kept it for his sake, thinking he drew meaning from rows of grassy *somalata* buried in earth? "You are very kind to consider my wishes," he said. "But that's not all I have left."

No, he had a fistful of memories of his mother, calm and tired; he had a book of botanical drawings he could not understand and notes he could not read.

He also had his existence. And he had a dream, finally: a wish for something grander than one hundred pounds and a steady clerical job.

And he knew where he must go next to bring it to life.

He would go alone, but Augusta would linger with him, the echo of her questioning voice in his ears. *It's not really a dream, is it?* It was now, dear fake widow. It was.

And she would become a dream too, especially the sharp sliver of time when she had told him *I want you very much indeed.*

It had not been enough. But it was far better than no memory of her at all. And seeing how marriage had treated the heiress who became Lady Sutcliffe—well, such women had good reasons to guard their hearts as carefully as their fortunes. Joss could not fault Augusta for protecting herself; he only wished he had been wise enough to do the same.

"I will see the plants destroyed," Lady Sutcliffe decided. "But it will not be enough to right matters. Too much else has already been destroyed in their stead."

"It won't be enough," Joss agreed. "But it might help. And Lord Sutcliffe is a positive fount of ideas. Perhaps he can think of other ways to make amends."

The baron sat up straighter. "Do you want to look through my spyglass, Celia?"

She frowned. "I sincerely hope that is not a euphemism."

"What?" The baron burst into laughter. "By God, Celia. You're a funny woman. I have missed you very much."

Her frown wavered. "I am glad you say so, even if you do not mean it. But I won't, you know. I won't touch your…spyglass. Not after you've been poking it in places it doesn't belong."

"What do you mean? A spyglass doesn't belong anywhere. Except in my hand, maybe."

The frown melted a bit more. "Then we shall let your hand tend to your spyglass for the foreseeable future."

Joss cleared his throat. "I should be getting back to my lodging. It seems the two of you have much to discuss."

The baron's thin face fell. "Will you be back?"

"Yes. I'll return later." *Much later.* "I'll help you find a good man of business to replace me. Perhaps Lord Chatfield could recommend someone, since he knows everyone else in the world."

"You'll stay," Sutcliffe decided. "You would miss me if you left my service. I'm the only family you have."

This was unfair to the baroness and her children, or to Sutcliffe's six sisters who lived in Lancashire. But Joss understood his meaning. "You're the only family I know well. But that won't be true for long, I hope. I have plans to learn about my Indian forebears."

Something about India had been so lovely to his grandfather that the late baron could not leave it behind entirely. Something about the language, the sun, the marvelous distance from England—Joss wanted to learn it all.

It would be, as Augusta had once said, an addition to the list of things he knew about himself. And the journey would begin—of all places—in the seaside town of Brighton.

Lady Sutcliffe's eyes were troubled blue pools as she looked up at him. "I ought to wish you godspeed,

Everett, but indeed I shall miss you. I live with three small children and a husband who acts like a fourth. Your sanity has been a blessing."

Before Joss could offer her thanks, a servant entered bearing the tea tray. When it was deposited on a table, Sutcliffe looked over the offerings and smacked the table with the flat of his hand. "Where's my hot water?"

"Do try some tea instead," said the baroness with polite formality. "And a sandwich or two, husband. How long has it been since you ate?"

"What?"

And with that, Joss bowed from the room. He had said all he could for today.

Mere words would not convince Sutcliffe to value his wife. Perhaps the blackmail attempt would, eventually, have a beneficial effect. Or the destruction of the conservatory. Sutcliffe was led by his purse and his *somalata* pouch; perhaps one day he could be led back to his family.

And for Joss, what now? An empty afternoon stretched before him as he descended the carpeted treads of the main staircase. If he returned to his rented room, the scent of sandalwood would make him light-headed. When the bottle broke, the golden oil sank into the wood planks of the floor.

For the first morning since reaching adulthood, he'd had none to daub on himself. He didn't mind leaving the tradition behind. It was a reminder of who he was, of the family that had built him, but he carried that knowledge far deeper than the surface of his skin.

Maybe he would return there after all. Or maybe he would take a walk in Sydney Gardens.

Slam. He collided with a smaller figure.

Or maybe he'd walk right into someone as he exited the house.

Taking a step backward to correct his balance, Joss found himself face to face with a maid, now rubbing at her forehead. She was a scrubby creature, with curly dark hair beneath her mobcap and avaricious light eyes.

This was the same maid who had delivered the last desperate letter from Lady Sutcliffe, then taken coin after coin to keep and break her silence.

So. Lady Tallant's maid was racing toward Lord Sutcliffe's house. Interesting.

But politeness first. "Are you quite all right, miss?"

Her eyes opened wide, and she dropped a crooked curtsy. "Yes, sir."

"Very good. If Lady Tallant should release you from her service after today's events, do let me know, and I shall give you Lord Chatfield's direction. The marquess would appreciate a servant with your sort of acumen."

He made to pass by, but she plucked at his sleeve. "Mr. Everett. It's you as I've come for. Mrs. Flowers—that is, Miss Meredith—is awake, and she's asking for you."

A soar, a plummet. How could he feel both at once? Joss paused halfway down the stone steps. "Is she, now? I suppose you are looking for a response other than 'Thank you for the information'?"

"Indeed, sir. I'm to fetch you at once."

What did Augusta intend to extract from him now? He would not be able to deny her again.

Or maybe he would. He had just shaken free of Sutcliffe, neither knowing or caring whether he would receive the promised hundred pounds at the month's end. Once he had pinned his future on the promise of that sum. But he didn't need it. He'd be fine.

And he'd be fine when he saw Augusta, too. Somehow. "Then lead on."

Twenty-two

"THE ONLY REASON I SHALL ALLOW YOU IN HER BED-chamber," said Lady Tallant when Joss entered the house next door, "is because she struck her head and cannot leave the room at present."

After extracting himself from the presence of the Sutcliffes, Joss was in no mood for further games. "How does that prevent her from leaving the room? Did she strike her head so hard that she forgot how to operate a door?"

"What a wit you are, Mr. Everett. But as it is for the sake of her health, I did not think you would be so cavalier," Lady Tallant tossed back as she preceded Joss up the stairs. To the drawing room, past it, to a story of the house he had never yet visited. It was familiar, though; a virtual twin to the one next door. All glossy wood and neatly papered walls, with soft carpets underfoot that must be a dreadful chore to take up and beat clean.

"Madam," Joss sighed. "I am deeply relieved that Miss Meredith is not seriously injured. But her recovery can have nothing to do with me. We have nothing more to say to one another."

"Perhaps you have nothing to say to her. But she has a great deal to tell you."

Having reached the corridor containing the main bedchambers, the countess knocked at a nearly shut door. Mentally counting off rooms in each direction, Joss recognized this as the equivalent to Lord Sutcliffe's spying room. The realization brought a thin smile to his face.

When Lady Tallant poked her head into the room, a murmured conversation ensued. Then the countess reemerged, rubbing her hands together. "You may enter now, Mr. Everett. *Don't* close the door. I shall be…well, I shan't be watching you, because I will return to the drawing room now. But—ah, you receive my meaning. Please treat her with respect."

This, he could answer quite honestly. "I would not dream of doing otherwise, my lady."

With that, the countess took her leave in a cloud of yellow muslin and self-satisfaction. And there was nothing left for Joss to do but open the door.

The first thing he noticed was how *brown* the room was. Nothing like the appearance of Sutcliffe's spying room at all, this had a dark trellised paper on the wall, a dark patterned carpet underfoot, and heavy drapes at the windows. In the bed—still dressed in her morning frock, but with a piratical bandage around her head—sat Augusta, half-hidden beneath a damask coverlet.

Brown, of course.

Yet a fire waved at him from the grate, and the drapes had been pulled back to greet the midday sun. "This seems a pleasant space to recover one's wits," Joss said.

Augusta was folding up some papers as he entered; when he spoke, she looked up with a smile. "That is exactly what I feel has happened. Do sit, won't you? On the settee, or maybe in the chair by the fire."

He perched in a feminine-looking chair near the fire, across the room from the bed. It squeaked as he rested his weight on its spindly legs, and Augusta's smile unsuccessfully tried to hide. For the sake of his dignity, Joss ignored this. "Shall I have the fire built up? You must be cold."

She shook her head. "I'm quite warm, actually." She blinked, then held up a hand as though checking whether it had grown its own glove. "How odd. I'm—not cold right now."

A reverie caught her up for a moment, and Joss waited it out until he could stand it no longer. "You wished to speak with me, Miss Meredith. What do you need to tell me?"

She sat up straighter against the mass of pillows behind her back. "I have decided to embrace my vulgarity."

"I am sure your vulgarity will be delighted, especially if you press it against your dockyard."

"Who wouldn't be?" she said with a little waggle of her shoulders. "It's my best feature."

No, it's not. But as he didn't want to begin with the giving of unwanted compliments, he only said, "I regret to admit it, but I find myself at a loss. To what do you refer, and what has it to do with me?"

She waved her handful of papers at him. "By now, all of Bath knows that Mrs. Flowers is really that red-haired cosmetic heiress Augusta Meredith. And your papers—thank you for the papers, by the way—gave me an idea for how to turn my deception to advantage."

He shifted his weight against the chair's groan of protest. "Specifically?"

"I shall never be welcomed to the heart of the *ton*. My money allows me passage to its edges, but my birth shall never allow me to proceed further. Because…"

"The nobility expects you to be vulgar?"

"Precisely." She grinned. "And what could be more vulgar than taking on a false identity only to advertise a new product?"

Joss considered. "Very little could be more vulgar than that."

Dropping the papers, she spread her hands as though laying out an advertisement. "'Try Meredith Beauty's complexion-brightening soap: a soap as transparent as your beauty.' Or maybe '*Shikakai* hair cleansing powder: the secrets of the Orient, now yours in England.' The copy needs a bit of work—"

"Rather."

"—but imagine: a new line of scents for men and women alike, priced exorbitantly to appeal to the elite. Sandalwood for men. The honeysuckle scent I use in my own soap; it could be manufactured in quantity. Maybe jasmine as well."

"You will slay every man in the *ton*. You want to unleash a whole ballroom full of women who smell like you?"

"Correct. And men who smell like you."

Joss groaned. "I've no doubt you will rule the polite world. But how is the embrace of vulgarity to help with this?"

"The pretense of being Mrs. Flowers was the vulgarity. The challenge now is to make people feel as though they were in on the charade, rather than the butt of a joke. With Lady Tallant's help, I hope to spread enough judicious gossip to convince the Bath-ites—"

"Bathonians."

"—that they knew I was deceiving them all along. That, in fact, they were really part of the deception, and that it was an excellent fiction which they enjoyed. That will bring them into the inner circle, so to speak. I mean, really; how could a name like 'Mrs. Flowers' be anything but an advertisement for soap?"

He pondered this. "What will the stuffy trustees of your fortune think of this scheme?"

"They will think I am being a silly woman again, no doubt. It has never occurred to them to attribute the steadiness of the company's profits to my silliness. Now that I am twenty-five, though, the terms of my father's will and the labyrinthine constructs of business would permit me to divorce my fortune from their care. And perhaps I shall. Or perhaps I shall do something else instead."

The look she cast him was so searching that he felt stripped by it, and he did not know what she meant by it. "If anyone can convince an entire city," he said, "I am sure it will be the combination of your determination and Lady Tallant's charm."

"I'm so enamored of this idea, I will not even point out that you just implied I have no charm."

"Or did I imply that Lady Tallant has no determination?"

"Surely not that." When she smiled at him, he could almost forget the number of ways in which they had rejected one another the night before. "Emily has agreed to drop a few blithe hints during her remaining days in Bath. I have taxed her goodwill much of late, but she has a generous supply. If she'll stand as my friend, I care not for the rest of the *ton*. An heiress with a powerful and kind friend can get away with much—especially if that heiress no longer cares whether a duke asks her to dance or whether Lady Stickler invites her to a ball."

Not for the first time, Joss wondered whether society's reluctance to deal with her—and with him— stemmed from their birth or from their behavior. These were the warp and weft of life's fabric: the family into which one was born, the choices one made ever after. Augusta's reputation could not be separated from her upbringing in trade, and perhaps the one could benefit the other. After this interlude as Mrs. Flowers, she could never again pretend to be anyone other than herself.

He hoped she would not want to.

But it could have nothing to do with him. For which reasons had they denied each other? He, because of the wounds of his birth; she, because of the choices that had hardened her heart.

There was no way around the chasm between them, and no way through.

Joss stood, the chair's old wooden frame letting out another groan as his weight left it. "My dear former fake widow, it sounds as though you have a marvelous plan in place. I do hope the information on the papers will be of great use to you. My best wishes for your future success."

"Wait, Joss. That's not all." She shoved back the coverlet; her ivory muslin gown was crumpled, her feet bare of shoes and stockings. He had not thought to see any part of her bared again—a sight so surprising, so intimate, that he had to look away to summon a mantle of calm.

"Oh?" He studied the elaborate carving of the chimneypiece. Acanthus leaves and putti.

"Lord Chatfield told me you did not plan to enter his service. So I thought—well, if he's helped you, which he certainly seemed to think he had, then he will be wanting help in return. In the form of information, for that's how he operates. And so I've written a letter to him to tell him of my plans for Meredith Beauty. He'll be the first to know, besides you and Emily."

"Fine."

"More than fine, you stubborn man. Don't you see? That's your payment taken care of."

Again, the gulf between them. It seemed to yawn before Joss, and he swayed, correcting his balance by grabbing the face of a marble putto on the chimneypiece. The smug little cherub. Lifting his hand, he turned on his heel to face Augusta again. "I'm sure you mean well, but it is not necessary for you to give me charity."

She snorted. "Charity? I've never met anyone who would stand for that less than you. I'd sooner try to…to sword fight with the prince regent than give you charity."

"You might win that sword fight. But what do you mean by this, if it's not charity?"

"Was it charity when you helped Lord Sutcliffe? When you took on a debt of honor to sort out his difficulties?"

"No. It was my job, and it was also the right thing to d—oh, are you making some sort of analogy? Damnation."

"Quite right." As she sat atop the bed, she folded her legs next to her. The bandage about her head slipped down, revealing an ugly bruise. When it covered her eyes…

…it reminded him of the cravat with which he'd covered her eyes, the ecstasy to which he'd coaxed her. It was all she wanted to take from him, but so much less than he wanted to give. "You don't owe me anything."

"I know." She tugged at the bandage, pulling it free over her mare's nest of still-pinned hair. "I don't owe you a thing. Which means anything I choose to give you is a gift, not a payment. And certainly not charity."

"What's the difference between charity and a gift?" Somehow his feet had crossed the room, and he stood beside the bed looking down on her.

"The difference is all in the intention. If I feel that I am better than you? That's charity. But if I feel that…" She drew in a deep breath, shuddering. "That you're the finest gentleman I know? Then it's a gift. Joss. I mean it as a gift."

His whole body seemed to vibrate, a tuning fork to the chime of her voice. "Then I thank you for the gift. I was not certain how I would pay my debt to the marquess, so—I—thank you."

"You're quite welcome." Even barefoot and messy-haired and bruised, she appeared gracious and dignified. "I'm sorry, Joss, that I ever belittled the size of your dream. It was yours, and therefore it is perfect for you. What do you intend to do after you leave Lord Sutcliffe?"

He sat on the bed next to her. It would not be improper, surely, because he would keep his boots planted firmly on the floor.

Right. And there was nothing improper in feeling the sway of the mattress beneath his weight or inhaling her faint, sweet smell of honeysuckle.

Or wondering why, now, at last, she was warm.

"Actually," he managed to reply, "I have a new dream. I intend to go to Brighton, where an Indian man by the name of Dean Mahomet has built a popular bathhouse."

Her brow puckered. "Dean Mahomet? I'm fairly certain that was the name of the man who operated the curry restaurant in London. The one I visited with my father. Can it be the same person?"

"Probably. Can there be more than one Indian man named Dean Mahomet in England?"

"Most likely not." She nibbled on her bottom lip, then nodded. "You wish to meet him, then? Do you want to seek employment from him?"

"In any capacity needed, yes. He cannot require more variety of me than Lord Sutcliffe did. And I will bring along my grandmother's book and ask him for help translating the notes written in the Hindustani language. I have ignored the Indian part of myself, and I should like to learn more about it."

Her hand slipped into his; sweet tension hummed in his fingers.

Maybe there was no chasm beneath his feet, after all. Maybe it was only unsteady ground, over which they would both have to pick their way.

"In the book," Joss added gruffly, "Dean Mahomet might find reference to some plants or receipts that would be useful in his health treatments. I intend that ours will be a business arrangement; I shall not ask him for favors."

"No, you would never do that." More tightly, she laced her fingers through his. "Do you not wish to offer him your grandmother's notes on *shikakai*, then?"

"No," Joss said. "Those are a gift. To you."

"Oh." The syllable came out as a sigh. "Then—I thank you. But there's one more thing I want to ask you."

"Of course."

She drew in a deep breath, then swayed closer to him on the bed. "I should very much like to marry you. Would you ask me, please?"

❧

She knew him too well to expect him to fall on her, pressing her with kisses, and exclaim his delight. None of that was particularly characteristic of Joss. A dry, lewd comment and a searing glance would be quite welcome, though. And she had hoped he would leave his hand in hers. She liked the feeling of his bare skin, of this small intimacy that made it easier to ask for a far larger one.

He did leave his hand in hers, though he leaned

away from her, fixing her with dark eyes under stern black brows. "This has a suspicious ring of familiarity to it, just as we began in the Assembly Rooms when you informed the world we were to dance. I ought to consider myself fortunate, I suppose, that you did not simply tell someone else we were to be married and force me to go along with your scheme."

Was that a faint smile on his lips? "I considered that approach," she said lightly. "But I concluded it lacked the proper romantic flair."

"Again you hold my reputation in your hands, then. But I don't wish to be used as your pawn, Augusta."

So he again called her Augusta; but it was only one word to bring them closer, the rest to distance them. "Oh. No. Of course not." She drew up her knees, making an untidy ball of herself atop the mattress.

He arched a brow, and the damnable, beloved expression of sly humor crossed his features. "I didn't say I wouldn't do it. I only said I wouldn't be used as your pawn."

"You silver-tongued rascal. Eventually I will remember to press you for a complete explanation of what you mean." She rubbed gingerly at her bruised forehead. "What *do* you mean?"

"That depends on you." He hitched one booted foot atop the bed. "Why do you want me to marry you, Augusta? And why now, when you could hardly listen to me talk of my regard for you yesterday? Am I just another way to help you flee your problems? Does Meredith Beauty require a sacrificial husband?"

"I deserve all of those questions."

"The answers matter very much to me."

"Lord Chatfield is not always right about the relative importance of questions and answers." Beckoning toward him, she said, "More. Tell me more. Whatever angers you or worries you. Whatever you think of me. I want to make sure I tailor my groveling to the proper shape."

He pulled his hand free of hers, pressing at the bridge of his nose. "I have already told you what I thought of you. You didn't handle it well."

"And for that, I am sincerely sorry. I was stupid and wrong."

"Go on."

"And...ungrateful. And cowardly. And unfeeling."

"Go on."

"You want to hear *more*?"

His hand fell, and his mouth bent into an unwilling smile. "I am still waiting to hear how *you* feel. That interests me more than the groveling. Although the groveling is acceptable too, and if it gives you pleasure, by all means, continue. Might I suggest the sonnet form as particularly pleasing to the ear?"

She could almost feel him teetering on this fragile moment. If she upset it, they would fall away from one another.

Or they would tumble together. "I don't have any poetry in my soul," she said, wrapping her arms around her rumpled skirts, her folded legs. "No sonnets. Not even a rhymed couplet. All I can say is that I love you."

The ultimate oblivion wasn't in losing herself at all: it was in giving herself. In thinking of someone else rather than dwelling on her own disappointments. To think about how Joss smiled, how his voice rubbed soft and low over her skin, how his laughter felt like her own joy.

"I love you," she said again.

He trailed a forefinger over the sheets. "That is a good start. Why have you come to this conclusion now, though?"

"Should I go through the groveling again? It *is* relevant."

"No need; I recall it perfectly." The tracing finger moved closer to her bare toes. "In what way is it relevant?"

"The cowardice is the most relevant, I think." Her toes curled into the sheet, anxious. "You would never be satisfied with anything less than honesty, and that terrified me. I had not been honest with myself for a long time. And in Bath, I was dishonest with a whole town."

"No one could accuse you of having little ambition."

"Indeed, no. I have always been given the best, whether I deserve it or not. And you, Joss—you're the best man I've ever met."

He raised one brow—one wicked, teasing brow—and she caught up a quick breath of delight. If Joss was arching one brow, that meant he was feeling…well…like *Joss*. And Joss loved her. He had said so, and he was always honest. "You have more poetry in your soul than you realize, Augusta."

"Do you think so? Let me add to my non-rhyming sonnet of your fine qualities, then. You saw me as worthy when I did not; you treated me with respect when I expected far less. And you also showed me the darkest bits of myself, the ones I hadn't wanted to face. My vanity and fear and fumbling—you saw that; you saw me just as I was. And I couldn't believe that you would love me even so."

"I could not bear to lie about my own heart."

"Yes. I know." Her arms loosened about her folded legs. "You have teased me, but you have always been honest with me too. I have not been brave enough to let myself trust you, or anyone, for more than a moment at a time. But—I want to. Because of you, I want to. I could not let you go without telling you that."

Her feet slid, legs straightening, and she looked him in the eye. "So—thank you. And I love you. And if you should ever care to ask me to marry you, I would say yes."

"It's not the answer that matters," he murmured. "Only the question. Isn't that right?"

"The question matters very much." The heat in his gaze brought a blush to her cheeks. "And the answer does too."

"Then here is my question, and my answer, and all the truth of what I feel." And leaning toward her, he cupped her face gently in his hands and covered her lips with his own.

Twenty-three

THE KISS WAS LIKE A BRIGHT TUNNEL, ONE INTO WHICH Joss could fall and fall forever and feel ever more shining and new. Her lips, her flower scent, her low murmurs of pleasure—or were those his? Intoxicating and endless, the way she whispered…

"Oh, drat."

"No." He caught her mouth again in a quick, hard kiss. "You've mispronounced 'that was marvelous, Joss. Please do it some more.'"

But then he pulled back, in case that wasn't what she meant at all.

She flapped a hand in the direction of the door. "'Drat' meaning 'The door is not locked. We need to lock it.' And then, Joss, please kiss me some more, because it was marvelous."

A shiver of heat shook him. "You imply that we shall be doing something for which the door would be better locked."

She blinked hazy eyes. "I certainly hope so."

"That is a highly intriguing implication. And yet I promised Lady Tallant I would treat you with respect."

"I have never doubted that you would. Not from the first time I swore you'd promised to dance with me."

"If you insist, then, I'll lock the door at once. You *did* insist, didn't you?" Without the tiniest pang of guilt, Joss slid from the bed and turned the door's key. "But if you truly intend to marry me, I must place a condition on the agreement."

She wiggled her bare toes at him. "I should have expected nothing less from a man of business. What is this condition? As a woman of business, I must hear it before I agree. Though I am almost certain I shall."

All peaches and golds and ruddy tones, she looked like a bowl of fruit he wanted to nibble up. But she must understand what he wanted before there was any more nibbling or tasting or stroking or…

He cleared his throat. "A solicitor shall draw up marriage settlements to protect your control of your own fortune, and especially to set aside money for any daughters we may have. I won't have you or any possible children suffering for want of money that ought to have been yours."

Her brows knit. "But that's quite generous and lovely. Why would I disagree with that?"

"For no reason, I hope. I just want you to understand how important it is to me."

"Yes." Her smile was bemused, watery. "Yes, I do. It's the sort of choice that makes you who you are."

"I only exist because my mother had no such resources."

"No, you exist because your mother had a loving, eager heart. It was no more her fault that she was tricked into thinking a dishonest man a good one than

it would be her fault if a thief stole jewels from her."
She blinked, her nose crinkling. "And that's true for
me as well. But there's one advantage I have, having
known a bad man."

"What is that?"

"I know how to identify a good one." Catching the
cuff of his coat sleeve, she tugged until his balance was
overset and he had to catch his weight on his hands.
With them planted on the mattress, only a few inches
away from her rumpled, bundled, beautiful self, it was
so easy to sway forward and kiss her again.

Just once. For now.

All right, twice. Or three times.

Really, anything under a dozen was demonstrating
admirable control.

"Have you any other conditions?" she said breath-
lessly when he pulled back.

"I don't know what you mean. Kiss me some more."

She laughed, that low, erotic sound that had captured him from the first. "I'm not going to make you
an indecent proposition, you know."

"Damn."

"Because…" She tugged at the knot of his cravat.
"There's nothing indecent about this. I trust you to
treat me with honor. Just as I shall treat you."

He didn't want to be a man like his father, who
took advantage of women; he didn't want to be like
Sutcliffe, careless and destructive.

And…he wasn't. For all that most people consigned
him to the shadows, Augusta saw him clearly; she
understood who he wanted to be.

"We're getting a license tomorrow. Today. As soon

as I leave this room." He shut his eyes and let himself feel: her hands playing over him, her breath, warm on his cheek; then her lips pressing to his brow, pulling gently at the lobe of his ear. Her hot tongue in the hollow behind his jaw.

His elbows went loose, and he clambered onto the bed. "I should take off my boots."

"Do you want to take the time for that?"

"No. Though since I do want you to be as naked as possible, I am willing to return the favor if you wish."

Her honey-brown eyes went wicked. "I most certainly do wish. Here, let me help you off with those."

It was not in Joss's interest to disagree. Instead, he yielded to her touch, helping her remove his boots, then tug free the knots of his cravat. After this, she shoved him back to the bed with delightful force. "My turn. Shall I cover your eyes, as you did for me?"

"I would consider that a great unkindness."

She laughed, and so he watched as she slipped free the buttons of his waistcoat and the fall of his trousers. Her hands were everywhere then, sliding beneath his shirt to explore his chest, over his belly until it twitched with eagerness—and then down, to wrap around the naked length of his cock. Up, then down, she worked him in her hands until he felt his tightly coiled control begin to crack.

"My turn now." Stilling her hands, he rolled to a seated position. "I ought to be more original in my choice of words, but I really cannot think when you start grabbing at my person in such a manner."

"If you can string together a sentence that long, I ought to grab at it a bit mo—*oh*." Which, as Joss learned, was the sound Augusta made when he ran a thumb over her nipple at the same time he kissed her neck.

After that, it was time for more discovery, and it was her turn to surrender. Quickly, though not as quickly as he wished, he unfastened her gown and stays. Her feet were already bare of slippers and stockings; admiring, he stroked the long lines of her legs.

In the bright spill of daylight, she was all curves and faint freckles, even more lovely than she had been by lamplight. Or maybe the extra beauty came from the way her eyes met his, the way her hands pulled him closer. So nothing was done *to*, but was instead done *with*.

"Are you ready?" he asked when they were both gasping, facing one another on the bed like naked, kneeling bookends.

"Yes. Are you?"

"You cannot imagine how much."

"Oh, I think I might be able—"

With a brush of his lips over hers, he cut off the sentence. Then carefully, minding her bruised head, he coaxed her flat on the mattress. When her hands laced behind his back, it felt like the most natural thing in the world—until he thrust into her heat, slow and reverent, and that feeling shook up everything he knew about pleasure. Never had it been like this, when love and trust and honesty were in place. He could unleash himself, laugh with her, whisper in her ear, sigh with the pleasure of each rocking movement. They could *be*, and together they stroked and urged each other on, nipping and thrusting until the climax built like a wave, crashing over them and leaving them gasping.

Afterward, he held her close. They were both far too warm, but neither wanted to let go yet.

Her hair was still in its pins, somewhat. As he cradled her, he plucked one pin free, then another, and worked his fingers into her glorious hair.

With a low hum of pleasure, she settled more tightly against him. "This is a shining moment," she murmured. "Right now, with you."

He didn't know the term she used, but he understood the meaning well enough. "Yes."

"I thought I'd never feel better unless I lost myself, but I was lost already. Then together, we found me."

"You were always you, even if you didn't realize it." Raising his hand to the window light, he let the bronze strands slip and play, then drift to cover her shoulder. "And you were always dear. My dear fake widow who shall soon be my wife."

And so they remained, body against body, talking of things important or inconsequential until the daylight began to slant and dim.

Joss could not turn off his racing mind entirely; the years had built a habit of details, of thinking ahead and preparation and contingency.

He knew there would be weeks to wait before their marriage. A scandal to quash. Sutcliffe to soothe and shepherd toward a new man of business. Plans that might never come to fruition.

But they had each other, and love, and a dream for what came next.

And they had this shining moment of contentment,

frail and lovely as a soap bubble. While it lasted, it was…good. Perfect. Precious.

And for the moment, it lasted.

And moments stacked on moments were the stuff of which life was made.

Epilogue

THE BANNS WERE CALLED, THE MARRIAGE TOOK PLACE in due course, and shortly after Easter, the Miss Meredith that had so recently been Mrs. Flowers became Mrs. Everett.

After the small wedding, the Bath-ites—or was it Bathonians?—could not quite recall who it was that had first suspected Mrs. Flowers was playing a part in the spring of 1817. The relevant page seemed to be missing from the guest book in the Pump Room. So perhaps she had arrived under her true name, and they were all in on the joke?

Perhaps so.

There was no denying it had been a bold joke, and the denizens of Bath were not sure whether they liked it. But they liked Lady Tallant, and she liked the new Mrs. Everett, and…well, perhaps one ought not to expect an heiress to a soap fortune, or whatever it was, to know all the rules of proper behavior.

She and her husband were gone soon enough, off to Brighton, or so rumor said, where they intended to work with a Hindustani man who called himself a "shampooing surgeon" and ran a most elaborate bath-house. The prince regent spent a great deal of time in Brighton and seemed to like it—but really, it all sounded rather exotic. The denizens of Bath were also unsure whether they liked the exotic or not.

But they did like the soaps that were soon stacked up in every chemist in their town and, from word that traveled into Bath with new visitors, across most of the south of England. These were soaps such as no one had ever seen: translucent ovals like great pieces of amber, delectably scented of honeysuckle. Or jasmine. Or sandalwood or lemongrass or sweet pea—and somehow, deliciously, there was an apple soap that smelled of the local orchards during the ripening season.

The price was exorbitant, but then, sometimes cost didn't matter, did it? So said Lord Chatfield and Lord Whittingham, both of whom had invested in this line of soaps, the latter after his ship did at last come in.

An unusual new product called *shikakai* appeared too; a sort of powder that smelled of fruit and, when worked into a paste, could be used to cleanse the hair. That was slower to catch on, though more than one lady's maid professed herself delighted by the ease with which she was now able to scrub the pomade and dust from *madame*'s coiffure.

Lord and Lady Sutcliffe remained in Bath for quite some time, as his lordship attempted to sell coal to Mr. Duffy of the city's iron foundry. The baron and baroness were not seen to spend a great deal of time together, though they appeared cordial. Lord Sutcliffe was recognized about town not only for the brightness of his coats, but also for the spyglass he inevitably carried. When questioned about it, he tended to adopt a sly expression and say that his wife had insisted his hand tend to his spyglass.

In future years, Lady Tallant and her husband and their two rambunctious sons again visited the house in Queen Square. Once, Mr. and Mrs. Everett joined them there with their young daughter, upon whom Lady Tallant was seen to dote with a rather misty expression.

As the two families promenaded in the garden of Queen Square, there was a great deal of chat and merriment. Upon one occasion, a grimy boy pulling a Bath chair overheard Mr. Everett being accused of "man flirting" with the board of advisors that had once served as Meredith Beauty's trustees. Whatever "man flirting" was, it inspired a great deal of laughter.

Counter to the recommendation of Lord Sutcliffe, none of Meredith Beauty's soaps nor cosmetics ever contained *somalata*.